Tenth Letter

the novel

KAYONA**EBONY**BROWN

THE UNITED STATES OF AMERICA

acclaim for
Tenth Letter

"A BREATH OF FRESH AIR. THIS BOOK HAD ME TALKING TO MYSELF, SMILING, LAUGHING, AND CLOSE TO TEARS. GREAT READ! PAGE TURNIN' AND POETIC."

- M.T. POPE, AUTHOR: *BOTH SIDES OF THE FENCE*

"THE COMPLEXITY OF THIS LOVE STORY IS A STEP ABOVE OTHERS READ THIS YEAR. THE CHARACTER DEVELOPMENT IS PHENOMENAL AND THE REALNESS OF THE STORYLINE STRIKES HOME. THE METAPHORS USED HELP THE READER TOTALLY EXPERIENCE THE PAIN IN REALIZING THE SHORTCOMINGS OF INDIVIDUALS. BROWN IS A NEW VOICE IN RELATIONSHIP DRAMA AND THE POWER OF STARTING OVER. I ABSOLUTELY RECOMMEND THIS ONE!"

- DELTAREVIEWER, *REAL PAGE TURNERS*

"IT'S THE BEST BOOK THAT I'VE READ SO FAR THIS YEAR! I REALLY, REALLY LOVE THIS BOOK! THE WAY YOU CAN CONNECT WITH THE CHARACTERS, THE PARELLEL MEANINGS... I MEAN, IT JUST GETS YOU THINKING. AND IT'S A GOOD STORY ON TOP OF THAT."

- TIFANY JONES, *SISTAH CONFESSIONS RADIO SHOW*

BROWN HAS PUBLISHED WHAT COULD BE THE BLUEPRINT TO UNDERSTANDING EXACTLY WHAT IT MEANS TO TAKE A RISK; NOT ONLY WITH LOVE, BUT WITH LIFE... PERIOD."

- SIMONE BANKS, *SCHEME MAGAZINE*

Dedicated to
Thelma and Veronica
[Grandma and Momma]

Kayona Ebony Brown entertainment products
600 Pennsylvania Avenue SE #15530
Washington, DC 20003
Visit the Web site at www.tenthletternovel.com

Library of Congress Control Number: 2006905155
ISBN-10 0-9786725-0-X
ISBN-13 978-0-9786725-0-8

Originally published in paperback by Brown'stone Literary Division, 2008.

Second independent published paperback edition 2014.

Book design and layout by Kayona Ebony Brown.

Manufactured in the United States of America

i got a light so bright i'm shinin'
i look into the mirror at myself and i'm almost blinded
i'm the moon, but God's the sun
so without His light
i wouldn't have one

-kayona ebony brown

She looked at the digital clock on the nightstand as the last of three big red numbers turned into a seven. 8:27 a.m.

I gotta get outta here.

The *last* thing she needed to do was fall asleep.

Get comfortable.

She turned over slowly to see if he was asleep. His back was to her just as hers was to his seconds ago.

I gotta get outta here.

She covered her face with both of her hands and whispered, "I gotta get outta here."

* * *

April shouldn't be so hot. Especially at night. But DC rarely has a good spring: it's winter to summer with no in-between. And the city is infamous for its humidity during this time of year, too. Hoochie-mommas and girls who *normally* look like they just came from a rap video shoot aren't the only ones in cut-off, homemade halter-top shirts and mini-mini-skirts. Women with long hair have it tied up in ponytails; the ones with naturally short hair wear their weaves and extensions in pin-up styles; and those who prefer the short look hurry to make appointments to get fresh shape-ups, trims, and clippings before summer's real due date.

Guys are no different, wasting no time stripping from even short-sleeve shirts to expose those wife-beaters, which they seem to take pride in sporting. The color of choice is almost always white. Some go as far as breaking out the sandals this early in the year—the ones that look like the bottom half of a tenni'-shoe... But then they defeat the whole purpose with socks.

89 degrees. 7:45 in the evening. Even at this hour, the windows of sedans and coupes are rolled down as far as they can go, and the cloth coverings of almost every cabriolet and ragtop are hidden somewhere in the back of the vehicles allowing the drivers to get an extra dose of that thick Chocolate City air.

Jaye sat watching this pre-summer scene from the roof of Black Girl Art Gallery where he'd been all day with his chin in his hands, and his head. . . somewhere in New Jersey. He took his time getting up from his seat on the rooftop of the gallery. He was comfortable up there. It was peaceful. He could sit up there forever, alone, and just watch the world beneath him. He'd be safer that way.

But he stood up anyway, stretched, and with a deep breath cleared his mind of the thoughts that filled it. This was supposed to be his big day—the grand opening weekend of Black Girl Art Gallery. *His* gallery. He was supposed to be happy. So he took off the sad mask and threw on the happy-to-meet-you face for the newspaper reporters, magazine journalists, and photographers. He had interviews to do, quotes to give, and pictures to take. Misery had no place at this party. Or at least it wasn't given an invitation.

Before he could get completely down the stairs and onto the gallery's main floor, he noticed that the place was covered with press who flooded the inside and front entrance trying to get pictures and quotations from the two young owners. He made his way over to Keyon who actually enjoyed entertaining them.

"I need to talk to you for'minute."

"Wait," Keyon told him, and continued his quotable speech: "You see, the art world *loves* to put people in a box. They want to applaud those who fit a stereotype. Well…" he said, "they gon' have to heckle us."

The people who heard him laughed. One female reporter's voice rose above the laughter, "Yeah right! Boo *you?*" as if she would fight the person who dared to heckle.

Keyon was Jaye's partner. Best friend. Almost twelve years ago, Jaye walked into his new living quarters for the first time at the Corcoran College of Art and Design in DC only to find a Boston native standing in the living room that almost looked just like him—a pair of crisp white Nikes, blue jeans, and a plain white t-shirt decorated his frame too. Even their hair was similar—cuts close, slightly faded and shaped up. His roommate stood just over six feet too, and had a similar lean build. He was a bit lighter in complexion though, and his eyes were naturally narrow and dark. They were both at the prestigious fine art institute to study the same thing—painting.

"I really need to talk to you for'minute," Jaye whispered again.

"One moment," Keyon said to the reporters. He turned to Jaye and asked, "What is it?"

Jaye sighed. "I'm sorry, but I'm not feelin' this."

"Feelin' what?"

"*This*, man," he said, referring to the atmosphere. "I'm not in the mood to deal with all these people right now."

Keyon sighed. "Look… This is the first night of the biggest weekend of your life. You can't let some…" He searched for the word: "*Stuff*," he said, "mess this up for you, man. Come on. Look at this."

Jaye looked around. Everybody was talking about the great art they saw:

"These guys have basically begun a new movement in the art world. Their work is brilliant!" one person said.

"They're more than just modern day neo-expressionists," another person said. "They haven't quite found a name for them yet—they're style. I don't know what to call 'em, but they're great!"

And not only were they talking, but they were taking pictures, jotting notes, trying to analyze and interpret the works... Keyon Braxten and JayMahr Cobain were the talk of the art world.

Jaye took Keyon's advice; this was his big night and there was no time for misery.

"You're right. You're absolutely right, man. I can't let this hinder me from enjoying my success."

"That's right," Keyon said. "You gotta get it together. There's gonna be tons of people in here this weekend. They're here to see you," he teased, trying to cheer his friend up.

Jaye tried to smile.

"Now come on. You got some reporters to talk to." Keyon threw his arm around Jaye's neck and guided him over to a swarm of media people.

Just like every other newspaper, journal, and magazine, *FACE Magazine*, a lifestyle, culture and entertainment publication, had sent their best writer to cover the opening of Black Girl.

"I fucking *hate* Georgetown," she said to herself aloud as she circled the block for the fourth time realizing that she should've taken a cab.

She leaned over so she could get a better look out the passenger's side window.

"'Scuze me, are you coming out?" she asked a wealthy white guy sitting in a Lexus.

The guy nodded, and no sooner than he did, a woman with similar blue eyes and blond hair got in on the passenger's side.

"Thank God," the young journalist sighed. And luckily for her, the two-hour parking rule was almost set to expire. She had seen all those people inside the gallery when she drove by and immediately doubted that she'd be able to get what she wanted if she had been limited to a time frame like that.

The guy moved and the journalist in her clean-for-the-summer-weather, champagne-colored coupe prepared to take his space. She threw her hand up thanking him as he drove off.

The place was quite large inside, so everybody had elbowroom, but that was about all they were allowed. She was immediately taken by some of the pieces, but she was reminded by the sound of cameras and rude writers to snap out of admiring the work and start working on her story. She had taken more than thirty pictures already, but all of them had been of the art; the rest were of the celebrities that were scattered about the place. No shots were taken of the owners; she hadn't any quotations either.

In the front, she saw two guys posing with the mayor of DC. She assumed that they were the men of the night. She snapped several good pictures of them.

She watched.

The guys were smiling, talking to the reporters, posing for pictures, and one of them was even signing autographs.

She watched.

After several photos were taken, the huge smile that covered the face of the darker complected guy disappeared as he separated himself from his friend and the politician. Most, actually all of the media people were still trying to talk to the mayor and the other owner; the one who had unknowingly revealed to the FACE journalist that his I-am-so-happy-to-be-here attitude was a fake made his way by several reporters and proceeded toward the front entrance.

She kept watching.

He went out, so she decided to follow him. When she got outside, she looked to the left, then to the right. Across the street. He was nowhere to be found.

"Damn," she said, thinking that she had lost him.

She wanted to go back, but the journalist inside of her wanted to find him. Investigate a little bit. She walked to the left, slowly. When she got to an intersection, an alley-looking spot, there he was—sitting on a milk crate with his chin on his fists. She hardly needed a full three seconds to examine him well enough to describe him to the police if need be. He had smooth, dark brown skin. His frame was well structured; he was tall, she could tell that much. His eyes were dark and his brows were even darker, and they were thick but naturally neat. His eyelashes were long, which made him appear even more innocent than he would have otherwise. He had full, soft lips that were accentuated by a low trimmed mustache, chin hair, and just enough facial hair to make side burns, but hardly enough for a full beard. His hair on his head was kept in a curly bush about a half-inch high, but purposely uncombed because of the style.

He wore a canary yellow button-up shirt un-tucked, and blue jeans made for wearing with boots, which fell perfectly over his white sneakers. Other than his watch, he wore no jewelry.

"I'm sorry, but I'm not answering any questions right now," he said, sensing her presence without having to look up.

This made her even more curious. She knew that she should've just left him alone and gone back inside the gallery, but again, the journalistic side of her took over.

"May I at least just ask you one thing?"

"You just did," he responded.

He was sarcastic she noticed. She said, "That didn't count."

With frustration covering his face, he said, "My name is Jaye Cobain, I'm from East Orange, New Jersey. I…"

"Whoa… Wait," she cut in. "I do need to know that stuff, but that's not what I wanted to ask you."

He said to her nicely, as he finally looked up to see who was bothering him, "I would really like to be alone right now. Just for a minute."

She was the complexion of a roasted peanut. Blessed with a five-foot, seven-inch stature and thickness proportioned only in the right places. Her eyes: brown. Her hair: curly and brown and very short, especially now because of the heat. Lots of ethnic looking costume jewelry hung from her wrists, neck and ears, complimenting the outfit—a baby blue, knee length, summer skirt made of a thin fabric that caused it to cling nicely to her hips and hind parts, and a blouse that fitted likewise.

When he looked at her—even for just that short amount

of time—he noticed each and every one of those features, but had no problem convincing himself to care less. His mind was preoccupied with other things.

"Just give me ten minutes," he said to her. "I'll be back inside. Just… I need some time alone right now."

"I see," she said, feeling sympathetic and not understanding why, but really wanting to know what was bothering him.

She came close to meeting his demands and walking away. But she couldn't. "I saw you inside and I noticed that ahh… You weren't exactly *into* this like your friend. I just came out here because I was curious as to why," she admitted. "That's all."

He didn't say anything.

"But if you really don't feel like talking about anything right now, I'll have to respect that."

Maybe there was a part of her that followed him because she was genuinely concerned for the stranger. But only part of that could be true; the other part, which was her main reason, had to do with her job and the story she had to get. Her boss was always talking about getting the first scoop, and she almost always obliged.

She only stood in front of him for a second, then she allowed the human side of her to take over and she began to walk away.

He sighed. "I apologize," he said.

She turned around and said, "Excuse me?"

"I need to work on my PR. I'm sorry. I'm not used to this."

"That's okay," she said, keeping a nonchalant demeanor.

He reached to his left and grabbed another milk crate like the one he was sitting on and placed it in front of him—his way of inviting her to sit.

She took him up on his offer by simply walking back and sitting on the makeshift chair adjacent to him.

He reintroduced himself by simply saying, "Jaye."

"Irony," was all she said about the coincidence that: "My name is J. J Llaureano. *FACE Magazine.*" She stuck her hand out for him to shake.

Jaye, still not smiling or looking sociable in any way, returned the shake and said, "Nice to meet you."

"That was convincing," she mumbled sarcastically, not joking at all.

He didn't respond.

"So," she said, "What's bothering you so much that you had to take a timeout from probably the biggest night of your life?"

Jaye thought about it. He thought about the truth—why he was really sitting outside on a crate pouting when dozens of media folk and celebrities had come out to meet and congratulate him and his friend on their success. Then he realized who the woman sitting in front of him was—a journalist. One of *them*.

"I'm just…" he started. He looked up at her and she was listening attentively. "I'm just really stressed out about this whole… This whole thing," he said. "I gotta keep sayin' shit over and over and over and… I'm not a celebrity, y'know? And I never wanted to be one. I am a *visual* artist. I prefer to be seen and not heard. My art speaks for me." He stopped for a moment and gathered his thoughts. "I just came out here to get myself together. I don't wanna go back in there."

The details of his elaborate excuse for being outside were true—but only partially. A smirk appeared on J's face because she knew—she could look at him and tell—that his lack of love for limelight wasn't holding that much weight. It was something more, something heavier. But she neglected to go "journalist" on him. She just said, "You better consider yourself lucky. We usually wait 'til artists die to give 'em this much recognition."

He smiled.

"There it is," she said, seeing him smile for the first time. "Now that wasn't so hard, was it?"

"It wasn't." He looked down, hating that he admitted that. "You are ruining my mad time. I'm supposed to be mad right now."

"No. You're *supposed to be* your ass in *there* enjoying yourself and talking to some other people like me."

"I know, but I don't feel like it."

She nodded. She couldn't make him go back inside if he

didn't want to.

"Okay," she said. "Well… You know what usually helps me clear my mind when I'm stressed out?"

"What?"

"I walk."

He looked at her—straight into her eyes.

"That's it," she said. She smiled.

Now Jaye was smiling. Again.

"Wanna go for a walk?"

8:27 a.m. She had to *leave.*

She looked at the digital clock on the nightstand as the last of three big red numbers turned into a seven.

I gotta get outta here.

The *last* thing she needed to do was fall asleep.

Get comfortable.

She turned over slowly to see if he was asleep. His back was to her just as hers was to his seconds ago.

I gotta get outta here, she thought.

She covered her face with both of her hands and whispered, "I gotta get outta here."

He heard the whisper. She had to get out of there. She was going to leave? She was going to get up and leave without even saying goodbye. Without even bothering to talk to him again. Without even ever seeing him again.

Who is she? What *is she?* He thought.

Thoughts about her went through his head; he didn't know what to think of this woman. Was she some type of harlot or something who was used to this—sleeping with guys and leaving? She could've been.

She could've been a completely innocent woman who just so happened to fall victim to his long sad face the night before. She could've been that too.

Or maybe she was neither. Maybe she was neither a slut nor a saint. Maybe she had just made a mistake too. Got caught up in the moment too.

So he said, "I'm sorry."

She lay on her back looking at the ceiling at the rotating

ceiling fan. A grimace was on her face after he said that. What was he apologizing for?

He said, "I shouldn't have taken advantage of you like that. I apologize."

This was strange. The grimace remained. "Taken advantage of" was a new one. That was a line she had never heard before.

She remembered asking him as they crossed the intersection of 29th and M, "Why did you decide to move back to Jersey if you had things going for you here?" She inquired about his post-college life.

He sighed as he thought about it.

"My mother. And my little sister." He thought about her and smiled. "Meka." He shook his head as he thought about Meka, a nickname for TaMeka. "I don't know. I felt I needed to be there for her. And my mother still needed help with a lot of things. She was working two jobs. I needed to be there. I wouldn't have been able to live with myself had I gone off to New York to pursue a career in art. That's what I was supposed to do," he said. "But I don't regret moving back home. I was there for Meka. She needed that." He thought about what he had said and added, "I needed it too. She keeps me grounded."

They talked about music.

Talked about food.

About places they wanted to go. Why they wanted to go there.

Life.

They talked about everything but Black Girl. He didn't want to, and though she was supposed to, she didn't.

Who is *this guy?* She thought. He didn't seem like the type who would purposely take advantage of a person, especially a woman considering how he talked about his mother and sister. So for a moment she actually considered accepting his apology. But then again, he didn't seem like the type who would sleep with a woman after knowing her for less than a day either.

"You didn't take advantage of me," she said.

"What?"

"I said you didn't take advantage of me."

Silence smothered the room.

"Look, you don't have any… diseases or anything like that or nothin', do you?"

"No," he said. "Do you?"

She shook her head implying that she didn't. "No," she replied. She sat up, avoiding eye contact with him. "I gotta go," she said as she began to put her clothes on.

"Leaving? But where're you goin'? It's…" He looked around for a clock to prove that it was a bad time to be leaving. "It's like 8:30 in the morn-"

"I know what time it is," she snapped.

She didn't mean to sound like she had an attitude. But then again, she really didn't care; she just needed to leave.

"This was a mistake and I am *really* sorry."

Why does he keep saying that?

So she wouldn't seem cold, she said, "Me too. That's why I have to leave."

"So when do you plan to get your story?"

She'd forgotten about that. "*I'll* worry about that," she told him.

He sighed and gently said, "Look. I think we should start over," after noticing how curt she was being.

"*What*?!"

She definitely needed to get out. The crazy apology was one thing, but now he was talking about starting over?

Start what over?

He followed her with the sheet from his king sized bed wrapped around his waist. She was already down the steps and standing by the front door.

"Hi," he said with a serious look on his face. "I'm Jaye Cobain." He extended his hand for a shake. "And you are?"

"What are you doing?"

"And you are?" he asked again, ignoring her question.

She sighed, reluctant to give in. She was stubborn.

She looked at his hand and thought about whether she should give him hers. Still reluctant, she put her hand in his and said, "J. J Llaureano."

There was an uncomfortable silence after her hesitant reintroduction.

"So what now?" she asked.

He sighed and said, "I don't know. I mean… we got off to a rough start."

She listened to him.

"And I apologize again for my part in that." He looked at her. "But… I can't… I wouldn't even be able to live with myself if I allowed you to just walk out and… never talk to you again, or see you again. I'm just not that type of person."

She wondered what type of person he really was. He was so confusing.

Jaye really wasn't big on bad first impressions. People saw him as this handsome, intelligent, cordial, and respectable guy. And he was. But a bone had just been thrown into his neat little closet, and quite frankly, he wasn't too pleased with that. So he did what any respectable man would do—he tried to clean it up.

After taking a few seconds to think about the situation, she said, "I yah… I feel what you're sayin'." She nodded her head. "Honestly, I would've just left and probably beaten myself up about this later, but ah… I see what you're saying."

He looked down at himself and became embarrassed after realizing his "attire."

She fought off a smile, and then asked, "So what now?"

He shrugged his shoulders and said, "I don't know. I… I don't know."

That uncomfortable silence covered the room again.

"Friends?" he suggested.

"*Friends?*" she asked, like that was the first, or maybe second time she'd heard such an insulting word.

"You know—friends. Be friends. Like *Friends*," he said.

"Friends." It even sounded funny after saying it so much.

"So?"

"And this is totally platonic?"

"Platonic," he confirmed, optimistically. "Yes."

She thought about it. "Platonic," she said again. That was another funny sounding, *new* word. "Platonic," she repeated. It felt more uncomfortable the more she said it.

She knew what friends were and she knew what platonic meant. But what she didn't understand was how or even why the two of them would incorporate either of those words into their lives with regard to each other.

So she told him, "Honestly? I really don't think that a friendship between us would work out."

"Why?"

"Because." She sighed. "I just don't think it's a good idea to do something like that after something like this." She didn't really know what to call it.

"Have you ever tried?"

She didn't have to think about it, but she hesitated to answer as if she did.

"Can't say that I have."

"Then how do you know it won't work?" he asked.

"Because I know…"

"You scared?"

"Scared of what?"

"Scared that it might."

She said, "I just know it won't. Okay?"

She was irritated now, and uncomfortable.

"Can you open the door, please?"

He looked at her, almost trying to see if she was serious.

She was.

A part of him was upset. Another part disappointed—in himself. A third part: angry—with her. He was embarrassed. But with all those parts put together, he still couldn't do anything about her decision. So he pulled the door open and let her walk out. He didn't even look at her one last time.

Who is Jaye Cobain?"

"What?" was all J could say as she tried to buy herself some time to think of a lie to tell her friend who sat on the couch staring across the room awaiting an answer to her question.

J walked into her house that morning after her night out, dropped her keys into her open purse, then tossed the purse onto the couch as she made her way upstairs to the bathroom, stripping. She washed away the faint smell of *Contradiction*. He wore only enough that night to be smelled by a hug recipient. Calvin Klein was all over her.

J bought herself three, maybe even five seconds when she asked, "What?" to the question Ty asked.

"Right here in the paper," Ty said, holding up the Arts section. "I've heard that name Jaye Cobain and… What's the other one?" She searched the paper to find the name.

"Keyon Braxten," J's other friend, Kenya, answered. "They just opened up a gallery in Georgetown." Kenya continued flipping through the pages of the latest *FACE Magazine* she'd picked up from J's coffee table.

"You know them?" Ty asked her.

"Well we have the same publicist. I bought some art from them once, about a year ago." She turned another page and said, "Real nice guys."

"And cute too," Ty added, handing Kenya the newspaper so she could see the picture.

J stood in the kitchen listening to the conversation, wanting to say something only so she wouldn't look like she wasn't saying anything. But she really wasn't in the mood. Her friends were at her house in Arlington, Virginia, just outside of DC. The three of them had planned to hang out that Sunday because they rarely saw each other these days. Tylia Aldridge worked a few miles north of DC toward Baltimore and she'd just started a practice with another psychotherapist, so she almost never had time. And Kenya Shaw was a music business executive; she ran a burgeoning independent record company.

J was two years younger than Ty and a year older than Kenya, and the three had virtually been sisters for the past ten years or so. They were the only family J had in the area, so she valued her relationship with them.

But despite the fact that they were family and knew more about her than she probably knew of herself, last night was a secret. Normally, she wouldn't care if they knew. Sometimes she would even tell them a story like this as if to brag about a conquest—'cause that's what guys were to her: conquests. But this time she didn't feel like it. She didn't feel proud. It felt more like a mistake. She might've even been embarrassed.

"J, didn't you go to the opening last night?" Kenya asked.

J continued searching the refrigerator for something and acting as if she didn't hear her.

"J," she called again.

J stood up straight with a small apple juice bottle in her hand and said, "Huh?"

"I said didn't you go to this gallery opening last night?"

"You interviewed them?" Ty asked.

J sipped her drink and thought fast. "Yeah, I went," she said.

They waited for her to say more. Ty even asked, "And?"

J was actually nervous. She started tapping her hand on the counter in the kitchen. "And," she said. "And it was nice."

Ty looked at Kenya who noticed too, but neither knew what they noticed. Now they were confused.

"The hell is wrong with you?" Kenya asked J.

She sighed. She grabbed up her apple juice from the counter and walked toward the living room where her friends sat.

"Nothing," she lied.

"Jesenia," Ty said, noticing the lie. She called J by her full first name. Nobody ever called her by that name except her mother.

"I don't wanna talk about it."

Ty concluded, "So it is something."

"Look, it's nothing. Seriously," J assured. "What ya'll tryin' to eat?"

Neither answered and neither planned to answer until J told them what was wrong. So they all sat there in silence. J, now relaxed on the couch pretending to care about what might be on TV, flipped through cable channels. Ty finished reading the article about Jaye and Keyon. And Kenya continued looking through the magazine.

Sick of the silence, J sighed and then blurted, "Something happened."

They let her finish.

"I was gonna tell you. Later," she said. "It was an accident."

"What was an accident?" Ty asked.

J furrowed her brow, thinking about how she was going to put this. She didn't want it to sound like what it really was, but there really wasn't any other way to package it. It was what it was.

"I was with him last night," she admitted, uncomfortably.

Ty asked, "With who?"

J thought about him: one second, she remembered watching him leave the gallery; the next second, she remembered finding him on a milk crate; the third second she was sitting in front of him; the fourth, they were strolling along the streets of Georgetown. And by the time ten seconds had gone by, she still hadn't figured out how exactly, from the sidewalk that night, she ended up in his bed that morning.

"Jaye," she answered. "I was with him last night."

Ty looked confused.

Kenya was shocked. She even had trouble exhaling. She scratched her head and asked, "Ahh… Jaye *Cobain?*"

J nodded. "And it's crazy… You know one-night stands ain't my thing."

"They aren't?" Kenya asked, joking—a little bit.

J shot her what was supposed to be a scornful glare, but she couldn't help but crack a smile at the joke herself. She thought about the situation for a moment as the smile slid from her face. She said, "I don't regret it though." She looked at the floor and not at her friends.

"Should I even ask why?" Kenya said, thinking that J would say something about the goodness of the experience with the chocolate Adonis.

"Well…" J thought and answered honestly, "I noticed that he looked miserable. Upset about something. I wanted to cheer him up."

Kenya said, "Yeah, I bet you cheered him up aw'right."

Finally, the laughter had come into their conversation. They joked about the situation now, even though J didn't mean the comment in the way that Kenya thought.

"So what are you now? Like the superwoman of sex or something?" Kenya asked, still laughing. "Do you, like, fly around and make sure the sexual needs of every man are met? You're like the sex defender of the world."

J said, haughtily, "Aye, I do what I can."

"You should advertise," Kenya said. Then she started

talking like an infomercial: "If you've been injured in a car accident, are experiencing the effects of a bad divorce, or have problems getting it up, call '1 800 J' for professional sexual healin'."

"Hey, that's an idea," J said, only partially joking.

They all laughed. Then they sighed concurrently.

"But seriously," J said. "Something was bothering him. I never found out what it was, but we talked for a while—off the record. Haven't even written my damn story yet."

Was it his innocence? His soft-spokeness? His benevolence?

"So you talked to him. Are you gonna talk to him again?" Ty asked. She knew the answer to her question; she just wanted to see if her friend would perhaps surprise her this time.

Though J didn't go around having one-night stands all the time, she had had similar encounters before—once or twice in college and another time when she was about 23. Truthfully, they weren't her style. A bit too risky. But even though one-night affairs weren't very prevalent in her life, she still lived by an unwritten one-night stand rule: she could never intend to be any more to the person than just a one-time hit. So she never spoke to the guys after that night. It just wasn't right.

"Mmm…" J hummed. "Last night wasn't supposed to be what it was. But it was," she said. "I've never slept with somebody and then tried to make something of it. What happened last night…" She paused to think. "What happened last night should remain just that—a thing of the past. It is what it is—a one-night stand—and it should be treated as such."

"Says who?"

Kenya and Ty didn't quite understand what J had meant when she said that last night wasn't supposed to be what it was, and they weren't familiar with this apparent "Rules of a One-Night Stand" book from which J continuously quoted. Neither Kenya nor Ty had had one before, but they were quite sure that there were not actually specific rules that applied to this game. Who said something couldn't be made out of what was supposed to be nothing?

J said, "That's just the way it is."

"That's just the way it is," Kenya repeated, almost disappointed about her friend's whole basis for not talking to the guy again. Knowing J though… she wasn't surprised.

* * *

Monday morning.

Jaye left the house headed for the gallery. He had planned to get there at ten, but it took him a little longer than usual to get out of bed and dressed this morning. Long weekend. His cell went off as soon as he locked the door. The display showed a picture of Meka, so he immediately answered the phone before it had the chance to ring any longer.

"Shouldn't you be in school?" he asked, not bothering to greet her.

"See, I'm not feeling well and you're being mean," she said.

He felt badly about attacking her. "Wha'sup with you?"

"Monthly stuff," she told him. "Hey, did you get the pictures?"

He smiled. "I got the pictures. I can't believe Ma let you cut your hair," he said.

Meka had gone from a typical 16-year-old hairdo—shoulder length, which she usually wore in a ponytail—to a shorter cut, worn down and bent on the ends from the previous night's wrap. She was chocolate like her brother and had the same dark eyes, same nose and full lips. She pretty much looked like a girl version of him, except she had her mother's short height.

He still couldn't believe how grown up his baby sister looked.

"Jaye, she's the one that cut it for me. She told me you was gon' be trippin'."

Jaye just continued walking. He didn't say anything else about it, but he couldn't believe how "adult" she was starting to look.

Meka said, "You know I can't wait to get down there and away from her."

Jaye smiled thinking about their mother.

"Did she ever nag you like she does me?" she asked.

"I was good," Jaye said.

"I'm good!" Meka proclaimed. "I got all A's and two B's on my report card this time. *And* my drama club gave me an award for best actress."

"Are you serious?!" Jaye asked, excited. "You didn't tell me that. That is so good! I'm so proud of you, Meek."

"Yeah, well, your mother told me that I need to focus more on bringin' those B's up instead of playin' around on the stage. This is my career we're talkin' about."

Jaye smiled at Meka's comment. "She doesn't mean any harm."

"Yeah right."

Walking the same streets he had a couple nights ago with J brought back memories. Good memories and bad memories. But he was on the phone with his baby sister, so he ignored the fact that he was starting to feel like turning around and going back home.

"I can't wait for you to come visit either," he told her. "I want you to see the gallery in person."

"I bet it's nice," Meka said. "The walls aren't white, are they?"

He smiled and said, "Gray."

"Yeah, you never liked plain white walls."

"Nope," he confirmed. "Only white canvases."

Meka sighed and said, "So… How are *you* doing?"

"I'm cool," he said, now standing outside of the gallery. He had answered quickly, almost missing her real question. He thought about what she really meant and he realized that the question wasn't as surface-level as he thought. He began to understand the tone of her question. He understood what she was asking him. He then said, "I'm… I'm get'n by, Meek."

Though Meka couldn't see him, she saw right through him. She only asked how he was doing just to hear what he would say. She knew the answer to her question just by how he acted—his tone. She knew he wasn't "cool." And she simply settled for the answer, "Get'n by."

She said, "Okay, Jaye."

He stood there listening to the silence over the phone, hating the fact that it was interrupted by the sound of buses and cars and walkers-by.

She said, "Look, that's my other line…"

"I thought you were sick."

"I never said that." She laughed and said, "Bye Jaye."

"Bye TaMeka."

Jaye walked in and greeted his potential customers and window shoppers as he made his way to the back to his office. This was his first real "workday."

"Good morning Mr. Cobain. You have…"

"Hold up. Wait," he said. "I told you that you can call me Jaye. Mr. Cobain is my grandfather," he said to his gallery manager.

Linda was a 34-year-old with seven years of motherhood experience and fifteen years of office management expertise. She was new to art, but she had already proven to Jaye and Keyon that she was able and willing to be more than just a helping-hand in Black Girl. Every minute they were there that hectic opening weekend she was there with them.

She smiled and said, "I'm sorry. *Jaye*. You have two messages. Your publicist called. Ebony Brown is coming Thursday. And Meka called. She said to call her back…"

"I just talked to her," he informed. He smiled at the thought of Meka.

"Hi. May I help you?" Linda asked, looking past Jaye at whom she thought was an approaching patron.

He hadn't noticed that someone was approaching the desk from behind him. He looked back just as J said, "No. I've found what I was looking for," referring to him.

"What are you doing here?" he asked, continuing his walk toward his office. "You need to get somethin' for your little magazine?"

She followed him.

"No." She waited until they got behind the door to say the rest. "I don't need anything for the magazine. Thank you."

He didn't say anything to her. He wanted to look like he

was busy, so he stood up behind his desk and began fumbling through some papers. He didn't really want to look at her. He was embarrassed because he felt he had played himself by asking her to be friends. He realized how stupid it must've sounded.

She noticed that he had cut the cute little bush she remembered from the other night; now he was nearly bald.

"Short hair is a good look for you."

"So why are you here again?" he asked.

She just stood looking at him, waiting for him to look up from the desk. After a few seconds of silence, he looked at her to see what was taking her so long to answer, or leave.

"Can we talk?"

He looked at her as if he were expecting a punch line.

"What are you talkin' about?"

"Well I... I want to apologize to you," she said. "For the way I acted the other day."

He looked down at the desk again as if a response might've been there on one of those papers. He thought about it.

"Apology accepted."

"Look, I wanna give this thing a try," she said. "If you still do."

He looked at her trying to see if he could detect an ulterior motive in her eyes; he tried to decipher the reason for her visit. He couldn't tell whether it carried the same weight in sincerity as his proposition or whether she had changed her mind for some other reason.

He thought about it as he looked back down at the desk.

"That's okay." He looked back up at her: "Shit happens," he said. He shrugged his shoulders. "I'm a big boy. I can live with that." He had grown to accept his mistake. "We ain't gotta be cool."

She had come to the gallery not expecting to really make a long-term friend, but to simply be able to say to herself—and Kenya—that she had tried. She was willing to try it.

"I know we don't have to be," she said. "But come on, it's worth a try. Can we give it a try?"

He didn't know what to think of her visit, but he didn't want to be a part of whatever her reason was for changing her mind.

"No thank you."

She was sure he would still be that nice, guilty guy from the other day who would do anything to erase the thought of something like this out of his mind. Apparently, she was wrong.

"So what are you saying?"

He said, "I'm saying… that I'm not interested in a friendship—in anything—with you. Anymore."

His comment had insulted her and he could see the excuse-the-hell-outta-me look on her face, so he said: "Look, you were right—a friendship between us would never work." He waited for her to respond. She didn't, so he added, "Why even waste our time?"

She knew he was right. But she never had a guy propose friendship though. What was friendship like? Where would it go? She was so curious to know. But she wasn't going to find out now.

"Look… I have a lot of work to do here." His way of telling her to leave. He was finished talking about a friendship that was never going to happen. It was time to move on.

K

enya's Memorial Day cookout had officially begun two hours ago and already the place was nearing crowded. Guests occupied the chairs—drinking, talking, and eating. Caterers worked the grills, preparing food for the people that were there and the ones expected to come, and the bartenders were already mixing up drinks that consisted of hard liquor and tropical fruits even though it was just after 3 o'clock in the afternoon.

"Jaye. Keyon," Kenya said as she made her way over to them. Her long, thick, dark brown hair flowed like the girls' in the commercials, and her milk chocolate complexion was flawless. She wore a summer dress that showed off just enough of her fairly fit frame, and the heels on her sandals boosted her to 5'6".

Jaye took her hand and said, "Kenya, it's nice to see you again." He leaned in and kissed her cheek.

Keyon agreed as he gave her a hug and kiss too. "When are you coming to the gallery to spend some more money?"

She smiled and said, "I'll be there, believe me." She saw Ty and signaled for her to come over. "I made plans to go this Thursday, but I gotta go outta town."

Keyon watched Kenya's friend as she made her way over to them with a smile decorating her delightful face.

"This is Ty," Kenya said, placing her hand on Ty's shoulder as soon as she approached. "One of my best friends. Ty this is…"

"Keyon," he said taking Ty's hand. He was immediately taken. He noticed Ty's naked ring finger. He also noticed that she had a gorgeous golden complexion almost the color of honey. He noticed that she wasn't thin, but couldn't be considered heavyset either; her height was average too. He noticed her naturally curly black hair, which she wore pinned to the back, and her beautiful baby-like adorable face that seemed to stand out because of the hairstyle. She wore little make-up. Not much jewelry. And all the right colors to make her glow. Breathtaking.

She shook his hand and said, "Nice to meet you," while still smiling.

"The guys from the newspaper," Kenya reminded.

"Oh yeah!" Ty remembered. "The artists. Okay."

"I'm Jaye," he said, shaking her hand. "Nice to meet you."

She examined Jaye since she already knew something about him. He was beautiful. That was the only word that could come to her mind to describe him. It had nothing to do with his physical appearance, though physically he was attractive; she was going by his energy and aura. She got a very good vibe from him. Both of the guys.

Kenya said, "There's tons of food in the back—burgers, seafood… Help yourself," she said to them. "I gotta make my rounds."

"Okay," Jaye said, smiling.

Kenya walked off and when he looked back at Keyon, he was indulged in conversation with Ty already.

He went to the back where most of the guests were— dancing to the music as the DJ mixed it up, eating and drinking, and conversing with others whom they had just met or hadn't seen since mayba last year's cookout. He decided to take Kenya's advice and get a plate, but before he made it over to where the food was, he saw *her* across the yard talking to a guy. The guy was awkwardly tall and lean like a basketball player, but not one Jaye recognized. And he looked older than her. At least ten years older than her.

He walked over to the buffet with his mind already made up. He glanced over at J and the guy who were just feet away from the food; she had her back turned so she didn't notice him. He still couldn't believe her. How self-centered could the woman be? She wasn't interested in anything when he asked, but he was supposed to jump at her offer, which he didn't trust. He didn't understand where this sudden change of heart had come from. But he didn't think too much about it. He really didn't care. And he wouldn't have been surprised if she was only coming back for that story. That's how condescending he assumed she was.

He got a burger, some potato salad, macaroni and cheese, and a soda. He sat at a table where there were already four women sitting, eating, and saying, "That is my *song*" to almost every record the DJ played. The only thing he noticed was the vacant seat; he didn't realize the company he'd be keeping.

As he concentrated on his plate, the conversation between the four women ceased. All eyes were on Jaye. They watched for a moment as he slowly and lazily scooped up some macaroni.

After looking up and noticing that his presence was probably an intrusion on what was probably "girl-talk" amongst the four of them, he spoke:

"Ahh… Hi."

"Hi," one of the women said.

She sat facing him on the opposite side of the table. He immediately assumed that she was the most outspoken of the four. But this was probably only because she spoke first.

"What made you wanna join in on our boring little conversation? Especially with all of these celebrities floatin' around here."

"Ahh… Actually, I just wanted a place to eat. I wasn't tryin' to join in your conversa-"

"It's okay," she said, smiling.

He forced a smile.

"I'm Simone," she said reaching over to get his hand. She immediately reminded him of Queen Latifah. Same face and everything; a hairstyle similar to one Queen would have, and she was sharply dressed. Because he thought Queen was pretty, he thought the same about this girl.

He said, "I'm Jaye Cobain," and took her hand.

They held hands while exchanging "Nice to meet yous" and smiles.

"I'm Heather," the lady to Simone's right said. She practically took Jaye's hand from Simone's.

"Hi Heather."

Heather had short hair, a tall frame, a light brown skin tone, and was thin—model thin.

"You wouldn't happen to be Jay*Mahr* Cobain, the artist, would you?" the lady sitting beside him on the right asked. This lady was obviously older than the others; she looked to be about 40. She too had short hair and light brown skin, but this woman was noticeably short in stature.

"Yeah," he said. "That's me."

"Wow. It is a *pleasure* to meet you," Heather said, more excited now by the guy who was not only incredibly good-looking, but was an incredibly good-looking celebrity of sorts. "I've been dying to come to your gallery to see what all the talk is about."

"I've been," said the woman to his left. She hadn't said anything the entire time he was there. She was an Asian woman. Chinese-American, actually; she didn't have an accent.

"Oh yeah?" he asked.

"Yeah," she said. "I purchased a print called 'Sunday Morning.' I have it in my office at work. It's the only piece I have up."

Somewhat of a blush struck his face because "Sunday Morning" was one of his pieces.

"Thank you," he said.

He took another bite of his burger and proceeded to indulge in conversation with the four ladies.

Across the yard, J continued counting to five in her head,

then smiling and nodding. This was now her routine as she stood listening to this guy who wouldn't stop talking. Well, she wasn't actually listening, that's why she had developed this whole "count to five, then nod" routine.

"That's why I usually drive one of my trucks instead of a car. I just got this complex about being low to the ground when I'm riding for a long time."

She sighed and said, "Look, Todd…"

"My name is Sean," he said.

She frowned. "Really?"

"Yeah," he said, almost upset.

"Wow. I thought your name was Todd. You look like a Todd. Are sure your name ain't Todd?"

He didn't find that funny.

"I'm joking with you," she lied. She really had forgotten his name. "Lighten up. Look, I have your number. I'm gonna call you."

He smiled.

"Look, I got some people I need to talk to. I'll call you."

"Okay," he said. "I'll talk to you later, J."

She sighed and walked away. She then looked over at the table where those four women were. And there *he* was—laughing and talking to them. *What could he have to talk about with them?* He seemed like one of those types of guys, she thought—the type that has women falling all over him. Little did they know. *Stupid ass bitches.*

"I'm Lisa Tsung," the Chinese woman said, shaking his hand. "CEO of L. Tsung Entertainment. We're an artist management company."

"Pretty successful, huh?"

"Very," she said. "We represent four multi-platinum bands, three rappers, and countless singers."

"Mm," he hummed, impressed by what he'd heard.

"Which is why you *must* give me a *personal* tour of your gallery someday," she said, handing him a business card with her personal phone number on the back. "I have a few walls that are in desperate need of redecorating. And what better way to decorate than with the work of America's premier artist."

"I wouldn't say all that," Jaye replied, modestly.

"I would," the older one said. "I've been dying to get to DC so I can visit."

"You should," he said. "My partner and I would love to have your business."

"Your partner," Heather said. "Is he *half* as fine as you are?"

Jaye blushed. "I don't... I don't know..."

"Are you single?" Simone asked. "I mean I'm just asking."

"Ahh... Yeah. I am."

"You mean to tell me that with all this success you've been having lately," Heather said, "and as *fine* as you are... You haven't been snatched up yet?"

Blushing more, he said, "Can't... say that I have."

"That's too bad," Lisa said with a phony look of pity mixed with seduction on her face. "What are you doing later?"

J went over to the bar area and got another bottle of Smirnoff Ice. She drank it straight from the bottle as she reluctantly glanced over at the table where Jaye sat with the women—all of who seemed to be taken by every word that left his mouth.

Bastard.

She couldn't believe what he had done. She had gone to his gallery—used her lunch break too—just to extend her hand in friendship. She went out of her way just to apologize to him for being impetuous with her decision to avoid trying to make things more than a one-night thing, and this bastard rejects her. She wasn't used to rejection. And she didn't like it.

"Hey girl. Wha'sup?"

J looked to her left as Salon walked closer expecting an answer to his question. Salon was J's friend from the magazine—the photo editor. He began his internship the same time she did, and both had been employees ever since they finished undergrad.

Salon epitomized a stereotypical homosexual male—exaggerated femininity: walked with somewhat of a switch, used heavy hand motions when he talked, he loved fashion and was an expert on what a woman should do with her hair.

"Not a damn thing," J answered once Salon was closer. "Finally got away from that motor mouth ass guy. He talks *too* damn much."

Salon laughed. "Girl, I saw you over there talkin' to him and I wanted to bail you out, but… I didn't know. I mean he *was* fine as hell."

"As *hell*," J agreed. "But I can't be fuckin' a brotha who can't shut the hell up. I don't wanna hear that shit."

Salon laughed harder.

J sipped her drink and shook her head, disgusted with the whole situation as she kept her eyes on the women at the table with Jaye.

Out of nowhere, he said, "Oh, I meant to tell you—you are lookin' *fierce* this evenin', Ms. Girl."

J chuckled at the compliment.

"Yes," he said looking her up and down. "And you are workin' those shoes, honey."

"Thank you, Salon."

She sipped her drink again and inadvertently glanced back at the table. For a few seconds, Salon watched with her.

"Who is that?" he asked. "Your latest prey?"

She shook her head. "No." She paused for a moment, then said, "*Hell* no."

She hadn't told Salon the story of her and Jaye and she hadn't planned to. Yeah, Salon was close enough to her for her to call him a friend, but she didn't tell him all of her personal business like she did, say, Kenya and Ty. Salon wasn't on that level and never would be. Not too many people were.

"He's… He's just somebody I know. Nobody special."

"Mm," he hummed, pressing his lips together, giving J a "yeah right" look. "Sweetie, we don't give somebody that's nobody special *that* much stare."

"Seriously, he's nobody."

"Okay. I have to admit, though—he is definitely eye candy."

J wasn't about to deny that.

"Here's a little FYI," Salon whispered. "You see that

skinny one with that *old* Toni Braxton cut?"

J looked over and spotted her immediately.

"Her name's Heather," he continued. "If I was you and he was just somebody *I* knew… I'd advise him to stay away from her. Ms. Thing is *hot*. She's burnin' brothers, okay. And she'll fuck anything with a pulse, you hear me?"

J simply nodded her head implying that she followed him.

"Better go save your friend 'fore Ms. Heather gets her claws in him," he said.

J chortled.

Salon smiled and said, "I gotta go get myself somethin' to eat, honey. I am *starved*. I'll talk to you later, girl."

"See ya," J said as Salon switched off toward the food.

Salon didn't know it, but he had given her an idea.

She looked back over at Jaye talking to hot Heather and the gang. The women were all over him. He wasn't even all that, she thought. And for a moment she hoped things would go for Heather like they had for her the night of the gallery opening. But that could be too good for him; he might wrap it up this time.

"So," Heather asked. "Do you rent or own?"

Jaye said, "Own. Why?"

"Do you have any kids?" Lisa asked.

"No."

"Want any?" she asked.

"Of course. One day."

"You are just too much," Heather said. "Well I'm looking forward to my trip back to DC to visit you. The gallery, I mean."

He smiled. The women were a trip.

"Jaye… Where've you been?"

He looked up only to see J standing beside him. Smiling. He was so confused.

"I've been looking all over for you," she said, pretending to pick something off of his shirt. She snatched a seat from the table behind her, put it beside him and sat down.

"What?" he said.

All of the women were confused too.

"Oh, I'm sorry," J said. "I'm Jesenia," she said, as if everybody at the table should've known her.

"Who?" one of the women asked.

She looked at Jaye, smiled and said, "You mean to tell me he's been sitting here all this time and he didn't tell you about me?"

"I thought you said you came here with your business partner," Heather said.

"I'll see you all later," the older woman said as she got up from her seat. She could tell that J was not his business partner, so she decided to leave before things got out of hand. "It was a pleasure meeting you Jaye."

J smiled. One down, three to go.

"Nice to meet you too, Jesenia."

Still smiling, J said, "I know," not loud enough for the woman to hear her.

"Call me," Lisa said to him anyway as she got up and walked away too.

He didn't know what J thought she was doing, but whatever it was, he liked it.

"So what happened to your partner?" Heather asked. She didn't believe he even had a partner now.

"Keyon?"

"Could you excuse us for a moment?" J asked the last two women at the table. They seemed as if they were going to be stubborn, so she figured she had to use this assumed "girlfriend" title to her advantage to get them away.

J just continued to stare at them. She gave a look as if she was waiting for them to leave. She even used her hand to shoo them away.

Though they both had J in height, they didn't want to cause any scenes, so they got up like she asked and left. "I need to check my makeup anyway." He was fine, but he wasn't worth fighting over at Kenya Shaw's party.

J was holding her stomach in laughter as they walked away. Mission accomplished!

Jaye smiled, but he was happy for different reasons.

"Thank you," he said. "You helped me out."

"What?" She didn't quite hear what he'd said. Or at least she didn't think she did.

He said, "I didn't want to just walk away, but I didn't know how to get away from them."

The smile slowly slid off her face. "Are you serious?"

"I'm dead serious."

Disappointed, she said, "You gotta be fucking kidding me."

"I'm not playing," he said, smiling. He understood now what she was trying to do, and how she had actually helped him despite the cock-blocking she thought she was doing.

She looked away, pissed off.

He smiled harder. "But thank you so much, J. You saved me the trouble."

She was so angry. The only thing she could think of saying to him was: "Fuck you."

She got up and walked away, very pissed off now.

He shook his head as he watched her walk away. But he started to feel bad about being facetious; she didn't mean any real harm, and she had helped him out by coming over to the table, even if she didn't mean it.

He got up and went after her.

"J," he called.

"What?" she said sharply before turning around.

"Look. I'm sorry," he said. "And I'm sorry about the other day too, okay. I mean, I didn't trust your reason for coming back to my gallery."

She crossed her arms while he spoke.

"So why did you come back?" he asked. "What made you change your mind?"

She looked down at the grass around her open-toe sandals trying to find a way to say this without it sounding like it meant something else.

"Because. I guess…" She looked up at him. "Guess I wanted to know you."

He felt sincerity for real this time. He nodded his head. He appreciated that answer. He said, "I guess I wouldn't mind knowing you too."

She smiled as she thought about all they had been through already and they didn't even know each other.

"Yeah," he said, smiling. She was alright in his book now, and he let her know this in his cool, kind of hood-sophisticated way of speaking, which she found rather sexy: "You ah'ight, J. That was real clever what you did."

She said, "Aye, I'm J."

He said, "What's that supposed to mean?"

"It means I'm J."

He smiled. She had a confidence that was out of this world! "Well look," he said. "Seriously, I wanna thank you. Those women are crazy as hell. Do you know one of them felt me up underneath the table?"

J just laughed at him. She was kind of happy she'd helped him now.

"I feel so violated. It's not funny," he said. He waited until she stopped laughing to say, "You saved me."

She just looked at him. Again, something in those eyes revealed more than he probably knew. He wasn't a bad guy. He wasn't a bad person. He was new.

She said, "Okay. I'll tell you what: I'll let you hang around me for the rest of the day."

"You'd do that for me?" he asked sarcastically.

"I will," she said. "I'll keep the molesters away from you."

"Okay," he said smiling. "And I'll make sure to keep all the tall, charming, retired basketball players away from you."

She laughed. "Deal."

J aye gripped the steering wheel of his three-week-old, black SUV as he cruised through a yellow light on his way to Home Depot hoping one of those stupid hidden cameras didn't get him.

As Keyon flipped past a basketball sneaker advertisement in the latest edition of Sports Illustrated, he said to Jaye without looking up, "You've been quiet about what's her name." He finally looked over at Jaye who was concentrating on the road in front of him. "J, right?"

Keyon waited for an answer. Kenya's party was more than a month ago; he knew that Jaye and the journalist had patched things up, but how much patching, he didn't know. He wanted Jaye to tell him who this girl was.

"What?" Jaye asked. "What am I supposed to say?"

"You s'pose to tell me *some*thing."

"S'nothing to tell. I mean... We talk," Jaye revealed. "Well, we don't talk like that, but I mean we speak on the phone sometimes. She's cool."

"You went out, right?"

"We didn't go *out*. You make it sound like a date."

"You went out," Keyon said. "You left the house and went somewhere with her. You went out!"

"We went to a sports bar," Jaye said as if the arcade-bar couldn't possibly be a place people go out to. "We played air hockey, drank beer, and ate Buffalo wings for two hours." He tried to simplify the night as much as possible. "We're just cool. That's it. It's nothin'."

Keyon accepted that answer. But he still wanted to know: "What's she like?"

She was a Chicagoan who wrote about arts and entertainment for a living. She was schooled at the finest HBCU of all Historically Black Universities—The Real HU—Howard University. She traveled a bit because of her job, and she loved it. She drank beer; she liked the way it accompanied some non-special occasions. She didn't have any kids; he never asked whether she wanted any. She wasn't religious, but she wasn't an atheist either. She was single. When the topic came up, she said, "No, I'm not in a relationship thing. And no I don't wanna be." He wondered why, but neglected to get too nosey.

Every generic adjective that could describe her came to mind—beautiful, intelligent, funny, outgoing, yada yada yada... Neither of them thought a platonic friendship could be real. But it was. That was good enough though, because anything more would be much too much.

Jaye paused for a moment as he gathered his thoughts about her. All he said was, "She cool."

"Your type?"

Jaye sneered at the question. "Type?" he asked.

He had eliminated that kind of thinking from his mind because right now he didn't want to be interested in anybody.

"No," he answered. "She's not."

He didn't explain why, and Keyon didn't bothering asking. He just looked back down at his magazine and left the situation alone.

* * *

J was the last to arrive at the restaurant, and she took her seat seeming exhausted.

"Starvin'. I think I'ma get the steak," she said before picking up the menu.

"Steak for lunch?" Kenya asked.

"Yes, steak for lunch. And speaking of lunch," J said. "You remember that guy Sean?"

Ty asked, "The one you kept calling Todd to piss him off?"

"Yeah, well, I found out that he knows how to use his tongue for more than just running his mouth."

Ty looked around to make sure no one overheard what J said.

J sighed and said, "I needed that."

"The guy from my party? I thought you didn't like him?"

"Girl's gotta eat. I'll have the filet mignon with the potatoes," she said to the waiter. "And I want it done well."

Ty stared at J, somewhat embarrassed by her outspokenness. She ordered, "Crab cake, no bread. House salad."

Kenya ordered grilled salmon and asparagus.

"So… How's your man doing?" she asked.

J sighed and gave her friend a look that said that she didn't appreciate the comment.

"Oh, excuse me, your *friend*," Kenya joked. "The one you've been hanging out with."

"Talkin' bout Jaye?" J rolled her eyes. "We don't hangout."

"You say that, but I bet you'd be jealous if he was hangin' out with some other chick?"

"Jealous? Look at me," she said, arrogantly. "J ain't got a damn thing to be jealous about. He and I are just friends," J said. "He can do what he wants, cuz you *know* I'm gon' do what *I* want."

"*Who* you want," Ty corrected.

"Damn right," J said.

Kenya and Ty both laughed at their friend. It wasn't surprising to either one of them because for as long as they had known J, she'd been this way. She called it: "dating like a man."

"Men do this shit all the time," she'd say. "They lead you on, get your head all in it and shit, and then what? Fuck you and bounce. Fuck that. I'm gettin' what I want from these guys and I'm out. I'm doin' what they do."

And that's exactly what she had been doing. J was 30 and hadn't had a serious relationship since... Well actually, she had never had a serious relationship. And as far as she was concerned, she never would.

"Speaking of which, Ty... How're things with you and Keyon?" J asked.

Ty smiled. Then she started to turn all pink in the face. She leaned forward and sipped her soda, trying to cover up her giggles and grins.

"Things are good. Great, actually."

"Mm. *Great,*" J said. "'Great' is generally an adjective used to describe..."

"Well I'm using 'great' to describe the *friendship* that we've established these last couple of weeks," Ty said. "Nothing sexual."

J smiled. "So is that the thing now-a-days—friendships?"

"Well I don't know about everybody else, but Keyon and I ain't playing no games. If things continue to go the way they're going, hopefully we'll have a beautiful and intimate relationship someday."

"Well excuse me," J said, smiling, happy for Ty. Playfully, she asked, "Don't you think you're moving too fast?"

Ty smiled and said, "Fast? No. You're just moving too slow. Actually, you're not moving at all, J."

The conversation was still light—not as playful anymore, but it hadn't turned into an argument. Kenya simply listened to this conversation, not interrupting, because she wanted to see where this was going.

"And what is that supposed to mean?" J asked.

"It means you're almost middle-aged and you've never had a serious relationship." She exaggerated J's age to help with her point. "You've finally met a man who obviously likes you, and who you like for reasons other than just sex, but you wanna play this... *stupid* ass game to 'get all the *brothas* before they get you'."

Ty shook her head, almost waiting for J to respond. She didn't.

"When are you going to just... just stop being scared and be loved?"

Ty waited again. No response.

"Ask Kenya," she said. "Love is a wonderful thing, ain't it?"

"A *wonderful* thing," Kenya agreed, nodding, despite not being in it herself.

"And you're scared that it's gonna hurt you."

"Love ain't *shit*, okay. I've seen you in relationships—motha-fuckas just downright disrespectin' you, cheatin' and lyin' and shit. I've seen people fall in love and get hurt and I ain't lettin' that shit happen to me."

"Let me tell you something: love ain't do a damn thing to me," Ty said. "Love don't hurt people. *People* hurt people."

J said, "Yeah, well I'm not gonna let *people* hurt me. Okay? I need to wash my hands."

* * *

"Are you a playa now, Jaye?"

"What?" The question caught him off guard. He had no idea what Meka was talking about, or even where that question had come from. They were barely in the house and she was asking off-the-wall stuff.

She was out of school for the summer and in DC to spend the remainder of her vacation with her brother. After he picked her up from the airport that morning, they went everywhere. She had never been to DC, and he almost showed her the entire city in one day. She met a lot of people he knew.

She said, "You seem to know a lot of women."

Jaye smiled—modestly though. "I have a lot of female friends," he said. "But you gotta understand that people treat me a little differently now that they wrote about me in the paper."

She smiled. She appreciated his humility. She still had questions though.

"That woman who was talking about different tints of blue… She was really into you."

He said, "Okay," heading to his bedroom, taking his shoes off. He hadn't noticed what Meka noticed. All he knew was that the woman was a wiz when it came to interior design and she was going to help him redo his basement. He couldn't handle a project of that caliber without help.

"So you never answered my question," Meka said. She was standing at the bedroom door still waiting for answers. He was sitting on the bed taking his socks off.

"No, Meka, I'm not a playa."

He laughed again because to him that question was funny.

Me? A playa? he thought. He couldn't imagine himself even living such a lifestyle. That wasn't his thing.

"Then who was that woman?"

"A friend, *Ma*."

"Don't call me that."

"Well that's who you're actin' like," he said. He got up and put his socks in the hamper, and proceeded barefoot. "She's a friend."

Meka didn't believe that.

"She's going to be helping me with the basement. She knows a lot more than I do about that stuff."

He went into the kitchen and washed his hands before opening the refrigerator.

Meka followed him.

"So that J girl that came into the gallery today—who is she?"

He smiled. "You're a trip," he said. He knew Meka would inquire more about J. That was her job. "I told you, she's a friend of mine, too."

Meka quickly realized that he would probably say she was the friend who was helping him with maybe the living room. "How long ya'll been *friends*?"

"Mmm… Couple months," Jaye answered.

"You sure have a lot of friends."

He said, "I'm a friendly guy."

"Mm-hmm," Meka hummed in distrust.

Trying to change the subject quickly, Jaye said, "We're going to the movies tonight to check out that new Kung-fu joint right?"

But Meka wasn't off the subject. She said bluntly, "I don't like her," referring to J.

Meka was always very straight forward with Jaye. He wasn't one that read between the lines very well, so when she wanted him to know something, she let him know.

"You don't even know her," he said.

"I know I don't like her," Meka answered. "She just had this attitude."

"What attitude? I didn't notice any attitude."

"Mm. There's a lot you don't notice."

His sister's older-than-her-age attitude was always funny to him.

"What is that supposed to mean?" he asked, still smiling.

She was smiling too when she said, "It's not funny, Jaye. I'm serious."

"I know you are. I just wanna know what you mean—there's a lot I don't notice."

"I have to point out everything to you," she said. "I have to look out for you cuz you don't know no better."

He laughed.

"You *don't*," she insisted.

The smile slowly disappeared from his face. He thought

about what Meka had just said. Once a woman was in, it was easy for her to steal his heart. Well, it wasn't actually stealing because usually he gave it to them willingly.

He smiled to cover up the fact that perhaps Meka knew what she was talking about.

"Look, Meek... I'm not about to be in a relationship with anybody right now," he said. "I'm just not ready for that."

She didn't say anything else to him about the women because she knew why he didn't want to be with anybody at the time. She just stood there watching her brother as he searched inside the refrigerator for God knows what.

"Well I'm glad you're taking this slowly, Jaye. I really am," she said. "Cuz I don't like to see you hurt. You're a nice person. And people know that. These girls," she said, "can see that." She let him think about it for a moment before she added, "But that's okay though. That's what makes you *you*."

He thought about what she was saying and how true it was.

"I don't wanna have to shank one of these broads."

He burst into laughter. He said, "Listen to you." She was funny, but he was happy to hear her passion to be protective of him.

"You know I will," Meka said, smiling.

"Yeah, I'm sure you will, Jersey girl." He was still laughing. "So what do you want to eat tonight?" he asked.

Meka sucked her teeth and said, "I don't know. Won't you get one of your women to come over here and cook for us?"

He closed the refrigerator and grabbed her and started tickling her. "Real funny, big head."

* * *

Dana Mitchell was ten when she met Hasaan Cobain. He was twelve. A boy from around the way—stayed a few blocks up from where she and her family lived in East Orange, New Jersey. They became boyfriend and girlfriend when she was fourteen, and she got pregnant when she was fifteen.

Hasaan had a job at a local barbershop sweeping floors and answering telephones for under-the-counter money, and occasionally he would make a few "runs" for the guy who owned the place. But when Hasaan was going to have a family to take care of, fifty or so dollars a week just wasn't going to suffice; he needed more money so his girl and new baby could live comfortably. He dropped out of school and took over a couple of corners, which put hundreds of dollars into his pockets every week.

Dana gave birth to a seven-pound baby boy that July. They named him JayMahr Cobain. Hasaan added "mahr" to Jay as reverence to Islam, despite being estranged from the religion most of his life. He had been promoted by the time his son was born, and in just a few years, he grew from a small-time errands boy, to a local dealer, to one of Jersey's biggest pushers. And though they had an on again off again type of relationship—real rocky—he and Dana were married on a warm summer afternoon.

Several years later, Dana was pregnant again, but Hasaan wouldn't even see the child born.

He went to a convenience store one Friday night to get milk for Jaye's breakfast, and Blunts for his.

"You want anything?" he asked Jaye, who sat in the passenger's seat playing with a plastic water gun.

Jaye looked up at his dad sitting across from him in the driver's seat. He wanted candy. He wanted popcorn. Soda…

"Don't spray that stuff. It'll mess up the leather," Hasaan warned, as he prepared to run in the store for his grocery.

"I want cand…" Jaye looked over at the side mirror watching the figure get closer by the split-second.

A guy dressed in regular street clothes—black jeans and a red t-shirt with a red bandana around his mouth—walked up to the car. And without saying a word, he lifted a small handgun and shot twice into the driver's seat. His movements were mechanical. His face was filled with madness. His wrath left blood all over the leather interior. And all over Jaye.

Jaye didn't understand the severity of what had just happened. But he lifted his little toy gun—disregarding what his father had just told him—aimed it at the goon and shot twice, hoping that it would have the same effect on him as his seemed to have on his father.

It didn't.

For years he didn't cry. Despite years of psychological therapy when he was a boy, it wasn't until he was a freshman in college that it really hit him. That's when he really understood who his father was; he was Hasaan Cobain, the kingpin. It was then he realized *what* his father was—a drug lord. And it was then that he realized his father would never see him become a father. Sometimes he hated his dad for being selfish and bringing death upon himself. Sometimes he just missed him and wished that he could be there to help him be a man. Many nights, he lay in his room at college alone and cried himself to sleep.

So how did you celebrate turning the big 3-0?" J asked, as she walked over and handed him the birthday dinner she'd prepared—fast food burger and fries on a plate.

He sighed as if his day had been too long and took a seat on the floor. He said, "I'm celebratin' right now. It's just the day after July 19th."

"None of your girlfriends from Kenya's party called you up to take you out?"

"Very funny." He gave a fake smile and mumbled, "Bringin' up that old stuff."

Out of sheer curiosity—or maybe just nosiness—J asked, "What's up with you, Jaye?"

"What do you mean? I couldn't be better. I've got my health. And my hair." He smiled at his own silliness.

She said, "No, I mean... How come you don't have a girlfriend?"

He shrugged. "I don't know," he said. "Girls don't like me."

J gave him a look that said she expected the truth. And she knew that wasn't it.

He said, "I guess I'm…"

She wanted him to say more. He always said very little.

"I don't know, J. I guess I'm just movin' really really slow. I ain't really tryin' to… get into anything right now, you know."

J looked at her food, which she hadn't touched yet, then back over at him. She had another question, but she almost didn't want to ask. She didn't know whether he wanted to talk about that right now.

To her, Jaye seemed like the type of guy who would find that woman who was right for him and eventually, one day, get married, have kids, and live happily ever after. She knew men, and this man didn't seem scared of commitment. She couldn't imagine Jaye saying that he didn't want a relationship because he wanted to "play the field some more," because in that case, he would've been trying to take advantage of time he spent with her. But he wasn't.

She remembered how dejected he seemed when they first met, and there was a part of him that hadn't seemed to change, as if to have gotten over it—whatever "it" was. She still couldn't tell whether something had happened to him more recently in his life, or whether his traumatic past was what hindered him from being happy now. All she knew was that he seemed fragile.

As a journalist, J learned to live by the saying: "You'll never know unless you ask." So as much as she wanted to know why he felt the way he did, the more she realized that she'd probably never know unless she came out and asked him.

"Why not?"

He picked up his cup and sipped a little bit of lemonade before answering.

"Because I still don't think I'm ready t…" He sighed. "Relationships can be a bit difficult and I think I need a little more time before I get into another one."

J said, "Oh. Okay," as if she were content with that answer, though it really didn't tell her anything. She wanted to know why he felt like this. But she decided to separate herself from the *FACE Magazine* employee inside of her. She was going to be patient. She was his friend, so it would only be a matter of time before she knew, anyway. She was going to just let him tell her when he was comfortable.

"I never told you about my girlfriend." And then he corrected, reluctantly, "*Ex...* girlfriend."

Obviously, he was comfortable now.

"We started seeing each other... 'bout a year and a half ago." He took a sip of the lemonade then sat it back on the floor. "She was perfect. She was the perfect girl: smart, beautiful, funny... And she had picked me," he said with pride. "She was perfect for me. And everybody thought so. I even told her so—that I had found my perfect woman. I was what you would call 'head over heels'." He looked down at the floor between his knees.

"Keyon and I decided that we were gonna open the gallery this year. DC was definitely the place. It was a dream since college," he said. "Well, Nia—that's her name; she came here with me to look for a place and everything. I'd asked her to move to DC and she said that she would. My house was supposed to be *ours*."

He paused again.

"She was supposed to come the day before the gallery opened. She was packed." He took another sip from his cup. Sighed.

"She came. Came all the way to DC to tell me... that she wanted to be with *him*."

He hated to talk about this. Every time he thought about it his emotions would get all stirred up. He felt like he should cry. He felt mad. He sometimes felt like if he just threw a few fragile objects across the room he'd feel a little better. But it had been months. He had cried all he was going to cry, and had thrown all he could bare to break. She was gone and there was nothing he could do about it.

"Military guy. I guess she never got over him," he said. "She asked me if I thought it was possible to love two people. Equally." He stopped. Then he said, "I told her that I wouldn't know. I usually give all of my love to one person."

J wasn't used to conversations like this. She wasn't used to hearing such talk from a man.

"I never said it—out loud, I mean—but Nia was... I don't think I'll ever find that again."

J had to interject: "Jaye, I don't think anybody's perfect."

"Nia was." And he knew what J sitting across from him was thinking—that if Nia was so perfect then why wasn't she here? So he added, "She just, she made a choice that... She chose somebody other than me. It was me."

"Well..." J felt like she had to say something. "Consider it a favor. She let you go, so maybe now you can find somebody that deserves you, and who can love you the way you need to be loved."

That was all she could come up with.

He appreciated that comment, but nothing could really change his outlook. This was something that he was going to have to overcome on his own. That saying, "Time heals all wounds" hadn't lived up to its words for him.

He picked up his burger and asked, "So what's your excuse?" and took a big bite.

"What do you mean?" J asked.

He finished chewing. "I mean, I've known you for a minute now and I've yet to hear you talk about somebody you've been seeing, or somebody you're interested in, an ex... What's up?"

"That's because..."

She had thought about this before—telling Jaye some more things pertaining to her past, personal life and lifestyle, especially since they talked so much. But she always avoided it.

"That's because I don't have a man."

"Why?"

"Because..." she smiled, thinking about how she was going to phrase this: "I don't think that everything is for everybody—relationships especially. I don't think that that's for me."

A grimace appeared on Jaye's face; he didn't understand.

He was a strong believer in love—in man/woman intimate relationships—so it was surprising to hear that somebody else, especially a woman, believed the complete opposite.

"Hold on." He sat his drink on the floor beside him. "Hold on."

"What?"

"Hold up. What do you mean you don't think relationships are for you?"

"I mean…" She finished chewing her food. "Like you said earlier: relationships can be difficult," she said. "And I've seen people get hurt…"

"Wait a minute," he cut in. "You've seen *people*? Haven't you had some experiences of your own to learn from?"

"Ahh…" She smiled, guiltily, almost ashamed or embarrassed to admit to him the truth. "Well… I've never really been in a relationship," she said.

Of course she had been in relationships before, just not the type sweet little JayMahr was familiar with. J seldom kept guys around for longer than a month—two tops. "Any longer than that," she'd say, "and they're ready to start claiming a sistah. Uh uh. I'm not havin' that." She didn't want to be called anybody's "girl," and she didn't like people expecting things from her. She didn't like those responsibilities.

But she liked sex. Correction—she *loved* sex. And guys were useful; it was especially rewarding when they were constructive—could fix a car, do things around the house, etc. So to avoid the drama of a long, drawn out situation when she was ready to move on to the next best thing, she'd just cut it off four to six weeks into it. None were serious, real, *loving* relationships; none were like those "things" Jaye was used to.

"You gotta be kidding me," Jaye exclaimed. "Why not?"

She shrugged her shoulders. "I guess you can say I'm a bit pessimistic. Pessimistic and reluctant," she added, smiling. Then the seriousness came back to her face. "It's hard to… to believe in something you don't see. Something you've *never* seen. It's hard—virtually impossible—to think something might happen for you if you've seen it fail for everybody around you."

"And that's how you feel—like it'll never happen for you?"

She thought for a second.

She looked him in his eyes, fought off a smile and said, "Yes."

He noticed J's slight tomboy-like attitude—the pride and the discomfiture that consumed her when they conversed about topics that were beneath the surface. She would cover up her emotions with arrogant, quick-witted responses or jokes. She was very in touch with her masculine side, but he could see right through the façade.

She thought about what she was going to say—how she was going to explain exactly what she felt to him.

"I date," she said. "I spend time. I talk to guys, and it's like... outta all the guys I've ever spent any amount of time with... none of them have come close to helping me change my mind about the whole relationship thing. Matta' fact, they contributed to the way I feel now." She smiled and said, "I won't *say* 'never'," (even though she felt and believed 'never'). "But I will say that I just... I gotta be convinced. Whoever he is—he gotta make me *want* to change my mind." She said, "And that's gotta be a *hellava* man."

She had told him this much—enough. She had phrased it right and said it in a way that let her friend know what she thought he should know. Of course, certain feelings were left unsaid, but that was only for the best. He was a friend, but he was also one of *them*—a man. He wouldn't understand her position in the game—because that's what it was. He wouldn't understand why she made the moves she made.

"Hm." Jaye thought about what she had told him; he had one last question. "So do you *want* to be loved?"

J looked at him with somewhat of a smirk on her face. She interpreted the question as meaning, in other words, did she want to keep playing this game with a never-ending story (a wishful belief that she could one day win) or did she want to forfeit—stop playing the game all together. The truth was: she hadn't really thought about the answer to that question—whether she really wanted to be loved. So she thought quickly right then.

Her answer: "I don't know. But to be honest with you, I haven't really been looking for it."

He could appreciate her honest answer this time though. He looked at her and said, "You don't have to look for love. All you have to do is wait for it. It'll come to you."

They talked until 3 a.m. She gave him a pillow and a blanket so he could sleep on the couch or on the floor in the living room. But he wouldn't stay.

"I gotta… meet with this artist from San Francisco at eleven," he said. He was obviously sleepy, because he talked slowly and he kept yawning. "We'll probably be puttin' some of his work in the gallery."

"Okay," she said. "Good luck with that." She walked him to the door and opened it. "Guess I'll talk to you later."

"Yeah," he said, standing in the door looking at her. Out of nowhere, he said, "Gimme a hug," still sounding sleepy.

"What?!"

"Come on. Gimme a hug." He wrapped his arms around her and squeezed her tight. "I love you," he said, as innocently as a child would. "You're a good woman. And a good friend." His words were innocuous. "And I hope you find somebody that will love and appreciate you."

She had told him that a man had never loved her. That was sad to him. So he hugged her. Tightly. He wanted her to feel the love he had for her, even though it was nothing more than platonic. He loved her nonetheless.

She was speechless. Embarrassed. She blushed and said, "Thank you, Jaye. You are so sweet."

He kissed her on her forehead and said, "I'll talk to you later."

"Hey," she called, catching him before he could get too far. When he looked back: "The perfect girl?" she said, "She will choose you too."

He smiled, which made her smile. And then he took off, and she stood in the door and watched until his car was no longer in her neighborhood.

Jaye had touched her that morning. Surprised her. No man had ever told her that they loved her. That meant a lot.

Autumn was here. The leaves had already taken it upon themselves to begin jumping from the branches of the trees in a race to see who could get to the sidewalks the quickest. And the weather was nice—wind breaker weather: not *too* cool, but not at all warm.

J had just returned home from a two-day trip to Atlanta. Tired, she virtually dragged her suitcase into the house and dropped it on the floor in her bedroom. She flopped down on the bed and looked over at her answering machine to see if anybody had called while she was away. It wasn't blinking. No calls.

RIIIIIINNNG!

Just her luck. It was as if the person on the other line was across the street watching and waiting for her to come home.

She noticed a Chicago area code, but didn't recognize the number.

"Hello," she answered with a sigh.

"Hi, may I speak with Jesenia ahh… Llaureano?" a male

asked, as if he were reading her name from a piece of paper or something.

"Who's calling?" she asked.

"I'm ah... My name is Gavin Lane. Her... Well she's my sister. Can I leave a message?"

She nearly stopped breathing. It was almost as if everything was in slow motion at that point. It wasn't that she didn't know she had a brother; it was just that she had never spoken to or seen him or his... *their* sister before. Her mother didn't even tell her until she was a senior in high school that she had siblings: a brother her age and a sister two years older. But J didn't have a relationship with her father, and she didn't care about some *half* brother and sister. She certainly never bothered to try to get in contact with them.

"Hello?"

She cleared her throat. "Yeah, I'm ahh... I'm still here. This is J."

"Oh. Did I catch you at a bad time?" he asked.

"What would've been a *good* time?" she joked.

He snickered, relieved that his first impression of her didn't consist of a bad attitude.

"I know this isn't exactly the most comfortable thing for you to hear right now."

Got that right, she thought.

"But I decided to stop procrastinating and being scared and just call you," he said. "I really want to meet you and get to know you. But the other reason why I'm contacting you is to tell you that... Well our father is in the hospital."

She was silent. She didn't know what to say to that, or whether she should say anything. She didn't know whether the news required a comment. Did they want or need something? was what she wanted to know.

"I was calling to let you know, just in case you might've... wanted to... I don't know. I just thought you should know," he said.

"Well thank you... Gavin... for the thought, but..."

"It's serious." He paused for a moment, then he added, "The doctors say they're gonna have to operate. Just thought

I'd… call you in case you—y'know—might've wanted to pay him a visit. I know he would love to see you."

Her high school graduation was the last time she'd seen him. That was more than twelve years ago.

"Gavin, I don't think so."

"I mean I can't tell you that I know how you feel," he said, "because I don't."

She said, "Yeah, he was there for *you*."

"I can understand if you have some hostilities."

J didn't say anything this time, just sighed.

"If you change your mind, give me a call."

She wrote down his phone numbers—home, work, cell—and hung up the telephone with the same blank look on her face that she had when he introduced himself as her brother.

For hours that evening she thought about it. She contemplated the pros and cons of going to Chicago to visit her father in the hospital. One side of her couldn't care less; the other side wanted to be mature and do the mature thing.

She picked up her phone and called her friend on the other side of the Key Bridge.

"How was your trip?" he asked.

"Oh, it was nice." She had forgotten all about her trip to Atlanta just that quickly. "I was actually calling you to get your opinion on something."

"What is it?" Jaye asked.

"Well…" she sighed. "I yah… I received a call today from…" She even felt funny saying it. "From my brother."

"Your brother?"

"Yeah. His name is Gavin."

"So what did he want?"

"Well… He says that Michael—*our* father—is in the hospital. It's serious."

"Oh, wow. Sorry to hear that."

"He wants me to come to Chicago. He thinks Mic… My *father* wants to see me." She stopped again as she thought about it some more.

"Well?"

"Well I wanted to know whether you think I should go."

Jaye knew how she felt about her father; they had talked about this situation time after time. And though he knew she didn't *want* to hear from him that she should go, that's what she *needed* to hear.

He said, "I know it's hard to put the past behind, but that's really what you need to do in a situation like this." Knowing Jaye, she knew what his answer would be—the politically correct one.

"I knew you would say that." She paused for a moment. She had something else to ask him. "Jaye…"

"Yeah."

"Ah… Would you come with me?" She cleared her throat. "I mean… I would feel a lot more comfortable if… if you were there with me."

"Sure," he said without thinking twice.

"Your mother won't mind?"

He smiled. "My mother," he said, knowing that she was referring to Meka. "Very funny."

* * *

Marien Scott was a successful independent filmmaker from St. Louis, Missouri. He had attended Howard University for undergrad where he was a film production major; he and J met the second semester of their junior years. At the time, she was the entertainment news editor for the *Hilltop* and he had just finished a documentary on Black college life, which had been picked up by a cable television network. Nearly every paper in the DC area, college and local, did a story on him. The two of them met when she interviewed him.

Their association now? Fuck buddies. He was the ultimate fuck of fuckable buddies, and had been for at least the past nine years. Marien phoned her that night; he was in town and he wanted to "see" her.

Marien was one of very few guys that knew where J lived. Playas almost never divulge the whereabouts of their living quarters. But see, Marien wasn't being played; they had an agreement—an understanding. An arrangement. They knew where their relationship stood.

There was a knock on the door around 11:45 that night. She knew who it was. She opened the door without bothering to look through the peephole and inspected him from head to toe as he stood on the other side looking just as good as he wanted. Just like she remembered. He stood about 5'9", and was a cinnamon-colored brother. He worked out, but he wasn't very athletic. He had dark brown eyes, close cut facial hair; the hair on his head was the same. He had on khaki colored cargo pants, a white collarless cotton shirt, a pair of sporty/casual boots, and a three quarter length black leather jacket.

"You gon' let me in or are we just gon' stand here and look at each other all night?"

She smiled and stepped aside so he could come in, then closed the door behind him. She looked at him again; he actually looked *better* than he did the last time she saw him, which was about a year ago. They usually saw each other no more than thrice a year, but when they were together, nothing even mattered. He never asked her if she had a boyfriend, she never asked him whether he had a girl. Their time was their time, and the life they had outside of it was just that—the life *out*side.

He took off his jacket and laid it across the couch. He didn't bother sitting.

"Anything new with you?" he asked.

"Not really. You?" she asked.

"Mm. Workin' on a new movie. That's why I'm in town. I was actually scopin' some places here and in Baltimore where I'll be filming."

Marien had had a few movies do pretty well with the critics, but still no real blockbusters. His last film actually got him some attention in Hollywood and had a few established actors wanting to work with him, so people were looking forward to seeing what he was going to do on this next project.

"It'll prob'ly be comin' out in about a year."

"Oh," she said. "What's this one about?"

"Nothing," he said as he came toward her. "Enough talking."

Nothing else was said. They began kissing and taking off each other's clothes right there as they made their way toward the...

"Steps. Why couldn't you get an apartment like normal people?"

* * *

Elsa, her two brothers, two sisters, and her parents emigrated from Santa Ana, El Salvador when she was thirteen and settled in Chicago, Illinois. For all of her life, she lived the typical lower class lifestyle; her parents did odd jobs here and there, and when she was old enough to work, she didn't have luck finding anything better. On the bright side, she learned to speak English quite fluently, so during high school she found jobs that embraced those abilities.

By the time she was twenty, office work had become her full-time gig. She was a receptionist in a dentist's office—Dr. Michael Lane, D.D.S. She wasn't working there a whole year before she and Dr. Lane were involved in a romantic relationship. Michael was ten years older than Elsa, Black, and married with a daughter. But she was in love with him. So in love that by the very next year, she gave birth to his child.

She named her Jesenia Lorena Llaureano.

Jesenia was Elsa's first and only child. She didn't even believe she could have children; she had miscarried three times before giving birth to a healthy baby girl. The only disadvantage to this dream come true was having to raise this child by herself, which she wasn't prepared mentally or financially to do. Michael already had a family prior to his affair with Elsa and he wasn't interested in another one. Sometimes though, he'd make a birthday party or some holiday if it was convenient, or maybe a Monday if he felt like he could spare a little of his time. But it was hardly *enough* time for Jesenia to get to know him—know who he really was. So by the time she was fifteen, she stopped caring. As far as she was concerned, she didn't have a father. She had gone from calling him "Poppa," to "Pop," and eventually "Michael." Before long. . . she didn't call him at all.

* * *

They arrived in Chicago the next day just after 7 p.m., and at her mother's house by 8. Well it wasn't actually a house; she lived in an apartment, the same apartment she had been in since J was about thirteen. And the place looked the exact same as it had all those years ago. As J walked by the red box where the fire extinguisher *should've* been, she sighed and shook her head in repugnance as she always did when she passed it. She hated that place, and she hated the fact that her mother had to live there.

"Sorry I couldn't pick you up," Elsa said as her daughter and her friend walked through the door. They had caught a cab from the airport. "I just got home about an hour ago, myself. Hi," she said, grabbing Jaye's hands. "You're JayMahr."

"Yeah," he answered, smiling, though it wasn't a question.

Her mother looked just like he had imagined. She was barely five feet, not fat or thin, skin tone just a shade or two lighter than J's, and the same dark brown hair. And she spoke with an accent. She pronounced J's name with an "H" sound.

"Jesenia told me about you. She said you were really cool."

"Oh I'm cool, huh?" he asked J.

"Anyway," J said, not paying his silly question any attention. "What's that smell? What are you cooking?"

"Just spaghetti and garlic bread. It should be done. Are you hungry, JayMahr?"

"Ahh… Yeah," he said as if he didn't know whether he wanted food now or not. He wasn't really hungry, but he decided to eat just because she offered. Just to be nice.

J followed Elsa from the living room to the kitchen. And she stood by the small, quaint, oval dining table and watched her mama put the finishing touches on the marinara-soaked ground meat that simmered in the big silver pot on the front burner.

All she could come up with to ask was, "Is that ground turkey?"

Elsa looked back making sure that J was talking to her. She hadn't seen her come in behind her. "Yes," she answered. "I have to watch my diet."

J looked down at the floor, and then back over at her mother. For some reason—maybe the smell of the garlic in the air was nostalgic—as she stared at the small Hispanic woman trying to hurry-up and get the food ready, it reminded her of when she was a girl in this same apartment, hungry and tired from a long day at school (or maybe not at school), and how her mama would come in after a ten-hour workday and make what seemed to be miracles in the kitchen just to keep her stomach from growling any longer.

She remembered how bad she was when she was younger—getting in trouble at school, not going to school, smoking, staying out all night and partying, and verbally disrespecting her mother. Elsa was a soft woman—easy to get over on. There was a huge cultural barrier and J took advantage of that too. Back then, she hated her mother simply because she was a foreigner and couldn't identify with her, couldn't help her become a Black woman. She hated her mother because she had made her different; she told people to call her "J" and she formally introduced herself as Jesenia Llaureano with an American pronunciation, not ("Hes-*sen*-neh-ya Lor-deh-yah-no" as it should've been pronounced) as Elsa intended when she named her. She didn't want to be Spanish; she didn't want to speak Spanish; she didn't want to eat Spanish food…

But as a senior in high school, when she began seeing less and less of her friends, and more and more of the doctors and nurses at the local hospital because of her mother's health… She had to get her act together. As she sat by a hospital bed holding Elsa's hand and talking to her—*really* talking to her—for the first time, everyday, she saw that her mama actually wasn't that bad. J had never noticed her mother's sense of humor before. But as she lay in the hospital bed making snide comments about the food or her inability to use the "pee-pot" properly, J realized that her mama was actually quite the comedienne.

Doctors expected her to get worse. But everyday that J came to that hospital—making it her second home as she did her homework and slept there many nights—she saw Elsa get better with each passing day. Their connection as mother and daughter, and as friends, grew stronger too. And one day… Elsa was able to get up and walk out of that hospital at her own will. And to this day, J took *no* day that she had her mother alive with her for granted.

Now, they talked on the phone at least once every single day, even if just to check in with each other, and she went to Chicago at least once a month to spend time.

J stood there watching her mother as she made sure everything was turned off. She walked over and placed her hand on her shoulder. When Elsa looked up at her, J smiled, leaned over and gave her a kiss on the cheek, and then wrapped her up in her arms, hugging her tightly.

"I got it from here," J told her, letting go. She realized that her mama hadn't even taken her shoes off yet.

Elsa held her daughter's hands and smiled, so proud of her every time she looked at her.

"Go and get comfortable," J said. "I got it."

They all sat at the kitchen table eating and talking. Elsa had a lot of questions to ask Jaye because…

"You're the only guy that Jesenia has ever brought home."

He looked over at J with a smile on his face after her mother said that.

"She said that none of the guys she date are special enough to bring home. I guess she considers you to be special."

"Come on, Mama. Stop tryin' to start somethin', okay. And I told you that Jaye and I aren't dating anyway."

"Right. I'll leave him alone." She took a sip of her water, then asked J, "So you're going to the hospital in the morning?"

"Yeah. Probably around ten," she said, still reluctant.

"I'm happy you're doing this. I'm happy that you are so mature, Jesenia."

She got up and kissed J on the head, then left the dining area to wash her plate.

J was about twelve or thirteen when she realized the situation between her mama and poppa. At the time, she didn't even really like her mama, and with that she lost all respect for her, which made it easier and internally excusable to be mischievous. She couldn't understand why a woman would live *knowing* that she will never be number one in the man she loves life and be content with it. That was stupid to J.

"She's washing dishes," she said to Jaye. Louder so Elsa could hear her: "Mama, I said I got it. You can rest now."

* * *

At 10 a.m., J was at the hospital standing outside the door to Michael's room.

"I really don't wanna go in there," she whispered to Jaye.

"You want me to go in with you?"

"No." She sighed. "No. I… I gotta do this. I might as well get it over with." She sighed again. "I gotta do this," she said again, softly.

The door opened and a young man their age, tall, dressed in a gray business suite came from the room. He closed the door behind him. He was handsome—well groomed; close haircut; had a peanut butter complexion and hazel colored eyes; stood eye-to-eye with Jaye.

He and J locked eyes.

"Jesenia?" he asked.

"Yeah?"

He smiled and said, "I'm Gavin."

They shook hands. And since it was appropriate, as well as mutual, they hugged.

"Nice to finally meet you."

"You too," she said. She wasn't half as enthusiastic as Gavin was, but she had a little smile on her face. She was happy to finally be meeting her brother. "Gavin, this is Jaye."

They shook hands.

Sill smiling, Gavin turned back to Jesenia and said, "So we meet. *Finally.*"

"Yeah. Thirty years," she said.

"Thirty years," he repeated. "Look, we have a lot of catchin' up to do. How long are you gonna be in town?"

"I planned to leave tomorrow morning at 11."

"How 'bout dinner tonight at my place? I can't really cook, but we can order in. I know this great Chinese restaurant that delivers," he said. "We can have dinner while we talk."

"Sounds good," J said.

"I can introduce you to my daughter."

J's eyebrows rose, surprised to hear that she would be meeting her brother's daughter. Her niece, technically.

"Don't you have a sister? Well... we?" she asked.

"Yeah. Michele," he said. "Michele is... Well... Michele isn't exactly..." he looked for the word, "*open* to meeting you. She can be a little... difficult sometimes."

All J could say was, "Oh." She didn't know Michele, so all she could do was take Gavin's word for it.

"Yeah," he sighed. "Well... Maybe she'll come around sooner or later."

"Yeah."

He looked at his watch. "I gotta get outta here. I gotta go to work," he said. "Well I should be home about seven. I'll give you a call then."

"Okay. I'll talk to you later."

"All right. It was nice meeting you, man," he said to Jaye before walking off, hastily.

J sighed.

She turned from Jaye and slowly twisted the door handle. She didn't know what to expect once she got on the other side of that doorsill.

Does he really want to see me? Will he know who I am? What will he have to say to me? She thought.

She wanted to back out; go home; forget she had ever even come to Chicago. But she couldn't; she was already there. And the door was already open.

"Jesenia," he said, as she slowly walked in. He had a smile on his face.

He was much older-looking than she thought he'd look, and though he was always a dark man, he seemed even darker now. She wouldn't have been surprised if he had problems other than the ones he was in the hospital for.

"Hi," she said, closing the door behind her.

Nobody else was in the room, which made her a little more comfortable, but she hadn't moved from that spot by the door where she had been standing since she closed it.

"You can come closer. What I have isn't contagious," he said, still smiling. He was so happy to see her.

She wasn't smiling. She still didn't know what to feel. She slowly walked closer until she was close enough for him to touch her hand.

"May I have a hug?" he asked.

She didn't want to, but before that thought of reluctance could process, he was on his way up for a hug. So she bent over to meet him halfway. He hugged her tight. She gave him one of those weak arm-wrap-arounds with the pat on the back.

"Pull up a chair and relax ya'self. You don't have to stand over me the whole time."

She hadn't planned to stay very long, so a chair, to her, was unnecessary. She pulled up one anyway and took a seat.

"You are so beautiful," he said.

It took her a moment to digest his words. "Thank you."

He looked at her, admiring his daughter he hadn't seen in over a decade.

"When did you get here—in town?"

"Ah… Last night. I spoke to Gavin for the first time on Monday. He told me everything and I… I came as soon as I could."

He looked at her with that almost-in-tears smile on his face and said, "Thank you. I really wasn't expecting you to come, but you… you did, and you made my day."

She had one of those fake smiles on her face, and a "yeah, whatever" expression in mind, wishing that she could find an opening so she could leave.

"Well… I'm sure you know why I wanted to see you." He said, "I want to apologize to you. I'm sorry for being a bad father. And I'm sorry that I waited until I was damn near dead to tell you that. But I am."

He stared at the wall just past his feet as if it would help structure his thoughts the way it did the room.

He coughed uncontrollably for a few seconds. Then he looked over at her. "I just want to… to spend this time admiring you and appreciating you. Because I've never done that before." He asked, "May I have the honor of doing that?"

She looked at him in the eyes—those watery eyes—and she said, "Why not?"

She felt as if a weight should've been lifted off of her chest—her heart—after the visit to the hospital. But as she looked out the cab's back window at the stores and the houses and even the children playing on the streets of her old stomping grounds, she realized that the weight was still there. That feeling that she had—that desire for answers—was still there. Her visit lasted over two hours. They tried to play catch-up. She let him know what she was doing in life; how she was living; what her plans were for the future; and she even introduced him to Jaye. But the question that every fatherless child wants to ask still lingered in her mind—why?

She just didn't know how to ask a man constrained to a hospital bed facing a life-threatening situation to state his case.

So just like the stores and the houses and even the children playing on the blocks of the Southside—not a thing had changed.

She went to Gavin's house that night; they ate; caught up. She met his two-year old daughter. They talked about their careers—his as an Information Technology Marketing Manager for a computer company. They talked about their lives—his as a single father of one. They talked as much as they could about the past; their childhoods; their father.

She sat on the couch in the living room at her mother's apartment that night beside Jaye with her head resting comfortably on his shoulder. He had his arm around her. He held her because he knew that that was what she needed at the time. He comforted her.

"It went well. He is really nice. And his daughter—she is *so* adorable."

"Did you get to meet your sister?"

"No."

She thought about it. She wondered, *Damn, will I ever meet her?*

Out of nowhere, she said to Jaye, "Thank you for coming all the way here with me on such short notice."

"You needed me. What was I s'pose to do?"

That meant that he'd be there for her. That was a good thing to know.

She looked at the television at Bugs Bunny for a moment, then she said, "Jaye."

And he said, "Yeah?"

And she said, "I don't know if I've ever told you this, but you are a good friend."

He smiled and said, "I try." Then said, "You ain't so bad yourself."

She smiled. And she watched television some more. She watched Bugs Bunny. She had more to say, but she watched Bugs. Like Jaye, he made her feel better.

When the cartoon went off, she said, "Jaye."

He said, "Yeah?"

She said, "Jaye... I don't want you to see other people." She stopped, but he could tell that she wasn't finished. "I had to share my father. I don't wanna share you."

* * *

She could tell that something was wrong even before she answered the phone. She had a feeling.

"The doctors said that the surgery went well. They don't know what happened."

She was barely in her house from the airport when Gavin called to tell her the news—their father had passed away that morning.

J didn't feel sad or upset. She didn't cry. She felt like a child would feel; somebody had died, but she didn't really know how to accept it. It was almost as if she didn't even understand the concept of death or what it meant to pass away. All she knew was that now he was gone forever. She couldn't miss him though. Because how could he be gone from a place if he was never really there in the first place?

M

s. Llaureano is here to see you. Should I send her back?" Linda, the gallery manager, said as she interrupted, buzzing in on the phone intercom.

"Yeah," Jaye answered.

Meka said, "That's my cue."

"Why are you so hard on her?"

"Jaye, I told you," Meka expressed. "I don't like…"

Meka stopped talking just as J tapped on the open door. She stood holding a dozen dark pink roses. She didn't hear what they were discussing before she came in, but she allowed them to finish before she said anything.

Meka was already standing, ready to leave. "Thanks for the money, big bro. I'll see you later."

"Whoa, wait. I want you home at a reasonable time," Jaye said before she got away.

"What's a reasonable time?" she asked.

"11," he said.

"I shouldn't have asked."

"12," he said.

"How 'bout 12:30?" she negotiated.

"How 'bout 12?" he said. "And not a minute later."

She said, "Bye," rushing by J so that she wouldn't have to speak.

Jaye sat behind his desk rubbing his face with his hands. He sighed.

"This big brother/daddy thing is more than you bargained for, huh?" J asked.

Meka had convinced Jaye to let her stay in DC with him to finish high school. After she found out about Duke Ellington School of the Arts, a place for the elite and most gifted young artists, as a young actress she *had* to go. Jaye gave in and said she could stay as long as she got in. She killed the audition.

"It's crazy," Jaye said. "I'm used to it, but she's getting older. I don't wanna talk to her like a baby… Never mind," he said when he remembered she was standing in his office with a bouquet of dark pink roses. Dark pink says, "Thank you."

"What's this?" he asked.

"I wanted to thank you. These are for you," she said, handing him the bouquet.

"Thank you." He took them from her hand. "But what for?"

"Come on, Jaye. Chicago? You took two days out of your schedule at the last minute just to go there with me. I appreciate that."

"Told you it was no problem."

"And I heard you when you said it. I just want you to know that the favor is greatly appreciated."

"Anytime," he said smiling, almost uncomfortable. Nobody had ever given him roses before.

"And another thing," she said. She ran her fingers through her hair before she made her second point. "I wanna apologize to you too."

He frowned with a question mark on his face.

She sighed. "I told you that I didn't want you to see other people. And that wasn't right."

He looked at her standing there in his office, nervous, as she tried to find all the right things to say. So he asked her, "Why wasn't it?"

His question threw her off. Only thing she could think of saying back to him was, "What?"

"Why wasn't it right?" he asked again.

"It was selfish."

"It was real," he said. "Bold as hell."

She wasn't expecting that response from him. As she thought about what she'd said to him, she too realized that it was bold. It took confidence to say something like that. Or blatant selfishness.

"Did you mean it?" he asked. "I mean is that how you feel? You were vulnerable, J."

"I wasn't vulnerable." Maybe she *was* vulnerable—a little bit. But it was how she felt. Of course, she had no idea what her statement actually meant though. If he didn't see other women and she cut off other men, what did this make them to each other—friends who didn't have any other friends?

"So… I mean… Where is this coming from?"

He was confused. He was also scared. If he said "yes," what did that mean? They were friends—platonic friends—who had already seen each other naked. Every day, he looked her in the eyes—the last person with whom he had had sex. That was more than most platonic friends could say. He kept wondering whether this was too soon for him. He was confused because he didn't understand why this had come about now. He was scared because he wasn't necessarily prepared.

"Jaye. I had to say how I feel," she said. She had left Chicago feeling the same way she had when she left the first time for college more than a decade ago.

"But why now?"

She shrugged her shoulders implying that she didn't know the answer, but she knew the answer. She finally said, "I went to Chicago and I saw a man who was *supposed* to be so much to me. He helped *make* me. I watched him die. I was in the room," she said, "while he was dying. I had so much to tell him, so many questions… I wanted to know why he treated me like shit. I wanted *him* to know how I felt about being *treated* like shit."

She took a deep breath, looking at the floor more than she was looking at Jaye.

"But, you know… I sat there in that room and I didn't say any of that." She regretted it. "So I said what I said to you," she told him, as she finally looked him in his eyes, "because I couldn't—I could *not*—pass up another chance to say how I feel."

He knew that her feelings were honest and real, and he appreciated the fact that she could articulate them.

She said, "I ain't never asked a man for nothin'. And I know it's a hellova start by asking one to give up other women, but… Jaye I know how I feel when I'm with you. I wanna be with you—all the time. And honestly?" She made sure he was hearing her when she said, "This friendship just isn't enough. Anymore."

Silence suffocated the room.

This was all new to her. But obviously, the way things were was old. She wanted something different—something more. So why not now? What was so wrong with now?

Jaye said, "Okay," and walked from behind the desk and sat on the front of it facing her. He asked her, "So what would this be?"

She looked in his eyes. She didn't know what this was. He was obviously accepting her proposition, but she didn't know what was next. What did this make her? What did it mean? Were they a couple? Was she a girlfriend?

She sighed. "Jaye… I don't know. I don't know, okay. Let's just do whatever this is slowly. Okay? Slowly," she said.

Though she had made the proposal, she was actually second to surrender. One man… The girlfriend… Exclusivity… She needed a little time for all that.

He took her hands in his. "Slowly," he agreed.

Unsuccessful relationships were becoming redundant. How much time is enough time to fully recover from heartbreak? A year? Nine weeks? Eight days? How about seven hours? It had been six months since Jaye's last relationship ended and he was still in the process of healing.

J had become a very good friend. He loved her very much, and he would've been lying to himself if he said that he never thought that she could be more than a friend, because he had. But his biggest fear was that things would never be the same if a relationship wasn't as successful as their friendship. He was afraid that his issues might mess up her first experience with a man capable of being so much to her. He didn't want his past to hinder him from showing her everything monogamy could be. What a man should be.

* * *

"Damn," she swore, quietly, yet with much frustration in her voice. A heavy sigh and her teeth smacking followed her swear. "Oh God!" She was fed up.

She decided to take a break. She pushed her chair back from the computer and went to the window to look out, hoping that maybe she would see something that would inspire her. She had been sitting at that computer for over an hour and all she had written was her name and a mere two sentences. She was up shit's creek because the essay was due the next day—all three-to-five pages.

The doorbell disrupted her concentration.

She walked downstairs to the door and looked through the peephole.

J.

She rolled her eyes as she pulled the door open.

"Hey," J said to her, walking in wrapping up her umbrella.

"Hey," Meka said, unenthusiastically, already walking back up to her room.

Meka wasn't fond of J. Not since the first day they met at her brother's gallery. Jaye said that she was "just a friend," but it wasn't a surprise to Meka that the two of them were an item now. Yeah, real convenient. She had no concrete reason for disliking J, she just didn't like her. Actually, she never cared for any of the women her brother dated. Some would act too nice by trying to win her over because they knew she didn't like them; others just ignored and avoided her completely as if that would make her go away. They were all intimidated by her, though they were usually more than ten years her senior.

"How are you?"

"I'm cool," Meka said with her back still to J.

J looked around. She could tell that Meka was home alone; the place was too quiet for someone else to have been there.

"Jaye hasn't gotten here yet?" she asked anyway.

"Nah," Meka answered. She continued up to her room and softly pushed the door behind her. She sat back at her computer and attempted to type again, but after two sentences, she found herself sucking her teeth and sighing heavily. "Ahhg," she grunted, aggravated. She would mumble what she thought she wanted to say in her paper, and then she would suck her teeth after realizing that it didn't sound good.

This went on for about five minutes before J got up and slowly walked upstairs to the room door. She could hear Meka from where she sat on the couch, so instead of just sitting and letting time pass, she figured this could be her opening to say something other than "Hey" today.

The door was half open, so J walked up and knocked softly. She could see Meka sitting at the computer from where she stood.

Meka looked over at her wondering why she was standing there. She looked back at the computer and reluctantly said, "You can come in."

J fell into a unique category. She wasn't scared of Meka. She never patronized her, nor did she ignore her; she always faced her head-on. She spoke to her—asked her how she was doing. She invited her places, genuinely. She asked her opinion because she really wanted to know. She wasn't intimidated by Meka. She actually admired her prowess.

J slowly walked in looking around because she had never been in this part of the house before. There was a twin-sized bed in the middle of the room; the head of the bed was against a wall decorated with pictures of all her favorite musicians, television and movies stars, and sports figures. She even had a spot dedicated to Aaliyah, whose music she'd just recently discovered. All of her furniture was maple wood. The computer desk was near the window on the left side of the bed where she sat.

As J looked around, she wondered what she was going to say. She had to say something quick or else Meka might've thought she was crazy for just standing there in her room for no reason, looking at her walls.

Meka sucked her teeth again and said, "Shoot."

This was J's opening. She asked, "What are you typing?"

Meka didn't answer right away, simply because she didn't want to. She didn't feel like talking, and she especially didn't feel like talking to J. But just so she wouldn't seem like she was being an utterly disrespectful, stubborn little bitch, she said, "A paper."

She was going to leave it at that, but that answer was vague. And rude. So she said, "I'm *trying* to write this stupid paper for English class."

"How is it coming?" J asked.

Meka really didn't want to answer. She really didn't want to talk to J. She said, "Look… It's due tomorrow so I don't really have time to waste." She looked at the computer screen and said, "Jaye should be here shortly."

J didn't understand why Meka hated her so much. She had hated people herself, but she had good reason—they were pricks and assholes. But she had never done anything to Meka to be considered either.

"What do you have against me?"

Meka rolled her eyes thinking she was never going to finish this paper now.

"Look, I don't have anything against you. I just need to fini-"

"You don't like me," J said. She shrugged her shoulders. "I mean that's cool." Meka wasn't the first and probably wouldn't be the last person to dislike J. J was used to living with the disapproval of others. "But your brother and I are close, and I wanna know why that bothers you."

Meka thought about an answer. She tried to find something nicer to say than what her real reason was, but she couldn't. Without regard, she just told the truth: "Because you're not good enough for him."

J said, "You don't even know me."

Meka looked at her and said, "I don't have to."

J didn't say anything. She couldn't. The words hurt like a bat coming across her face in mid-swing. She wanted more than that—an answer with more basis. But she got the bare-naked truth.

Meka looked back at the computer and continued trying to think of something to type.

"Okay," J said, accepting Meka's answer. She didn't like it, but she was fine with it.

"You know," Meka said, "I might've come off rude, but I'm just being honest. And I know you were just trying to be nice, but I have a paper to wri-"

"Right," J said. "You got less than a day to write this paper and you're sitting across the room insulting a professional writer." J let that sink in for a moment.

Meka sighed and relaxed in her chair. She realized that she had probably burnt a good bridge, and for no reason. What did she have to lose? The paper probably wasn't going to get done any faster if J left, so…

"So what does the paper have to be about?"

Meka gave in. "*If Beale Street Could Talk* by…"

"Baldwin," J finished. "That's a good book. What do you have to write about it?"

"Well," she sighed. "I chose to discuss the role of relationships: man and woman relationships, black and white, family relationships," she said, lazily. "It has to be between three and five pages and I can't even get a paragraph."

J walked over to the side of the bed nearest the computer and took a seat facing Meka and the desk.

"That's a pretty good topic. You got a thesis yet?"

Meka looked at her with one of those "yeah-right" expressions on her face.

J said, "Okay, we can start by coming up with a thesis. That might make things a little easier."

Meka sighed once again, bit her bottom lip and shook her head. Her face was long and blank, and she looked like she was holding back tears. J could tell that something else was bothering her besides the three-to-five-page paper.

"Aye," J said, softly. "You wanna talk about it?"

Meka shook her head implying that she didn't, then threw her right hand over her eyes. Tears rolled down her face. She wiped them away and said, "Sorry. It doesn't have anything to do with this."

J looked at her. She didn't know what to say.

Meka continued to wipe tears. But it seemed like the more she wiped the more they ran. She grabbed a tissue from the desk drawer and proceeded to wipe them away. She said, "I'm sorry."

"It's okay," J said. But she had to ask: "Boy problems?"

Meka sniffed and wiped some more.

"He broke up with me today. Over the phone," she said. She sniffed. "One year of my life wasted. *Jerk.*"

"What happened?"

"Another girl," she said. "Said he was lonely cuz I'm in DC."

J didn't say anything. She didn't know what to say to that.

"He was supposed to help me with this stupid paper and now I'm stuck with…" She stopped and wiped her eyes. "I can't believe he cheated on me. Guys are so… *stupid!*"

"Not all guys. You just gotta… You gotta find ah… *Wait* for a good one to come along."

J felt weird even thinking this, but she had to say it for the sake of Meka; she wouldn't have wanted to agree with her and have her thinking such a thing, regardless of how true the statement may have been.

Though she had no idea what to tell a young girl in a situation like this, they talked. She had to wing it.

"I know you really liked him," she said in conclusion, "but believe me—there are gonna be so many other guys… Good ones too."

J thought about how parents must've felt having to talk about Santa Claus.

"Especially when you become a big time actress," she threw in.

Meka started to look a little cheered up after J said that.

"See," J said, smiling too. "You know what I'm talkin' about."

"I guess," she said. She looked at J and she said sincerely, "Thank you. Really."

"Anytime."

Meka looked J up and down as if she were inspecting her. She said, "I guess… I guess it's okay if you date my brother."

J laughed.

But Meka was serious when she said, "But *don't* hurt him."

J stopped laughing. The words pierced her chest and hit her right in the heart. They almost took her breath away. She had no intentions of hurting him, but hearing Meka say it brought "what if" thoughts, and for the first time ever… Meka scared her.

All she could say was, "Okay." She cleared her throat and said, "Now let's finish up this paper."

Ｉt was Friday and Jaye had spent the day in his art room working on his latest piece he had yet to name. Around 8 o'clock, he put the paint up for the night so he could do one of his most favorite things in the world—watch a good basketball game.

He had just taken a break to get some more chips and another beer when the doorbell rang.

She was standing outside looking apologetic and nervous and cold all at the same time. She asked, "Can I come in?"

He moved to the side and welcomed her in, quickly closing the door behind her.

She untied the wool belt that was the same material as the coat and allowed the knee-length cold-protector to slide off her back and into Jaye's hands. He hung it for her on the coat rack.

He knew she would come to her senses and talk about it.

He figured the reason for her actions might be a little deeper than what he knew, so he wanted to allow her some thinking time.

Without bothering to walk to the living room and get comfortable, she stood right where she stopped in the foyer and said, "About yesterday..." She shook her head and sighed. "I wanna apologize for the way I acted."

Yesterday after a highly needed visit to her hairdresser's, J made her way to Georgetown to meet Jaye at the gallery. And like she did every time she went to Georgetown, she spent more than ten minutes driving around looking for a place to park and yelling at the nine out of ten drivers on the road whom didn't deserve licenses. So by the time she got inside, she was rolling her eyes and swearing heavily under her breath, still frustrated with what she just had to go through, again. She walked in and went straight up to Linda behind the desk.

Linda asked, "Georgetown traffic, huh?" before J could even say anything.

The fact that Linda saw right through her made her snicker a little bit. "Yeah," she admitted. "How you doin'?"

"I'm fine."

"Jaye around?"

"He's in the back," she said.

"Thanks."

J made her way down the short hall to his office. When she got there, the door was slightly ajar and she heard laughter. It was the laugh of a woman.

The laugh was followed by Jaye saying, "Aww... Stop."

"Seriously," the woman said. "You are *fine*. You should think about modeling."

"Come on," Jaye said modestly, obviously blushing.

"You never thought about it?"

"No," he replied, probably still smiling.

Suddenly, J's heart sunk to the bottom of her shoes. She pushed the door open slowly and walked into the office with pain and one of those no-the-hell-you-didn't-bitch looks covering her face.

"Hey. I wasn't expectin' you until later," Jaye said, looking at his watch. She usually took longer in the hairdresser. "J, this is Autumn. Autumn this is ah..." He looked at J. "This is J," he finished.

"It's nice to meet you," the woman said, throwing her hand out in front of her.

J looked at it and decided to shake it only for the sake of good manners. She looked the woman in the eyes thinking all sorts of things about her. The woman was shorter than J; dark skinned; short curly hair too; wore a gray business suit and a smile. Very pretty.

"Well I'm about to get outta here. I'll see you later," the woman said to Jaye. She didn't leave before throwing in, "Cutie."

The woman left from his office closing the door behind her.

J took a deep breath, trying not to display her anger and pissed-offness.

He walked over to her and kissed her on the cheek, then asked, "What's up?"

She had come to the gallery to meet him for dinner. She was a half-hour early.

She looked away from him deliberately. She wanted to keep her cool. She asked, "Who was that woman?"

He sat on the edge of his desk and answered, "Autumn? She's a frequent costumer. Good buddy of mine. Loves art. I mentioned her before."

J didn't remember no Autumns.

Autumn was a decorator who worked mainly with the interior décor of houses owned by people in the DC area with lots of money. There were several galleries that she purchased from for her customers and Black Girl had recently been added to her list.

"Yeah, well... What was she doin' in here?" J asked.

He looked at her with a question mark lingering on his face. It was accompanied by a slight smirk.

"What is this?" He was almost laughing now.

"What is what?" She didn't find anything funny.

"This," he said. "This emotion you have. Is this jealously?"

"Jealous? I don't get jealous," she said. "I just wanna know who the hell that woman was hit'n' on you, that's all."

"Hitting on me?"

"You're fine? You should think about modeling? She called you 'cutie'!"

Jaye snickered, not believing what he was hearing.

"You don't call that flirting?" she demanded to know.

Holding back the smile, he said, "No. I don't. I call it one person giving another person a simple compliment. She was joking, mostly."

That wasn't what it was to J. She became more irate because he wasn't admitting to it, and said, "Fuck that. I *know* what flirting is. That... *wo*man," she said, holding off from calling her something else, "was tryin' to get with you."

He was still smiling.

"And why the hell are you laughin'? This ain't funny, Jaye. Do I look like I'm laughing to you?"

Still smiling, he got up and walked over to her and said, "You're serious about this. That is so cute."

"What? What the fuck is cute?"

"You," he said. "I never seen you this way. It's cute."

He tried to kiss her, but she moved her head. "Don't touch me," she demanded. "You just sat there and let some bitch come on to you. What would've happen if I hadn't come in?"

The only thing J could think about was that woman and what she was saying to him before she walked in. Yes, he was fine. But how long would he remain so modest? Women loved him. When would he realize all of this and start taking advantage of it?

He sighed and stopped smiling. "J. She was not flirting with me."

She rolled her eyes and looked away so he couldn't see her face.

"Come here," he said, finally realizing that she was serious. He wanted to hold her close. "Come here."

"Don't fucking... Don't touch me."

She stormed out the door before the unspeakable happened. She couldn't let him see that.

"J!" He jumped up to follow her. He didn't want to yell in the gallery, so he just walked fast behind her until they got outside.

"J, come on. J!"

She ignored him and continued walking. He followed her.

"J." He slowed down realizing that she wasn't going to stop for him.

"J!" he yelled again, but the only response he heard was the sound of cars and buses on M Street and his own voice echoing through the night.

When she got inside her car, she took a few deep breaths, and it worked a little bit, but her heart was still pounding. Still pounding. Still...

She felt like she couldn't breathe no more. She closed her eyes.

She opened them and there it was. The unspeakable.

The salty water ran. Unstoppable. Down her face.

She sat in the car, steadily trying to wipe them away with the complimentary napkins she had taken from fast-food restaurants and stuffed into her glove compartment. She started her car and drove off without looking in the rearview mirror once.

She went home that night, took a hot shower, and crawled into her queen-sized bed with the intentions of going to sleep. Instead, she lay there all night thinking. She thought about the woman; about Jaye; about the tears. The tears said everything. She wasn't a very emotional person; she didn't shed tears easily. She maintained a hard shell on the outside, but on the inside she couldn't deny what she was—a woman: aka, an emotional creature. She cried. The fact that he didn't even know that she felt that way about him was what made her cry. He thought that it was a joke and he brushed off everything she said so easily. He took nothing she said seriously and that bothered her. He offended her.

But the tears—the tears let her know that it was her own fault that he didn't know these things. When they ran down her face, it was confirmation of her feelings for this man. She hid them so he wouldn't see them though.

He called her one time that night, but she let her answering machine pick up. He never left a message. He hated talking to machines.

"I'm sorry," she said. "I'm not a jealous person," she assured. "I'm not," she reiterated, making sure he understood her point.

She looked at him for the first time since she'd come into his house to explain and he was staring back at her with inquisitive eyes. She could tell that he wanted to know more.

She sighed. "I don't know what that was, okay? I'm not used to this."

"I know you aren't." He stepped closer to her. "I know," he said. "Autumn is just... an art lover," he explained. "She's a friend. She buys from the gallery a lot."

"Jaye, you shouldn't have to explain yourself to me."

She wasn't bothered by the woman's identity, but by her own.

"She didn't know who *I* was." Her voice was filled with concern. The woman should've known who she was. Why hadn't he told her?

He looked her in her eyes. "J, we been together for how long?" he asked rhetorically. "Baby, *I* don't even know who you are."

They were stuck between friends and a hard place.

He said, "I don't wanna introduce you as my friend. But I don't feel like I *can* introduce you as my lady. We're not there yet, right?" The question was rhetorical. "We don't see other people, but... I still don't know what that's supposed to mean, J." He looked her in the eyes, looking for answers. "Who are you?" He wanted her to say it.

She had an expression on her face that was soft, almost apologetic because she completely understood what he was saying. She had confused him. And she felt sorry about that. But it was so difficult to want so much... But at the same time, know so little. She wanted him. But she didn't know who she wanted him to be. She wanted to *be* somebody to him. But she didn't know who she wanted to be either.

"Jaye... This is hard," she said. Because of him, many of

her feelings had been tested. Cynicism wasn't so easy anymore. Neither was promiscuity. He was exposing her to a side of Mars she thought she'd never see.

"This is new to me," she continued. "Maybe I should've…" She sighed. "Maybe you should know more."

Uncertainty filled her voice because she didn't know whether she should say more—tell him more about her past. Yes, he should've known more about her. But would he feel the same after knowing? *Would he still want this?* she thought about herself.

"It won't change anything," he promised. He wanted her to feel comfortable saying anything she wanted to him.

She was so confused. She didn't know where to start. What to say. How to say it.

"This wasn't supposed to happen. I wasn't supposed to know you. I used to wish that I never met you. That I never had to do the story on the gallery. That we never slept…" She stopped and looked at him knowing that he was confused by her words. "After I got over the fact that I couldn't rewind time—couldn't change what happened… I accepted it. I accepted you," she said. "And that was scary. Because even though we said we were just friends… I was never satisfied with that. I always wanted you to be… mine." She looked in his eyes and said, "I wasn't ready to be yours. I was too scared."

He looked at her and softly asked, "Scared of what?"

She thought about all the things she was afraid of and chose instead to just say, "Monogamy. So much shit comes with monogamy," she said. "Never thought I would have it. Never really thought I could handle it."

He wanted so badly to ask her why, but if she wanted to explain, she would. And if she didn't? He trusted that if she didn't then she had her reasons for that too.

She sighed, knowing that there was so much more to this story. "Look. Jaye… I'm not like most women," she said. "I've lived a very ah… a very complex life. I'm really fucked up. I just want you to know that."

He smiled. "You're not any more fucked up than the rest of us."

She looked in his eyes and saw honesty. Sincerity. Just like in Chicago, he was there for her. He comforted her. Everything about him was new to her. He struck cords emotionally that she didn't even know she had. But it felt good.

She tried hard not to let her guard down though. She wouldn't give him the key. But she watched as he picked the lock—did all the right things and said all the right words that made her open up.

"So what now?" he asked. "What's next?"

She said, "I just wanna be with you. That's all I want. Okay?"

"Okay," he answered, nodding his head and smiling, both relieved and happy. "We can be together."

She nodded. "I'm not gonna be a coward anymore. I'm gonna do this."

She never saw herself actually settling down and being somebody's woman—being with just one guy. She thought she was supposed to be a single woman forever. The life she was used to living was very different from the one she was trying to live now. She didn't quite understand what to do. All she knew was that she liked him. A lot. And if that meant playing the role of girlfriend, which she hadn't rehearsed for… Then she'd improvise.

"This means no so-called art fans hanging around either."

He began to smile. "She wasn't flirting with me," he insisted.

"Whatever, Jaye."

"She wasn't," he said. "J, Autumn is a lesbian. And married. I know her wife."

He started to laugh. J had to laugh too. She said, "Hey, don't rule her out. You might have what it takes to convert her."

Still smiling, he shook his head and joked, "Mm-mm, I tried. It didn't work."

She grabbed a handful of his t-shirt and pulled him in for a kiss. "Don't fuck with me."

Optimism.

Jaye was optimistic now. Not that he was ever pessimistic.

He just wanted her to say exactly what she wanted from him. He wasn't going to see other people anyway so she needed to say more than that. And tonight she had. Tonight, she gave him optimism.

She never told a man so much. She had never been jealous—so genuinely jealous that she didn't know what to do. She had never been so insecure because she wanted to live up to so much; she never wanted *so* hard to be *so* much to somebody. She was used to only living for herself; if J was happy, J was fine. But now, she wanted to be so much *for him*. She wanted him to be happy with who she was. She used to not care what people thought of her. Now she cared; she wanted him to think of her a certain way—highly. She wished she were perfect for him—not so tainted.

Truth was though: she *wasn't* perfect. She *was* tainted. But there wasn't a thing she could do about that now. That scared her. She knew that the closer she got to him, the more he'd know. And even though he said that things wouldn't change regardless of what she told him about her licentious past, it was hard for her to believe that.

* * *

"To be this close," Ty said, "is already scary. To be even closer… is even scarier."

Her friend's words echoed in her head.

But the pleasure can be so hypnotic. It can make a person forget their name if it's good enough.

Oh, and it *was*. It was *real* good. Just like how it was that night they met.

Better.

She inhaled and let her eyes roll back as they closed. She bit her bottom lip to keep from screaming out.

Damn! It was so good!

"See, it's not that I don't wanna do it," J told her friend. "I do," she insisted. "I'm just… It's like I'm scared."

The word "scared" had changed the direction in which the conversation was headed. Now, it wasn't that J didn't *want* to have sex with him; she was just *scared* to. J, a woman who had looked at sex as a sport since her teen years and who had been drafted before she was able to legally drive a car, was now scared to take a swing. She had been in more consecutive games than Cal Ripken Jr. and now life had thrown her a changeup and she was scared to even try to hit it. The changeup was a tricky, off-speed pitch. She was used to a fast one straight over the plate, a slider, a sinker, or even an occasional curve, but not the changeup. Not too many guys had the balls to throw a *changeup*.

His pace had smooth, long, timed strokes that almost caused her to convulse from too much too-good. She couldn't seem to exhale right. He hit it *right*—in every vulnerable spot. In every place that seemed tender and ignored, he gave special attention.

Her back arched tightly almost like she was trying to get away from him. But getting *away* was the farthest thing from her mind. She wanted to—

"Come again," Ty said. "You're telling me you're afraid that sex will change things?"

J nodded. "I am. Yeah."

"How do you think things'll change?" Ty asked.

He felt her slipping away, so he gripped the mattress and pulled himself into her more, bringing tears to her eyes.

"I wanna be able to have sex with him… and maintain what we have right now."

"That's understandable," Ty said. "Why don't you think you would be able to have what you have now if you bring sex into the picture?"

"Because sex makes stuff different."

She turned him over on his back. Pinned his arms down with her hands. And straddled him. She became the aggressor. She leaned forward and grabbed the headboard for some leverage and support, and she rode slow… and hard. And with ease. And with rhythm.

She leaned down and kissed him.

"After I have sex with a man… I usually lose interest." She sat up in her chair changing her posture as she explained her case to her friend over lunch. "I don't really wanna be around them anymore. I don't want them around *me*... What's the point?"

Ty concluded, "So it isn't necessarily sex that changes things; it's you that change after having sex."

Silence covered the room for a moment.

J thought about her first encounter with Jaye—him sitting on the crate outside of the gallery; the walk they took; the conversation they had. He was an incredibly beautiful man, inside and out, and even though she neglected to admit it to anybody, or to herself, she fell for him that night. She had valid reasons for wanting him around after sex—he was irresistible. And he still was.

And now, for the first time in their relationship, they were having sex. She had held out far longer than she wanted to. Longer than she expected. Months.

Jaye was patient though. If she'd announced a newfound lifestyle of celibacy, he would've stayed beside her until the day she was ready. But she couldn't take it anymore. She was ready now!

He grabbed her hips and followed her lead in the ride. He breathed slower and slower like it was difficult for the air to escape or enter his lungs. He kept his eyes closed, afraid that if he opened them the sight of her naked body on top of him would be too much.

He couldn't go first.

He had let her have her way with him for long enough now. She giggled as he put her on her stomach again. It was a competition now—who can make who scream first.

She was winning.

"You know what I think?" Ty asked, rhetorically. "I don't think that you're scared that you'll lose interest in Jaye. You're far past that stage. If you were gonna lose interest, I think you'd've lost it by now," she said. "Loss of interest is not your problem. I believe your problem is: you think that if you have sex with him, it would be more than sex; it would be somewhat of a validation that your relationship has officially moved to the next level. That's what scares you. To be this close," she said, "is already scary. To be even closer... is even scarier."

And just like that... he won.

J's plane landed at 5 o'clock p.m. that Monday. She had spent the last couple days in Chicago for personal as well as professional reasons, and now she was glad to be back home, and anxious to see Jaye. He had offered to pick her up from the airport, but because he had gotten up at 5 a.m. to take her the day she left, she insisted on catching a cab home.

After she paid and thanked the cab driver, she grabbed her two bags and lazily made her way up the driveway. She was always tired after flights. She finally got the door open and walked in, dropping both bags onto the floor where she stood.

Before her nose even told her brain that she smelled food cooking, the sound of Jaye yelling, "Hey! How was your trip?" from the kitchen nearly scared her half to death.

She looked over at him with a huge question mark lingering on her face.

He just stood there smiling and waiting for an answer to his question.

She didn't answer. She walked toward the kitchen,

dropping her purse onto the couch on her way. She looked at him, still with that wrinkle-browed expression on her face. She looked into the pots that were on the stove; mashed potatoes were in one, peas and corn in the other. She looked in the oven—pork chops smothered in gravy.

She scratched her temple. "Mmm… I would ask what you're doing here, but it's quite obvious what you're doing," she concluded.

"I just wanted to surprise you. You know—make you dinner and all that," he said, smiling. "I got some massage oils…" He would've continued because he had more to say, but he could see that she wasn't exactly *into* what he was saying.

"What? What's wrong?" he asked.

"Ah… I ah… I know I gave you the keys. But… that was for shit like emergencies."

A frown appeared on his face because he didn't understand.

They were at her house in her bed when she gave them to him.

"I keep forgetting to give this to you." She handed him a little brown bag too small for any gift he could think of.

He asked, "What's this—a belated Christmas present?"

She smiled. "Not quite," she said.

He stared at the bag for a moment before taking it, wondering what was inside. He took the bag from her hand still looking at it and her skeptically.

He looked inside. To his surprise, there laid two shiny gold…

"Keys?" he asked.

"Yeah," she said, smiling. "I mean I thought it would be a good idea if you had a set just in case… you know—I get locked out or somethin'. Emergencies. I don't really know anybody else who lives as close as you do and who I would trust with a key to my place."

"Wow," he said. "I guess I'm supposed to say thanks, huh?"

She leaned over and kissed him, and said, "You can show your gratitude another way."

Now, he didn't understand *what* she was saying. "What?"

She said, "I'm sayin' that the keys are for emergencies, like say if I got locked out or I lost my-"

"I know what an emergency is," he said with a sharper tone.

He couldn't believe her. He placed the dishrag that he was holding onto the counter top and walked toward the door, upset. He wanted her to say something—apologize or something. She didn't. She didn't say anything, even though she could see how he was affected by her reaction.

He knew what she had told him when she gave him the keys, but he assumed that she was just saying the word "emergency" and really meant "here's the key to my place; this is my way of letting you get closer to my heart." He thought that giving him her keys was her way of saying something without actually saying it. Obviously he was wrong.

"Enjoy your dinner," he said, grabbing his coat without looking back at her and walking out the door. He waited on the other side for about five seconds hoping that she would come out looking for him.

She didn't.

She continuously asked herself, "When the hell did 'these keys are for emergencies' start meaning the same as 'come over and let yourself in whenever you feel like it'?" She fell asleep with the phone beside her after she ate that night. He didn't call.

He continuously asked himself, "When the hell did 'emergencies' start actually meaning *emergencies*? Especially when sex shortly follows the statement." He was pissed off that night. He didn't bother calling her.

The rest of Monday passed. Then all day Tuesday. No calls. No visits.

Usually on Wednesdays, they ate dinner together. Whether it was take-out or cooked, they always ate dinner together on Wednesday, Friday, and Sundays, so she didn't want to break what was already a little tradition of theirs.

She showed up at his house at 6 o'clock sharp and knocked softly using the doorknocker. Meka opened the door almost immediately.

"What's up?" she said to J.

"Nothin'," J answered. "What's up with you?"

"Same," Meka said, walking back into the kitchen where she was before she answered the door.

J walked in taking her coat off.

"So what we eatin' tonight?" Meka asked.

Hanging her coat in the closet, J said, "I don't know. Where is your brother?"

After swallowing the juice she had in her mouth, Meka said, "In the other room. He's workin' on somethin'. And you know how he gets when he's workin' on somethin'," she added, referring to his almost annoying insistence for solitude when he's in one of his creating "zones."

"Yeah," J said.

When Jaye worked on his art, he would lock himself in his private art room—sometimes for hours at a time—and he would paint or sculpt or do whatever he was inspired to do. But whatever he did, he preferred not to be disturbed.

J went up to the room where he was and softly knocked on the door.

He looked at his watch. It was after 6 so he had an idea who it was. He got up, walked over to the door, twisted the knob just enough for the door to crack open, and walked away without even greeting the person on the other side.

When she walked in, he was already sitting back down on his favorite chair—the soft, red leather, cushioned one, with no wheels and no arms. It was like a desk chair and he preferred to use while working on his art. He continued painting.

She closed the door behind her and slowly made her way over to where he was.

Quietly, she watched him paint for a moment.

After the silence became unbearable, she began to pace, slowly. She understood his "zone" and usually preferred not to violate it, unless she saw no other choice. Dinnertime was approaching and she needed to know what he was having.

He looked up at her to see what she was doing and whether she was going to say something, then back at his painting.

She stopped pacing. Sighed and said, "What are we having for dinner?"

He stopped what he was doing, continuing to stare at the canvas on which he painted. He couldn't believe that that was all she had to say after not seeing or talking to him for more than twenty-four hours. He wanted to say something to her—talk about why they hadn't spoken in over a day. But it didn't seem as if she was worried or bothered by the situation, so he chose to not bring it up and avoid conflict. He didn't want to seem like he was dragging on a situation that didn't need to be dragged on.

He didn't look at her. He looked down at his hand—at his brush.

"You can just make some cold cuts," he said.

Yeah, he decided to drop it. She had already, anyway.

"Oh, I can, huh?" she asked, smiling.

He smiled.

She leaned over and put her face in his and kissed him on his lips.

"I missed you," she said, kissing him again. As he sat in the chair looking up at her, she came closer putting her legs over him, straddling him before she sat down on his lap with her face in his, talking to him close and quietly between kisses.

"The whole time I was in Chicago..." she said, kissing his lips. "All I could do was..." She kissed the side of his face and said, "Think about you." She kissed his left ear, and then slowly kissed his neck. "Every day. All I could..." she rubbed his chest and continued slobbering on his neck, "could think about was you," she said. "Inside of me," she whispered.

And that's exactly where he wanted to be right now. He was already *ready*. He slid his hands underneath her blouse and rubbed her back while kissing her neck and chest. She smelt so good. And she was so soft... He became more and more ready with every touch. Every kiss.

He slowly slid his fingers under her bra strap and unhooked it.

She stopped.

"What? What? Why'd you stop?" he asked.

"Meka's in the other room."

"Damn," he said. "I forgot."

She kissed him a few more times before she got up. She adjusted her clothes while giving him one of her infamous charming and flirtatious smiles. She leaned over and kissed him again, then said, "Cold cuts it is."

I t's me. Call me back."

He had called her twice already; this time he decided to leave a message. She had caller I.D., which, to him, defeated the purpose of him leaving a message. His number wasn't unlisted; it would show up on the little screen and she would know he had called. But he had grown a bit curious as to where she... No, he was worried about her. He hadn't talked to her since some time the day before, and even then they only spoke briefly. He didn't have to think too much about it, he was conscious of the fact that they hadn't been together or talked very much in the last few weeks. He'd call; he usually caught her on her cell phone. She'd be in the middle of something. On her way somewhere. Doing something. Never in the right place to talk to him. It just wasn't the right time. Before, if he caught her at a bad time, she would make an effort to make that time the right time to talk to him.

It was nearly midnight now. 11:32 exactly. A Thursday night. He forced himself to leave a message.

Though he knew he wouldn't be able to sleep well until he heard from her that night, he crawled into his bed and pulled the sheets up over his shoulders and got comfortable. He put the phone on the pillow beside him and placed his head on the pillow beneath him as he fought off Zs. He wanted to be awake when she called. He put up a good fight, but after flipping through hundreds of cable channels and not finding anything in particular to watch—though bits and pieces of a lot of things—he was defeated at nearly 1 a.m.

"It's me. Call me back." The screen read "11:32."

She sighed and flopped down on the bed, then looked over at the clock to see what time it was now. It was one thirty a.m. She was home when he called, but she didn't feel like talking. She took a nap around 8 o'clock that evening just after she finished doing her household chores, then started on her article that was due in a few days. No mood to talk.

She debated whether she was going to call him back tonight. It was late and she really didn't feel like answering the "Where were you?" question. But that was a question she'd have to answer eventually, whether it be tonight or tomorrow or whenever she talked to him again. So she picked up the phone and pressed the number 1 and waited for him to pick up.

"Hello," he answered, sounding only half sleep.

"It's me. I'm just returning your phone call, but you're asleep, so…"

"No," he cut in as he cleared his voice. "Nah. I'm up." He made himself comfortable in the bed with the phone next to his ear.

Before he could say or ask anything, she said, "I yah… I been kinda busy lately. We're workin' on the fourteenth anniversary edition of the magazine and I've been… Just really caught up with a lot of stuff the last few days."

"Mm."

"We have the ah… anniversary banquet coming up that we're get'n ready for too." She sighed. "It's just so much shit goin' on…" She dreaded thinking about it. As much as she loved being at the banquet, she hated the pre-banquet drama. "I gotta find something to wear. You're my date, so you gotta help me."

"I am?"

"Yes. You are."

She had said something to him about it in January and it was March now, but she never mentioned it again. So since she had forgotten about it, so had he.

She said, "Jaye."

"Hm?"

"Why don't you come over here?"

He looked over at the clock on his nightstand. 1:35.

"Now?" he asked.

"Yeah."

He thought about it. He really wanted to see her; he hadn't seen her since Sunday.

"What do you have to do tomorrow?"

He thought. "Nothin', really."

He had actually planned to wake up and put the finishing touches on his latest painting. He told J that he wasn't doing anything.

"So what's stoppin' you?"

He was quiet for a second. Then he said, "Ah'ight." He got up and put on sweat pants, a t-shirt, and sneakers, grabbed his jacket and keys and headed for the door. He left a note on the counter so Meka would know where he had gone.

"You sure got here quick."

"I miss you," he said, kissing her on the side of her face as he came out of his jacket.

She said, "You smell so good." She was all over him. It was obvious what she wanted to do and she didn't waste any time letting him know that. She began kissing and sucking on his neck, while caressing his back underneath his shirt.

He tossed his jacket onto the couch as he took her up on her offer—becoming the aggressor in the process. He grabbed the back of her thighs, lifting her up, and wrapped them around his waist as he somehow managed to get them both up to her bedroom.

The light of the sunshine through the window woke him up that morning, but he kept his eyes closed to block them from being burned by the brightness. He immediately realized that he wasn't holding her close, as he would've liked to be, so he turned over with his arm already in position to embrace her. Surprisingly, his hand fell onto the sheets instead. With his eyes still closed and the belief that he had simply missed her, he moved his arm around in search of some sign of her. He opened his eyes immediately to make sure that his hands weren't lying to him. She wasn't there.

He sat up quickly with a look of tiredness mixed with confusion on his face. He sniffed the air to see if maybe she was downstairs cooking or something. But even he knew that was just wishful thinking; J never made breakfast. She might go out and buy something from the pancake house, but she damn sure wasn't cooking breakfast. He looked at the clock—11:37. He got up, still squinting from the bright sunlight, and headed downstairs to see what she was doing, and why she was up so early. When he got to the first floor he didn't hear anything. Or see anything. He looked around for a moment. Looked out the window; her car was gone.

He sighed and went back upstairs, sat on the bed, and then grabbed the phone. He called her cell phone and waited for her to pick up, while wondering what he was going to say and how he was going to say it.

She answered, "Yes, Jaye."

"Where are you?"

"You didn't get my message?"

"What message?"

"The note I left you on the nightstand."

He looked over and sure enough, there was a note. He picked it up and read it: "Lock up when you leave out," it said.

The words on the note caused him to suddenly be consumed with anger.

"Look. I'm in a meeting right now," she said. "Let me call you back."

He didn't say any more to her. He hung up the phone before she did. Bit his bottom lip. Sighed. He could barely digest what had just happened. In fact, he didn't want to. He just wanted to go home.

Around 1 o'clock that afternoon, he miserably strolled

into his place, dropping his Nets gym bag onto the floor.

"Hey, Jaye," Meka said, pouring herself a cup of water.

Though he knew it was early, he looked at his watch anyway so he'd know the specific time to which he was about to refer. "What are you doin' home?"

"Half day, remember? I told you I had a half day yesterday." She shook her head and said, "What's wrong with you?"

"Nothin'," he lied. "I just forgot." He picked up his bag, but neglected to move toward his room where he desired to be, in his own bed, asleep.

"I got your note," Meka said, grinning devilishly.

"Mm."

"Booty call, huh?"

"What?!"

Her question caught him off guard, probably because he knew but didn't want to admit to himself that that was what it was. He hated the fact that even his little sister could see what was going on.

"Watch your mouth."

"Please," she said, flopping down onto the couch. "I just call it how I see it."

He didn't say anything else to her, just continued to stare at her for a moment as she flipped through the channels in search of a good music video. He shook his head and proceeded to his room.

It was clear to J what was going on; she knew what she was doing. A month ago, she had come home one evening and a man was in her house. Cooking for her. The entire scene scared her, horribly. She wasn't used to coming home and having somebody there waiting for her. It suddenly hit her: she was really in a relationship. In relationships you do things; you have to share things. And she was willing to share a lot of things with him. Her house, however, was not one of them. Not yet, at least. This was her space—her place to be when she wasn't with him, or simply didn't want to be.

She needed time alone.

She used the magazine anniversary as her excuse for not

being available, but the truth was: she really just wanted time to herself—a vacation from this relationship. Things were moving a bit faster than she wanted them to be. So she had taken a time out (but hadn't told him). She needed to step outside of this life for a moment and perhaps evaluate it from another angle. However, she understood how much her distancing act was affecting their relationship. She could feel his anger when he hung up the phone that morning. She knew he would've preferred her to be there with him, in bed, instead of at some meeting, or anywhere else. Perhaps he would've cared less about her being at the meeting hadn't she been avoiding him the past few weeks.

She showed up at his place that night with an apology of sorts.

"Jaye, I know you're kinda... mad at me 'cause we haven't been spending any *real* time with each other lately," she said. "So I apologize for that. And I wanna make it up to you..."

* * *

It was a Friday. DC's weather still hadn't made up its mind whether it wanted to let winter stay or kick the old man out so spring could make her grand entrance. One day it was nearing seventy degrees; the next it was freezing. With the fluctuation in temperature, many people ran to local drug stores in search of the right cold and cough concoction that they hoped would help rid them of their sicknesses. J was one of those people. She wasn't buying the medicine for herself though; it was for Jaye. He had been sneezing and blowing his nose all night, so as soon as she got up that morning, she went to the store to get him something that she hoped would stop the sickness from attacking him any further. The *FACE Magazine* banquet was that night and she needed him to be there for her.

The drugs didn't take hold soon enough, or at all for that matter, but he went anyway—sniffling, sneezing, coughing, aching, stuffy head, fever and all. He went. Everybody who was anybody in entertainment had come out to show their support for the magazine and its staff for fourteen successful years in the old and new media business.

J had looked forward to this night, and like always, she spent it rubbing elbows with the stars—many of whom she had met during interviews she'd conducted. Most of the people there were familiar with Jaye because of the publicity he had gotten when the gallery opened a year ago. But with pleasure, she introduced her "date" to all of her co-workers, the magazine's advertisers, and entertainment industry folk who had not had the opportunity to meet him.

* * *

They walked into his house after catching the ten o'clock screening of America's latest artsy independent flick to hit theatres.

"Where's Meka?" she asked.

"Friends'." And that's all he said. He had been giving her responses like that all night.

"Jaye, what is wrong with you?"

"Nothing," he said, hanging his jacket in the closet by the front door. "I'm goin' to sleep."

She sighed. She could tell that something was bothering him, but as usual, he chose not to discuss it. That's how he was; that was something she discovered even when they were just friends—he never liked to discuss his problems, but he would always offer to lend his ear to somebody else so they could discuss theirs. Sometimes, he nearly forced others to talk, yet he always refused.

He proceeded up the stairs without waiting for her.

While downstairs, alone, she went into the kitchen, pulled a glass from the dish rack and filled it with water from the refrigerator. It was quiet. There was no television on, no radio, no sounds of someone else in the house, even though she wasn't alone. The silence allowed her the chance to think. She walked over to the living room, placed the glass of water onto the coffee table before her, and flopped down on the couch. She sighed again, thinking about what she was going to say to Jaye when she got upstairs. They needed to discuss this because there was obviously a situation.

After about ten minutes of sitting in quietness, she got up from the couch, sighed once more, and headed up the stairs.

The bedroom door was partially closed, though the glow of the television could be seen from the hall. She pushed the door in slowly and softly closed it back behind her. Jaye was lying underneath the sheets with his back to the door. But she didn't care whether he was asleep, he was going to wake up and talk about this "situation."

"Jaye," she called, softly.

"Hmm?"

After realizing that he wasn't sleeping at all, she took a moment to gather her words. She stood at the foot of the bed so he wouldn't have to do much moving when it came time to look at her.

"I think we need to talk about why things have been... so..." She sighed again. "I don't know," she said. "I wanna know what's wrong with you. What's up with the small talk?"

Now he sighed.

Before he could answer, she said, "I mean, I kinda figured it was because I canceled on you yesterday. And I apologize for that. I just needed to-"

"J," he interrupted, turning over to look her in the face. "If you think that that's the only problem that we have, then... *you* have a serious problem."

Her brows wrinkled and a confused look covered her face as she tried to understand what he meant.

"Excuse me?"

This time he sat up in the bed and switched on the small lamp that sat on the nightstand. Looking at her with his eyes narrowed and a question mark covering his face, he said, "You just don't get it, do you?"

Calmly, but with much attitude now, she said, "No, Jaye. No. I don't get it. Would you please explain the shit to me? Please. 'Cause I'm lost. I don't know what the hell is wrong with you."

In a calm and inquisitive tone with anger *hidden* inside it, he asked, "Why does something have to be wrong with me?"

"*You* tell *me*! You're the one that's actin' like a..."

"A what? I'm actin' like a what?"

"A child, Jaye. You are acting like a goddamn child. I mean: half talkin' to me all day? What? What kinda childish shit is that?" she asked, rhetorically. "Maybe if you talk to me and tell me what you feel some goddamn time I would have a clue."

"That's the sad part about this," he said, still calm. "You don't know *what* the fuck is goin' on. I shouldn't have to tell you everything."

"And you've done a fine job of not sayin' shit. That's your problem: you always want me to read between the lines."

"Read between the... J, making lines for you to read between is implying. I don't imply shit. I seldom even show my anger, so when you can *see* that I'm upset I think that as my *girl* you should *know* what's bothering me, 'specially when the reason is because of yo' ass."

"Because of... I mean *damn*," she said, shaking her head, "I am not a psychic fucking friend. I don't read minds, okay. If you got something to say to me, I would prefer if you just said it."

He looked her right in the eyes and said, "I love you."

Earlier that week on her birthday, April 1, they found themselves in his bedroom, watching television and talking. Surprisingly, she didn't want to go anywhere to celebrate.

"I probably saw every episode of *Martin* three or four times and I can still watch these reruns and laugh at 'em."

"Yeah," Jaye agreed. "Me too."

They were in his bed—his arms were wrapped around her. This was the way he liked to do things; he liked to stay at home and relax, preferably with her in his arms.

After the show went to commercial, he said to her, "You know what? Your big head kinda reminds me of Gina's."

"What?!" she said, jumping up and slapping him in the face with a small throw-pillow.

"I was just playin'!" he shouted, laughing.

"That's okay, Tommy."

"Tommy?" he asked. "Why you call me Tommy?"

"'Cause you ain't got no job, man!"

"Aww!" He grabbed a pillow and smacked her one good time across the head with it. They began to pillow fight on the bed. He pinned her down and held her arms as she giggled. He tickled her.

"Let me up," she said through the laughter. "Come on. Let me up before you make me wake Meka up."

He let her up. Then he moved in and kissed her lips and her neck as his hands moved slowly up to her breast.

"Jaye," she said. "I can't right now."

"Oh," he said, stopping, knowing why she couldn't.

"But you know what? I'll hold you."

He burst into laughter. "You gon'…" He buried his face into the pillows on the bed. "Oh my goodness. You'll hold me?"

"I'll hold you. What's so funny about that?"

He calmed down to answer her question.

"*You* wanna hold *me*?"

"Yes. I wanna hold you," she said again. She couldn't believe that he was surprised that she'd said that.

He was always the one doing the holding; she could almost never sit still long enough to even be held, now she wanted to do the holding? He couldn't believe it.

Smiling, he said, "Okay, J. You can hold me."

She said, sarcastically, "Thank you, almighty King Jaye, for allowing me to hold thee."

They crawled back under the sheets, laughing at her silliness. She lay down with her back up against the pillows that rested behind her. Before he made himself comfortable, she put her hands on his face and asked with playfulness still in her voice, "May I please have a taste of thy luscious royal lips?"

"Only if you ask without talkin' in that dumb voice."

"Boy, you better bring them damn lips here."

He laughed as he moved over and pecked her on the lips. "*Damn*, I love you," he whispered, still smiling. He meant the words he said, though the phrase had slipped out. He wanted to tell her this, but he wanted to do it in a more romantic manner, not while playing.

Before he could even expect a response, she said, "You know I don't like those little pecks. Come here."

She laid a real kiss on him this time.

As he proceeded to kiss her, he realized that she didn't say it back.

She didn't say it back.

Once the reality of what had just happened calculated, they had stopped kissing. A perplexed look covered his face as he made himself comfortable.

She had heard him loud and clear, and though he said it playfully and during a playful situation, she knew that it wasn't just something he was saying because maybe it sounded good. He meant it and she knew that and she knew *how* he meant it. But love… To say those three words, to her, was totally different from simply displaying the actions. Saying them required her to admit her submission to vulnerability, which was something she didn't want to reveal at this point in her life. So instead of saying it back like she knew she should've—and like inside she wanted to—she said to him, "Now I can hold you," referring back to the completion of the kiss she had asked for.

It was obvious that she wasn't making any attempts to say it back.

And now an eerie silence covered the room. Before she could even respond to the statement, for the second time, he grabbed his keys from the nightstand and held up two particular gold ones.

"Have I said enough?" he asked.

She looked at the keys for a moment, then right into his eyes, which were filled with pain—looked like disappointment, mixed with anger and exasperation. He placed the keys back onto the small table and looked back at her.

She took in some air and let it out very slowly. And with a somewhat frustrated look on her face, she said softly, as if she was looking for some type of sympathy, "Jaye. Come on. You know how I feel about you. I can't believe this. And we been through *this* before," she said, directing her hand to the nightstand as she referred to the key situation.

"We been through this before? We never solved anything. We just didn't talk about it."

"Okay," she said, taking a seat at the foot of the bed with her body positioned to face him. "You wanna talk about it. Let's talk about it." She had sarcasm in her voice. "Why are those keys such a big problem for you?"

Sensing that sarcasm and not liking it one bit, he looked at her and said, "They're not a problem for me. You're the one that has the problem with 'em. Why are they such a big problem for *you*?"

The change of direction in the question surprised her; she hadn't planned on being the one answering it.

"Jaye, when I gave you those keys, I told you what they were for. *You* took it upon *yourself* to use them the way you wanted to," she justified. "I can't help it if you misunderst-"

"No. You send mixed signals. You *knew* what I thought those keys meant. I thought the keys meant you were ready to really put something into this thing, but-"

She sighed again cutting him off as she got up from the bed. "Damn," she said, completely irritated by the conversation. "It's like every time I think I'm making some type of progress, *some*thin' new comes up."

"'Cause you half steppin', J. You tell me you're ready to do shit when you really ain't ready at all."

"How the hell you gon' say I'm half steppin'? Just because I'm not movin' as fast as you are, or as fast as you *want* me to, don't mean I'm not tryin'. Shit."

"You tell me you wanna do this—be with me and not be scared and all that—but it seems like for every step forward you make… you take two steps back," he complained. He noticed last week at the banquet how she introduced him as her "date," but he didn't say anything about that. "You tell me I don't say how I feel, but obviously you don't either."

"But Jaye, you *know* how I feel," she said. "I wouldn't be going through all this shit if I didn't care about you?"

"*Care* about me, J? I never said that I didn't think you cared about me. I just wanna know how come you can't tell me you love me? Why won't you express to me the extent of your feelings for me, huh? Or is that as far as we have gotten in this thing—caring?"

Jaye was willing to take things slowly like she had requested in the beginning, but things seemed to have gone from slow to damn near dormant.

He asked her, "What are we doing?"

She sighed.

"Am I just Jaye Cobain?"

She felt much more than that for him. "I turned my whole life around. For *you*," she said. He just didn't understand how much she had changed to get this far.

He thought for a moment about what she had said. "But what does that mean?"

"You mean a lot to me."

He looked at her for a couple seconds to see if that was all she had to say. When it seemed as if she was finished, he concluded that since she couldn't say it then maybe she really didn't love him.

She thought about it. There was no doubt in her mind; she wanted to be with Jaye, but she wanted to do things on her watch—when she was good and ready. But when would that be? A month? Three months? A year? Maybe two. As she stood there and these thoughts ran through her head, she wondered what would happen if she told him that she couldn't say it—if she told him that she wanted to wait a little longer. She could see him leaving that night. She could see him saying to her that he didn't think they should be together anymore. She could see him separating his life from hers. And she could see them not being a part of each other anymore—forever. That's not what she wanted.

So to avoid any of these unwanted reactions to her real feelings, she looked him in the eyes and said, "I love you. I love you. Okay? I. Love. You."

She said it three times, and each time she said it, she realized how much she meant it. She looked at him, realizing that she was looking at her first love—the first man she'd ever said those three words to. She was so mad though. She was nearly in tears. She took a deep breath and managed to hold them in. She was mad because she had not only said it at a time when she didn't really want to, she also didn't say it the way she would've had it been a time when she was more sure that it was something she wanted to say.

He could see what had just happened; he had virtually forced her to say it. And the "Are you happy now?" tone in her voice and look on her face when she said it only made him feel worse. He made her say it, but he realized that in his demanding request, he never told her *how* he wanted her to say it. He wasn't at all happy with her delivery; however, she had given him what he thought he wanted. Not the *way* he wanted it, but it was what he asked for nonetheless. And because of this, his opinion about her remained the same—she was still half steppin'. But... he still loved her.

He got up from the bed and walked over to her and wrapped his arms around her.

The Orioles were hosting the Red Sox, and Jaye and Keyon had seats right behind the dugout. The game didn't start until 7. Keyon wanted to get a new Sox jersey before they got there to support his home team, so they stopped at a sporting goods store just outside of Baltimore.

He grabbed the one he wanted, then looked over at Jaye and said, "Anyway, you were sayin'..."

"Yeah," Jaye remembered. "It's like... she got pissed off when I told her she was half steppin', but..."

"Why is she half steppin'?"

"I don't know," he said. "She told me that she was ready to... to stop being scared, and that she was ready to move forward and all this, but..." Jaye shook his head. "Feels like we're in the same place. I don't know what the hell we're doing."

They approached the checkout. Keyon paid for his jersey and proceeded to talk as they left the store.

"You love her, right?"

"I do. But…"

"But?"

"But. . . I don't do shit like this. When I'm in, I'm *in*. You no'm sayin'?"

"Yeah," Keyon nodded.

Jaye sighed. He thought about past relationships. His agenda hadn't changed with J; he just wanted to love her. He knew that she had never been loved before. And now that he was trying to love her, genuinely give her his heart, she didn't seem to want it—not the whole thing anyway. He didn't understand why she didn't want the whole thing.

"I mean… is it me?" he asked. "Do I just attract woman that don't wanna be in relationships?"

"I don't think that J doesn't want to be in the relationship." Jaye listened attentively to Keyon. "Maybe she's taking baby steps in this thing, man. Maybe she's just being careful—don't wanna let her guard down too soon." He looked at Jaye to see if he was following him.

He was.

"You're impatient."

"No I'm not," Jaye denied. "I just know what I want."

"Do you?" Keyon asked. The look he gave Jaye hit him harder than any punch could've.

Keyon had been there through all of Jaye's failed relationships, and if there was one thing he knew it was that Jaye did not know exactly what he wanted.

Jaye didn't respond to Keyon's rhetorical question.

"Look, all I'm saying is: you should try to be more patient with her. You know her. I don't think you should force-feed her." Keyon asked, "Do you really love her?"

Jaye shook his head: "Yeah." He thought about it. "Yes. I love her."

"Okay well… I know it might seem like the right time for *you*, but you really can't be mad if it ain't the right time for her."

Keyon smirked and shook his head as he thought about Jaye.

"Maybe this is what you need. Maybe it's a good thing she's not letting you love her."

"How's that good?" Jaye asked.

"'Cause it's slowing you down. It's making you think about things," he said. "Just give the woman some time, Jaye. Give her some time. She'll come around. But don't rush her."

Jaye took in every word.

* * *

"I'm tellin' you..." he said, looking at the back of a package of individually sliced cheese. "They're puttin' it in everything. Can't even eat cheese now." He put the pack of cheese back and shook his head as he moved on.

"What's it called again?" J asked.

"It's called potassium sorbate or sorbic acid depending on which form of it they use," he explained.

"Hm." J shook her head, smiling. He could be so silly sometimes, even when he was serious about something, like this potassium sorbate thing.

They were in the grocery store shopping generally, but specifically trying to find something for dinner that night. This was their first time actually grocery shopping together, and it was here that she found out that her guy was a quasi-health freak. Yeah, he ate chips, cookies, and ice cream, just so long as it didn't contain potassium sorbate. Or sorbic acid.

"I'm tellin' you—this stuff is in the butter; it's in the syrup..."

"So what is it?"

He looked at her with a smirk, surprised that she was actually interested.

In actuality, she wasn't that interested—not in the potassium sorbate, anyway; she just enjoyed hearing him talk. She enjoyed watching him as he picked up stuff and skimmed the label. She enjoyed simply being there while he was there. She listened attentively as he answered her question.

"It's just a preservative. An old biology professor got me all nervous about it, so... I just try to stay away from it."

"Hm," she hummed as if what he was saying was so interesting. She followed him with her eyes.

"That's why I get my cheese from the deli," he said. "Look at this. It's in these muffins."

She giggled softly at him. He was serious, but he was funny.

It was right then that she realized not *what* she felt for him, but more so how *much* she felt it.

"I'm in the mood for seafood tonight. I think I'm gonna get a lobster from the-"

"Jaye."

"Huh?" He turned and looked at her to see what she wanted.

She looked at him, admiring everything about him. "I love you," she said.

His face suddenly had an obvious glow, but one of those inquisitive looks as if he couldn't believe that she had just said that—and said it right there in the grocery store—accompanied the glow.

"Jaye, I do. I *really* love you," she said again, just so that he would know she wasn't playing the first time she'd said it. She rested her arms on his shoulders, wrapping them around his neck as she moved in closer to say it again. "I love you," she said, smiling as she kissed him.

Right there in the bakery in front of the blueberry muffins, cookies and potassium sorbate filled birthdays cakes… they kissed.

J had done some serious thinking after she had told him she loved him in that horrible way the first time. She knew she'd had feelings for him, but she never knew what to call them. She didn't want to make the mistake of dubbing them "love" when they may have actually been something else—like *like*… During that argument though, she said it to him as a last resort—because she didn't want to risk having him not want to be with her no more if she didn't say it at all.

She then thought heavily about her strong desire to be with him; that desire to not want to be *without* him. She didn't know what being in love was supposed to feel like; all she knew was that it was "a being." No one could actually give her a definition, only descriptions. It was like asking somebody what a car was and their response being: "It has four wheels and ah... it uses gasoline, and it has doors... Yeah, doors." Characteristics, but not a definition. She wanted a concrete answer, but after she realized that she couldn't define what being in love actually was, she concluded that she had to evaluate things on her own.

She came up with so many different reasons as to why she could probably call what she had for Jaye "love," but the one that seemed to stand out the most was the fact that, at this point in her life, she couldn't imagine in a million years ever living without him. He had become so much to her that... well, when she thought about being with him, she knew that she needed to be a better her. She *wanted* to be better. He deserved a better her. And whenever she thought about where she'd be or imagined her life in the future, he would always be in those dreams with her.

And with that, she couldn't help but tell him... She loved him.

J was headed to Los Angeles for a few days for a conference, and while she was out there she was going to meet up with one of her old friends from Chicago, Alicia Morris, who lived there now. She met Alicia in her freshman year of high school and to this day they were good friends, despite the fact that they went to college on opposite ends of the country. They remained fairly close throughout their college years, though they saw each other rarely and spoke on the phone once every two or three months at the most. Now, they mostly kept in touch via email.

J and Alicia were like peas in a pod. They probably clicked so well because they had the same mentality about life, relationships and men: "*Won't* live with 'em; can't live without 'em."

Alicia remained in L.A. after college where she worked as Wardrobe Coordinator for numerous motion pictures. It was the middle of June now; the last time the two had spoken was sometime in January. Alicia's life status as of then: she was still childless, her career was coming along wonderfully, and she was still single by choice. Now, instead of having flings with the *average*

Joe, she was having them with Joe the movie star, Joe the football, baseball, or basketball player, Joe the record or movie industry exec, or Joe the recording artist.

"Li Li!"

Alicia had gotten out of the car so that she could get a good look at her friend who she hadn't seen in years. "J! Girl you look good."

"I know," J said, as they hugged each other tight.

"You haven't changed one bit with yo' arrogant ass," Li Li said.

Alicia, or Li Li as J called her, didn't look one year older than she did the last time J had seen her. She was the same beautiful, chocolate sister J remembered; the only difference was: she had longer hair. It rested on her shoulders now instead of being cut close and shaved on the sides and back. Li Li's measurements were pretty much identical to J's—same height, about the same weight. She was always fond of fashion, so it wasn't surprising to J that Li Li didn't want to come to Howard with her, though HU itself is one big fashion show; Li Li wanted to go someplace where she could get a great internship or job during the school year in her desired field, and then go right into her career after graduation. Like J, Li Li was always very ambitious; she wanted to get right into what she wanted to do.

"You look great yourself," J added. "Hair all long now."

"Girl," she said, running her hand through her hair, "I wanted something that could blow in the wind when I got the top down on this thing." She was referring to her car—a late model, black Ford Mustang convertible.

"This is nice," J said. "Well come on, girl, let's go in. I'm starving."

J and Li Li sat at a table for two catching up on the things they neglected to write in their emails.

"So is there anything new goin' on with you, Ms. J?"

J was a bit hesitant to say because she had predicted her friend's reaction, but she said it anyway. "I'm seeing this guy..."

"Just seeing?"

J almost didn't want to tell her friend her good news;

she knew what the reaction would be—the same reaction she would've had if Li Li told her something like this a year ago.

"Well... I'm in a relationship."

"A re-what?"

J smiled. "We've been together for... It's been eight months."

"Eight..." Li Li sat her glass down. "Eight months, J?"

"Eight months," she confirmed.

"So it's serious?"

"It's *very* serious."

Li Li looked at her with a smile on her face. "J, stop pullin' my finger."

"It's your leg."

"I don't care. Don't pull anything," Li Li said. "We all no your playa ass ain't in no steady relationship."

J's mouth fell open in surprise. She was surprised that Li Li wouldn't believe her. "I am."

"J, you are not the relationship type and you know that."

"I didn't use to be because... I don't know. I didn't have any belief."

"So this guy made you believe?"

She nodded before saying, "He helped me. Yeah."

"Get the hell outta here!"

"I'm serious."

Li Li sighed. She didn't believe J—not one bit—but she had to put her thoughts aside and simply play along. That's what friends do.

"Can't believe this. I'm losin' my girl?" she asked in a whiney tone.

"You ain't losin' your girl. I mean I..."

"Don't tell me you went a got 'L' on me. Don't tell me that, J."

J knew exactly what she was talking about. "L" meant "in love"—something the two of them vowed they'd never ever, ever do. "That shit is for the birds and them hopeless ass romantics," they'd say.

J started blushing and laughing. "Li Li..."

"J," she said in disappointment. "*J...*" she wined.

"I love him," she said, somewhat reluctant. "What can I say?"

Li Li shook her head. "You're serious about this," she concluded. "You lost your game, didn't you? I know that's what it was. My girl lost her... You lost your game, so now you fallin' back on *that* shit like a softy. I thought you was bettah than that."

J smiled to cover up the fact that she didn't like to hear Li Li saying that about her.

"It ain't like that," she said.

"Yeah it is."

Li Li smiled periodically because she was talking playfully, but she was dead serious.

"We were s'pose to be different from all these bitches out here hopelessly lookin' for shit that ain't there, and won't ever be there."

"Why are you so pessimistic?"

"Pessi... No, I'm *real*istic. You *used* to be." She sipped her wine and looked at J, serious this time. "You know men ain't worth shit. Never have been and never will be. Can't even get a good fuck out of some of 'em." She sipped some more and added, "Ain't worth a damn."

J thought about Jaye. She had to defend him. "Not all of 'em."

"What is this?!"

"Alicia, come on."

"No, J, *you* come on. You changin' on me."

"No, I'm just doing things a little differently," she corrected.

"Isn't that what change is?" Alicia asked, proving that she was right.

The table was quiet for a moment as J thought. She wasn't doing anything wrong by changing. Not one thing.

"So you don't miss... You don't miss it at all?" Li Li asked.

"What? Fuckin' around?"

"I was gonna say being single but... Yeah. You don't miss

just having sex?" Li Li asked. "A lot of shit comes with havin' a relationship. You don't miss not havin' to wake up with the same mothafucka all the time?"

J smiled as she thought. She sometimes missed not having to be so… together. She was always with Jaye. She went to bed with him. She woke up with him. She ate dinner with him… Sometimes she did just want him to have sex with her and then leave her alone, but she could never ask for that. Sex was more than that now.

She said, "Yeah. I know what you mean."

Li Li said, "See."

"But this is better," J said. "I like the fact that he's there when I wake up, and not just because it's his house," she added, as they both laughed.

"So tell me about him."

J smiled, happy that her friend had stopped badgering her.

"What's so special about this *guy* that's got you all… fucked up in the head?"

J's face immediately lit up. She thought about him. Everything about him. But no words could come to mind. She had been so busy being *in* this life with him, she hadn't really stopped to think about a question like the one her friend had just posed.

"He is just…" J thought some more and smiled some more. She tried again: "I'm tellin' you. He is just…"

Alicia began smiling and shaking her head realizing just how far gone her girl was. "Is he like that?"

"He is *like that*," J confirmed, relieved that she didn't have to keep searching for words.

"He got money?" Alicia asked. "What does he do?"

J didn't want to tell too much of his business. "He does his thing."

"Well, damn. Who *is* he?"

Any other time J would've been more than excited to get into all that—to brag and boast. She just said, "You wouldn't know him," knowing that, in fact, her friend would know him. But she didn't need to.

"Well, whoever he is, if he's got you open I bet you gotta beat the bitches off with a stick don't you?"

J just laughed and shook her head at her crazy friend.

Li Li said, "Well, Ms. J, I know you on lock down and shit now, but…"

Blushing, she said, "I'm not on lockdown."

"*But*," Alicia continued, ignoring her, "We're gonna have some fun tonight."

J was in the mood for fun. She could never turn down a good ol' party.

One of L.A.'s hottest radio personalities was having his birthday party at the city's hottest nightclub, and everybody was going to be there. Li Li, of course, was one of those people who knew everybody, so obviously she was on "the list." She and J arrived at the club around midnight and they walked right in and squeezed their way to the VIP room. There were so many people inside the club that they literally had to suck in their stomachs and walk sideways to get to their destination.

It was dark and the music was blasting throughout the place—so loud and so bassy that she could feel it in her chest and under her feet as she walked. The club was filled with people, young and not so young, who danced and grinded to the beat, which made the air humid from all of the sweating and breathing that was going on. Hairdos had frizzed and outfits were wet from perspiration, but as the DJ threw on hit after hit, the people just danced harder. Some chose to sit at the bar with their drinks if they could find a seat, but most people didn't bother to look; they just held their glasses over their heads as they gyrated and vertically humped each other on the dance floor.

After what seemed like a walk across the Amazon rainforest, they finally arrived at the VIP room, which wasn't as crowded and hot as the rest of the place; it was almost like a separate club inside of the larger one. Everything was nicer and it wasn't as rowdy.

"Aye, I'm gonna walk around," Li Li informed.

"Do what you gotta do. I'm 'bout to have some fun," J said, as she started dancing with a dark-skinned dude.

After dancing non-stop for about twenty minutes, she

became extremely thirsty, so she went over to the bar where she immediately and surprisingly found a seat. Even the seats at the VIP bar were usually occupied. She decided to order something light because she knew Alicia would be drinking.

"I'll have a Coke," she said to the bartender.

"On the rocks?" he asked, flirting.

She smiled and said, "Sure."

He was cute—caramel colored brother, short, nice build. She looked away and began snapping her fingers and seat-dancing to the song that played.

"Is that all? Just a Coke with ice?" a male voice asked, talking close to her ear.

She turned to see who it was. It was Marien, her movie-making friend from college—her infamous tango partner.

"You look like you just saw a ghost," he said.

"No, I'm just… I'm surprised to see you," she said, still in shock. "How is… everything?"

"Everything is good."

Marien still looked as good she remembered. He was dressed in jeans, black casual shoes, and he had his black, short-sleeve linen, button down shirt open, exposing the white wife-beater he wore underneath. His neck and chest were decorated with platinum jewelry—one thin chain and a Scorpio zodiac charm—and the diamonds in his ears reflected the spotlight that zipped back and forth across the room. The club lights also caused a twinkle in his eyes that only seemed to occur every time she stared into them.

"What are you doin' in L.A.?"

"Oh I have a conference to go to tomorrow, so…"

"Rum and Coke," he said to the bartender referring to his drink. He turned back to her and asked, "How long you gon' be here?"

She looked at her watch.

"Not *here*. I'm talkin' 'bout L.A.."

"Oh. Ahh… I'm leaving Sunday."

He wasted no time asking, "Wanna have dinner with me tomorrow?"

Whenever Marien invited her to lunch or dinner or

anything else that they *never* did, it always, without fail, meant, "Do you wanna fuck?" That was his way of saying it without saying it.

A slight blush struck her face as she looked at him and said happily, "I don't think that'll be a very good idea."

He gave her an inquisitive look and gesture, which implied the question, "Why not?"

"I'm not doing that anymore," she said.

A look of shock took over his face. He raised his eyebrows just before saying, "You gotta be kidding me. No offense, but… *You?*"

She smiled and said in a sweet tone, "I'll see you around, Marien."

He picked up his drink and asked, "Sure?"

She made the mistake of looking at him again, from head to toe and back up again. She said, "Ah… Yeah."

"Ah'ight," he said, giving up. "I guess I'll see you around then."

He walked away, and she continued to sip her Coke and snap her fingers to the music.

Just one hour into the night, she became unbearably tired. It was the flight that did it.

She left Li Li four text messages, and then went outside and tried calling her cell phone, but she got no response to either. It was one thirty now and she was ready to go back to her hotel room. She had been trying to get in touch with Alicia for the past twenty minutes.

She was outside of the club on her sixth text when Marien walked out and stood beside her.

"Leavin' already?" he asked.

"Yeah," she said, keeping her eyes on her cell phone just in case it rang.

"Where's your ride?"

"Well, I came here with a friend of mine and…" She was still looking at her phone. "I think she's still in the club. I can't find her."

"Hm." He gave the valet his ticket and the man went to get his car.

She dialed Alicia's number again and put the phone up to her ear. "I am ready to go. I'm jetlagged like shit."

"I'll drive you back to your hotel," he offered. "Where you stayin'?"

She gave him one of those "yeah right" looks and said, "No, thank you."

He snickered. "J, if you're tired and ready to go, I will drop you off at your hotel. You can call your girl when you get there and let her know where you are. I won't bite," he said suggestively. "I'm just being a gentleman."

She thought about it for a moment. She was so tired. The party was supposed to go on until three and she knew that Li Li was famous for staying the whole time. J knew she wouldn't be ready to leave now anyway; they had only gotten there an hour and a half ago. She considered taking Marien up on his offer. She didn't say anything. She just stood there beside him as he waited for his car to come around.

A silver BMW 3 series convertible pulled up and Marien said, "That's me. Sure you don't want me to drop you off?"

She sighed and looked at her watch. It said 4:40, but that was only because she had forgotten to set it for the time zone. She looked at her phone again to see if she had received any messages. None.

"Okay."

She got in on the passenger's side and closed the door as he pulled off. The ride to the hotel took less than fifteen minutes, and they didn't say much of anything to each other the entire drive.

The car stopped and she opened the door in an obvious attempt to rush away from him.

"Aye," he said, stopping her. "How come you don't wanna see me anymore?"

She sighed. "Look, I have to go, okay. Thanks for the ride."

He smiled. "Okay."

And she got out of the car and walked into the hotel without looking back once.

As she stood in the shower under the cool water washing the smoke smell out of her hair, she kept thinking. She still couldn't get that question Li Li had asked out of her mind. She just kept thinking about it, and thinking about it... *What was it about Jaye that was so special?* She began to remember how they met. The alleyway where they talked. The milk crates on which they sat. The walk they took. The impulsive sex they had that night after knowing each other for an hour and a half. At that point, she began to think about all the men she had been with in the past and how her life was before that night. She would've never guessed that the actions she considered fun would come back to haunt her in such a way.

Who am I to deserve such a beautiful thing? she questioned numerous times. She had lived her life a certain way—one with which she was very comfortable, considering its contrast to that of "normal" society. She had understood her place; she knew who she was; she understood how she lived and how her life and lifestyle differed from those of her friends, and many, if not *most* other women. She was comfortable with that. Women, regardless of race, nationality, or creed wish to find a good man, marry, have kids, and live happily ever after until death does them part. J's wishes were different; there was no ultimate goal to have the ultimate man, the ultimate wedding, and the ultimate whatever else bullshit. She wished to enjoy life while alive and simply leave it when she died. And between that time she would do whatever made her happy.

And up until the previous year—until she met Mr. Cobain—she had been enjoying this life as a female Don Juan, so to speak. A man like Jaye was not what she had wanted. Not in a million years. She thought about all the women who had stopped trying to find a man like him and had simply given up or settled. Which actually made her feel bad about having him.

J believed heavily in the saying, "Anything worth having is worth working for." And in this case, she had not worked for what she had gotten. *He* had simply fallen into her lap, almost literally, which was why she was so reluctant to let her guard down; she was paranoid—couldn't even believe that it was real. Because loving him was so easy. She was afraid of disappointment.

There was a part of her that was still cynical. She was afraid he would eventually do something typical of a man. Though she was convinced that he was a good man, in the back of her mind, she didn't think fate would be that nice to her. She didn't think she would be allowed to live happily ever after even if she wanted to now.

After her cool shower, she lay in her hotel bed still thinking. There was another part of her that wished that none of the stuff in her past had ever happened. If her past were different, she thought, then perhaps she wouldn't be so paranoid now. She felt like a kid who had cheated on a math test, gotten an A, and got away with it. She felt undeserving of Jaye, and she felt guilty for having bypassed all the heartache that everybody else goes through to find that special someone. She felt like she had been admitted into this elite group without having pledged. She felt that she hadn't worked for what she had gotten.

* * *

Jaye got up extra early to make Meka breakfast this morning. He had been thinking a lot about her and he realized she was all grown up. She was sixteen-years-old now. It seemed like just yesterday, she was a little bigheaded kid who loved taking rides on his neck and watching him paint. He couldn't go anywhere without her; she wouldn't let him. She would cry if he ever left her side. She cried for two weeks straight when he went away to college. She was only five so she didn't understand why he had to leave and why he couldn't take her with him.

He wanted that back.

"Hey," she said, coming into the kitchen not sounding particularly happy. Not sad. Not anything. She sat at the breakfast bar.

"Hey," he said. "Is everything okay?" His face was filled with concern and worry.

"Yeah," she said, wondering why he thought something would be wrong. A grimace appeared on her face as he placed a plate full of food in front of her.

"How's school goin'?" he asked, realizing he hadn't asked her that in a while.

She shrugged, "It's school," she answered, unenthusiastically. "Syrup, please."

He handed her the syrup and took a seat across from her so he could look at her as they talked. He wanted to talk with her. They used to talk all the time about everything, but they hadn't done that lately. He wanted to be more informed about her personal life, since she had one now. She used to tell him everything, though then there was really nothing to tell. But he loved that she felt comfortable talking to him about the boys she liked or the ones she had talked to over the phone. He used to know her feelings. He used to know everything she was doing, and he was confident that he knew the things she wasn't doing.

Now, he didn't so much feel like he didn't trust her, but he just felt as if they had been distanced from each other. He didn't think she felt like she could come to him like she used to.

"I guess school is fine. I'm just tired. I'm ready for summer, ya know?"

"Yeah," he said, understanding how she could feel that way. Duke Ellington students had several extra hours tacked onto their schooldays. She sometimes didn't get in until eight or nine at night and still had homework to do.

"Meka," he said, looking over at her, "How come we don't be together like we used to?"

"What you talkin' 'bout?" The question caught her off guard.

He put his fork down and reiterated, "How come we don't hang out like we did back in Jersey? We used to always watch the Nets games together. We ain't done that since you been here."

She smiled with an inquisitive look on her face. "I don't know," she said.

He had to ask, "You don't like being with me anymore?"

"Jaye," she laughed. "Come on."

"Really, Meka, I wanna know. Am I not fun anymore?"

"You're fun," she confirmed.

He thought for a second. Scooped up some scrambled eggs as they exchanged glances across the table. He said to her,

"Do you remember that night—I think you were in fourth grade—and I was tucking you in, and you asked me why were boys so mean?"

Smiling, she said, "I remember."

"You said that there was this boy you liked, but he kept pinchin' you and throwin' paper at you."

Meka laughed.

"And remember in sixth grade when I went shopping for a dress with you for the dance? You told me everything about the guy you were goin' with. How he wrote you a note that said that you were pretty, and how cute you thought he was."

Still laughing, she said, "Oh my gosh, Jaye, why are you bringing this up?!"

"Because, Meka, we used to be tight," he said. "I wanna know how come we ain't tight like that no more."

"We tight."

"Nah. We ain't like we used to be," he said. "I really felt like I knew you then. Now I feel like we're just roommates or some'n."

She sighed. "Jaye, I think we're tight, it's just that... Well, honestly, lately I haven't had very much to talk about. I'm usually in school rehearsin' all day long. And... Well, don't take this the wrong way, but... you're a boy."

"Okay?"

"No, I mean... I don't know. You're a guy. And not just like any guy, but you're my brother," she said. "We used to be like friends, but I look at you as like an adult now. I don't know. It's weird."

He wanted to understand. "So I'm more of a grownup than a brother to you now?"

She thought for a second, and then said, "Yeah."

He didn't want to be an adult; he wanted to be her brother and her friend.

"Well how can I change that?"

She shrugged her shoulders.

"I want us to be like we used to. I want you to feel like you can come to me with anything. I want you to feel comfortable with me."

She saw how sincere he was and how much he really wanted this.

He said, "I want you to feel like you can ask me whatever you want."

She nodded her head and continued eating, trying to think of something to ask to take him up on his offer. "All right, big brother. Tell me about J."

Somehow, he knew that Meka would get on the subject of his girlfriend and he was prepared to tell her what she wanted, or *needed* to know.

He picked over his food and asked, "What do you wanna know?"

"Do you... Are you in love with her?" she asked.

"Yeah, I love-"

"I mean do you *really* love her, Jaye?"

He looked at Meka and said genuinely, "I do. I really love her."

"So she's serious?"

"She's... She's serious."

"Good," she said, chewing and smiling, "'Cause I like her too."

"And to think—there was time when you hated her."

"I didn't *hate* her, per se."

Jaye looked at her as if to say "yeah right."

She laughed, then changed the subject back. "So... Where is this going?"

"What do you mean?"

"I mean is she just another girlfriend or is she..." Meka thought about exactly what to call it. "Is she gonna be more?"

"By more, you mean?"

Meka sighed. "Come on, Jaye. Don't try to act like you don't know what I mean. You *know* what I mean."

Jaye was smiling, only making Meka anticipate his answer more and more.

"I know what you mean?"

"Yes," she said. "So?"

He made her wait a little bit longer for an answer by eating some of his food before answering. "Well, TaMeka, if you must know," he said, "yes, I think she could be more."

Meka sighed. "Jaye, that's not telling me anything."

"What should I be telling you?"

"You should be telling me whether she'd make a good wife for you."

"Wife?" he asked as if she were speaking a foreign language.

"Yeah, as in the woman you marry and have kids with and all that type of stuff."

"Yeah, I know what a wife is."

"So could J be that?" she asked.

Meka knew her brother. She knew that he was a good guy. He treated women with nothing but respect; he was always honest; he was a gentleman; and of all the relationships he had been in, he had never once cheated on a woman. So she knew he deserved a lot more than he had gotten out of his so-called loves.

Jaye was a man of stability; he hated the volatility that the single life imposed upon him. Meka knew that sleeping around wasn't something he did. He liked having a woman in his life—someone to love and trust and protect and be there for. He couldn't have that as a single man—always seeing different women, not trusting any of them, not ever really knowing who they are. She didn't want him to keep being exposed to these women that weren't good for him; they might corrupt his mind, causing him to lose faith in something that he, to this day, still had so much belief in: love.

Instead of giving her a yes or no answer to her question, he simply said, "I'm very happy with J. *Very* happy," he reemphasized. "But I'm trying to take my time with this now. I love her. A *lot*. A *whole lot*," he said. He smiled. "And I don't wanna mess anything up. I need to take my time with her."

Meka understood him and didn't ask any more questions, and though he really didn't give her the yes or no answer for which she was searching, his response was good enough. She always hoped that he would find the right woman soon. His wife. She had been there through all of his heartbreak, heartache, and pain. Women had hurt Jaye on many occasions—disappointed him.

There was no "playing his cards right;" he had continuously just been dealt bad hands.

* * *

She had just come back into the hotel room that evening from the conference, and before she could even settle in, take her shoes off, and relax because she was still tired, there was a knock on the door. She assumed that maybe somebody had just made the mistake of knocking on the wrong door. If they had, she was simply not going to say anything or open it. Then she hoped that maybe it was Jaye. She knew that the thought was nothing more than wishful thinking, yet she walked over to the door a little quicker to see who was there.

Oh my God! What the fuck is he doing here?

She stood by the door for a moment wondering whether she should open it. He didn't have a reason—that she knew of—to be at her hotel room. She looked through the peephole again hoping that he had walked away, but he hadn't. He was still standing there.

She decided to open the door, reluctantly.

"What the hell did you do—follow me to my room?"

He said, "Please. Come on, J. A high-end hotel? I have friends."

She just continued to look at him, waiting for him to state his case.

"I got all the way home last night," he said, "then looked in the passenger's seat and saw this lil' jacket." He held up her jean jacket that she had left in his car.

The only reason why she didn't realize that it was gone was because she really didn't have any need for it. It was L.A.

She took it from his hand and asked, "Is that all?"

He grinned devilishly. Said, "I don't get a thank you?" She didn't say anything, so he said, "I just saw you not even a year ago. Since when do you not '*do* that anymore'?" referring to what she had said last night when she refused to "dine" with him.

"People change," she said.

"Yeah, *people* do," he agreed. "But *you*? You were never the relationship type. I'm assuming that's what you mean by *change*."

She looked down at her feet thinking about what he had said, but trying not to let it get to her. She didn't want to look him in the face—in the eyes. The entire reason they had begun their "relationship," so to speak, ten years ago was because he was "so fucking sexy," as she remembered thinking when she first laid eyes on him. It was the same thing she was thinking now. As much as she tried not to, she couldn't help it.

"Look, I'm... I'm trying to..."

"What *are* you tryin'? Tryin' somethin' new? I'll believe that. Change? Hell no," he said. "You ain't foolin' nobody but yourself."

She looked up at him and said, "I couldn't be like that anymore."

Her real reason for falling in love had nothing to do with her not wanting to "be *like that* anymore." The reason was because she had emotionally fallen for a guy—something she couldn't have fought even if she had tried hard enough. She actually had put up a fight, but loss, gracefully.

"So now you're tryin' to be somebody you're not?"

"I'm not tryin' to..."

"J. We both know what you are. And to be tied down..." he said. Moving his head so that he could look into her eyes better, he concluded, "That ain't you."

She took a deep breath and looked away.

Marien placed his hand on her chin and guided her face to look up at him. He could see the fear in her eyes. It covered her face. It was in her heart.

He moved in slowly and kissed her lips.

She didn't want him. She didn't want to see him. Didn't want him standing there in front of her hotel room door. But at the same time, she wanted him *so* badly. She always wanted him.

There was enough time for her to move and reject this kiss. Reject him. But she couldn't, though nothing held her there physically. If she were strong enough to say "no," then Marien probably would have respected her choice and simply left her alone. He might've actually believed that she perhaps was a changed woman. But she didn't. And he didn't believe for one moment that she had changed.

She let him enter...

Looking in the bathroom mirror, she hated what she saw. Once vain and self-assured, now all of those beliefs were unsubstantiated. For the first time, she didn't see a woman in the mirror that she was proud of. As she looked at her own puffy eyes and unkempt hair, she even realized how much she didn't like her. She wished she didn't know the bitch she saw.

Her head was pounding; she barely felt like blinking as she remembered the event in L.A. with Marien—the kissing, the touching, the rubbing, the sweating, the climaxes… the carelessness, the selfishness, the tactlessness, the thoughtlessness, the inconsideration… Suddenly, her entire body, her mind, and her heart became consumed with shame. Regret. And though Jaye knew nothing of what happened in L.A., she knew that she had hurt him, terribly; thus, she had imposed pain upon herself.

The doorbell interrupted her daze. She knew it was him. She wiped her eyes and slowly made her way to the door.

"You look like you were asleep. Did I wake you?" He was carrying a grocery bag as he walked in, smiling—happy to see her and happy to be there helping her over-come her "sickness."

"No. I was just waiting for you," she answered, closing the door behind him. She watched him as he walked to the kitchen, noticing that he had on crisp white sneakers with no socks. She loved that. She loved how he looked in his Nets basketball jersey and jean shorts. His legs and forearms were so hairy. She loved that too. She loved *him*.

"You could've used your key," she said, almost as if he should've known that.

He glanced back at her as he made his way toward the kitchen, but he didn't say anything. He just thought of what she said as another one of her small steps forward.

"Sorry I took so long. I know I told you I'd be here twenty minutes ago."

"It's okay."

"I'm gonna make you…" he said grinning as he took the stuff from the bag and put it on the counter, "my grandmother's remedy for headaches."

"What is it?" she asked, curious to know what he had bought.

"It's a love-shake."

She smiled—for the first time in 24 hours. She asked, "A what?"

"It's a milkshake—a love-shake." He looked at her, smiling, seeing that she wanted to know more. "It's a vanilla milk shake, with whipped topping, just a little bit of chocolate chips, and a few dashes of cinnamon."

"And what is that s'pose to do?"

"Well… When my head used to hurt and it was hot out… like it is today… she would make me one of these here 'love-shakes,' lay me down, and I would sip it through a big straw. I always fell asleep when I finished, but when I woke up… I was cured."

"So why does she call it a 'love-shake'?"

"Oh," he said, forgetting that he left out the most important ingredient. "Because you have to make it with love or else it won't work. I'm puttin' a lotta love in this one."

The smile that covered her face slowly disintegrated as she stood near the counter watching him. She didn't say anything, but thought: *He loves me so much that now he's putting it in my milkshakes.* A knot formed in her throat and she got all hot again, and anxious. She didn't want to talk because he would hear the shakiness in her voice, so she just walked away.

"Want me to help you up the steps?" he asked.

She just shook her head implying "no."

She wondered how long this would last—the nervousness, the guilt, the feeling like shit. The crying. She had cried more in the last day than she had her entire life.

No sooner than she crawled into bed, Jaye was in the room with the love-shake.

"Here you go." He placed the glass onto the nightstand.

"Thank you."

"This'll get rid of that headache."

He crawled onto the bed and got comfortable beside her.

"Jaye, I love you." Her back was to him and he was on his side right behind her.

"I love you too."

* * *

A whole week had passed since J's visit to The Golden State and she wasn't feeling any better. The average illness seldom lasts more than a few days, so in order to not look suspicious she pretended to be okay after a couple. With the help of a few love-shakes and some medicine, she had pretty much gotten rid of the headaches, but the anxiety symptoms still existed. They hadn't really gotten to the point where they could be labeled as "attacks," but she had to do something soon or else the sickness would consume her, causing her to result to serious medication.

It was the following Monday now. She had called Kenya that morning and requested her time for lunch. She needed to talk, and she needed to do it in person, and it needed to be with Kenya. Of course she didn't tell Kenya anything over the phone. She had simply called and said, "Clear your schedule. We're having lunch today." She didn't show any signs of *needing* to be with a friend.

By noon, she was walking through the doors of The Brown'sTone Recording Company's corporate office with two salads, bread sticks, and drinks.

"Hey," Kenya said as J walked in, placing the bags of food onto her desk. She closed the door behind her and placed the golf club with which she was using to practice her swing back inside the bag. "Is it hot enough for you?" It was nearly 100 degrees outside.

J sighed and gave her a look that answered her question. Then she said, "I got you creamy Italian. They didn't have regular." She began taking the food from the bags.

"That's cool." Kenya walked over and took a seat behind her desk as J made herself comfortable in the seat facing it on the other side. She looked at J with inquisitive eyes and said, "Something's wrong. You're too quiet."

J sighed again. She shook her head while looking down at the salad on the desk as she squeezed the dressing from the packet over the lettuce almost strategically. It took her a moment before she said anything, but finally, she answered: "I wanted to tell you Saturday, but..." She sighed again, then looked at Kenya. She shrugged her shoulders, lazily. "Just wasn't the right time."

That Saturday was Kenya's annual shindig. It had been a year since her last celebrity-infested cookout, now everybody was back at her rented palace again to simply party, drink, talk, and have a good time. And celebrate Memorial Day. They arrived just after four-thirty that afternoon.

Kenya looked at her watch and said, "You two sure are here early. I wasn't expecting you until like seven."

J looked up at him with a slight smile on her face. "He was rushing me. He hates to be late."

"Well, you need to ride with him more often 'cause you don't know how to get anywhere on time," Kenya said, as she and Jaye laughed. "Where's Meka?"

"Oh, she's in Jersey. She's leavin' for London next week so my mother wanted to spend a little time with her before she left."

"London?"

"She's goin' there for a summer studies program. Six weeks."

"Oh okay," Kenya said, glad to hear the news. "Well, help yourself. There's plenty to eat. You know I gotta run around greetin' everybody. So…" She sighed. "I'll see ya'll around."

"Okay," J said, as Kenya walked off to greet a group of women who had just arrived. "Let's find a seat."

Almost as soon as they sat down, Jaye said, "I'm 'bout to get somethin' to eat. You want me to fix you a plate?"

"No, I'll get it," she said insistently as she jumped up from her seat.

He frowned and slowly sat back down. "J, I don't mind. I'll…"

"No. Don't worry about it. I wanna get it for you," she said. "I'll get it." She smiled.

"Well…" he thought about what he wanted on his plate. "Well, you know what I like."

"I do." She smiled at him seductively and walked off.

Everything seemed to be okay today; she hadn't had any flashbacks, the heart palpitations weren't as severe, no cold sweats… She was feeling a little better. It was just past 4 o'clock and not once all day had she thought about…

Marien!

As she stood there holding an empty plate, about to get some macaroni and cheese for Jaye, there he was, also about to get macaroni and cheese. They locked eyes for a moment—both looking slightly nervous and surprised at the same time.

"J, I don't want any potato salad." Jaye interrupted the three-second silence with his presence.

"Do you two know each other?" the woman standing with Marien asked. She was fairly short, had long, flowing brown hair, and looked to be about their age—thirties. She was golden brown, wore just a little make-up, and had on a pastel colored summer dress, which was more than appropriate for the weather.

She was petite and pleasant-looking as she smiled, waiting for an answer to her question.

"Ah… Yeah," Marien said, smiling now, still looking at J. "We went to school together."

The woman smiled and then tried to nudge Marien discreetly, but it didn't work so she spoke on her own. "Hi."

Marien said, "I'm sorry. Ah… Tori, this is J." He smiled, but J wasn't smiling at all. He looked at J and introduced Tori. "And… This is Tori. My fiancé."

As soon as the words left his mouth, J felt like punching him in his face. She could feel her blood pressure rising and fists tightening. It had nothing to do with his fiancé, per se; she seemed to be a very nice woman. It was the fact that this was the same guy who had told *her* that *she* wasn't the relationship type. Had he been single it would've been one thing, but a damn near married man telling her that *she* wasn't the relationship type pissed her off, especially because he was exactly what he told her she was not.

Tori threw her hand out as an offer to shake theirs, while concurrently trying to show off her rock.

To be nice, Jaye shook her hand and said, "Congratulations."

"Thank you," Tori said. She was smiling so hard that each and every one of her teeth showed. "And what's your name?"

"I'm Jaye."

"Thought you looked familiar," she said. "You're the artist right? Jake Obain."

"*Jaye*," he corrected. "Cobain."

"Your gallery is beautiful." Before he could thank her, she had turned the conversation back to herself. "Yeah. After five years, we're finally gonna do this."

Jaye stood behind J, so he wasn't able to read her face. She had a smirk that could've been mistaken for a smile of happiness for the happy couple, but she was really thinking about all the shit Marien had told her in the hotel a week ago about her "trying to be somebody she's not." It all applied to him now and she was somewhat laughing at him inside.

Marien was the only one who understood the smile. He didn't appreciate it because J was never supposed to know about Tori. That was a violation of their rules. With a special relationship like theirs, there was never supposed to be any mixing of these two worlds.

J turned to Jaye and said softly, "I got you. You can sit down."

"Okay," he said to her. He looked over at the guy and girl: "Nice to meet you…"

"Marien Scott," he said, stating his name for the first time.

He reached out to shake Jaye's hand and J saw this, so she quickly put her hand in Jaye's and said, "No potato salad. I got it." She didn't want Jaye to touch his hand.

Not realizing what had just happened, Jaye said, "Ah'ight." He nodded to Marien and Tori, and then walked away.

"Well, it was nice to meet you, J," Tori said.

"Nice meeting you too." She didn't say anything to Marien and he didn't say any more to her. She decided to go to the grill first, just to separate herself from them.

She asked Jaye if they could leave early; she told him that it was the heat and that she was beginning to feel light-headed. But in reality, the anxiety was beginning to overwhelm her, and her emotions were, again, uncontrollable. She had excused herself several times to go to the bathroom inside to cry. She couldn't stay at the party feeling like that.

"What was it that you wanted to tell me?" Kenya asked.

J looked from the salad and into her friend's eyes. She said, "I…" She stopped, sighed, and thought about what she was going to say. "K, you're the only person I feel I could… could…" The tears began to form again—a reflex she had been unable to control for the last week. "Kenya… I…"

Kenya's face showed concern now as she wondered what could possibly be wrong with her friend who, to this day, had never cried in front of her. She said softly, "J, what is it? You're scaring me."

The tears were rolling down her face now.

"J…" Kenya got up from her chair and walked to the side where J was, grabbing the box of tissue on her way. She knelt beside J's chair, wrapped her arms around her friend and brought her close, hugging her, allowing her head to rest on her shoulder. She didn't know what was wrong. All she knew was that her best friend was in need of *her* best friend, which was all that mattered.

J began to compose herself as she lifted her head from Kenya's shoulder. She wiped the tears from her face and looked down at the floor as she prepared to part with her eight-day-old secret.

"Kenya… I fucked up." Her pitch was equivalent to a whisper. "I…" The thought of saying it evoked the thought of what had happened and she began to cry again. "I don't know what the hell I was thinking. I fucked up. I fucked up, Kenya."

With a concerned look covering her face, Kenya asked, "What? What happened?"

J shook her head. "I fu… I slept with Marien…" She looked at Kenya who had a look of shock mixed with sympathy in her eyes. She then looked back down at the floor. "I don't know what the… How could I be so goddamn stupid?"

"Aye, you're not stupid," Kenya said. She put J's head on her shoulder again. "You're not stupid. You just made a mistake, that's all. Everybody makes mistakes."

"And what the fuck was he doing there Saturday anyway?" she said, lifting her head, suddenly mad at her friend.

Kenya calmly said, "J, I don't send out invitations." She had someone who did that.

"I know," J admitted apologetically. "I know. I'm sorry. It's not your fault. *I* fucked up. It's my fault."

After a full minute of crying freely, she began to speak in a low, almost monotonous tone. "I have a good man." She looked at Kenya and shook her head with tears still rolling down her face. "I have a good man. Jaye is… Jaye is everything to me. The world. He's been through a lot of shit, and all he wants is to be loved. That's it. And I love him." The tears ran faster. "I love him so much. And I don't know what I would do if I lost him."

She took some more tissue from the box Kenya held so she could wipe her nose. "I don't know what to do. But I can't… I *can't* keep on like this—the heart fluttering, the hot flashes, the… the crying… I can't sleep. I'm going crazy." She sniffed.

The room got quiet and it seemed as if J was finished. She was still patting her eyes constantly and sniffing. "I'm sorry."

"J, it's okay. That's what I'm here for," Kenya said. She handed J a few more tissues. "I yah… You know I'm bad with stuff like this. I don't know what to tell you."

J tried to smile. "That's okay. I chose to tell you because I knew you wouldn't say the *wrong* things. Or judge me." She paused for a moment as she got herself together. "I feel bad enough as it is. Please don't tell Ty."

"I won't," she said as she got up and made her way back to the other side of the desk.

J looked down at her hands for a moment, then over at Kenya and asked, "What would you do?"

* * *

DC, on July 4, is always filled with the scent of gunpowder and burning charcoal cooking almost every part of the pig, cow and chicken, and vegetable/soy combinations for those who didn't eat meat. People from all over the country come to visit relatives, celebrate the holiday, and enjoy the Independence Day festivities, whether on the Washington Monument grounds where the *big* fireworks are or in a neighborhood where every kid and many adults engage in setting fire to flammable toys.

It was nearly 9 p.m. and the fireworks downtown were about to begin. Jaye had already set up the lawn chairs on the roof and positioned them to face the direction in which the celebration would be taking place. He had chosen a great spot where they could see the fireworks as they went off.

He was just about to go back in to bring the drinks out when he nearly collided with J who was on her way up to meet him.

"Hey. I didn't hear you come in."

She smiled and said, "I was tryin' to surprise you," and kissed him on his lips. "Hot out here, ain't it?"

"Yeah." It was still 90 degrees and the sun had already gone down. "You okay?"

She was holding her finger, which was obviously in pain. "Broke my nail." She had a look of pain on her face as she continued to squeeze her index finger as if that was the only way to relieve the soreness. "Shit hurts." She put her finger in her mouth. "Where's the nail clipper?"

He shrugged. "I don't know. Check the drawer."

"Okay." She was still in pain. "I gotta go get it."

"You know the fireworks start in a few minutes," he warned.

She went back inside the house and into his bedroom to search for the nail clipper. She gave the room a quick skim, looking on top of every flat surface—the television, the nightstand, the chest, the dresser, and even the bed. She didn't see it. So she decided to look on the floor. Nothing.

She walked over to the nightstand on her side of the bed and opened the top drawer. All she saw was a bunch of her stuff she'd left over: a comb, some back up lipstick, nail polish and nail polish remover... No nail clipper. The bottom drawer: no clipper. She went to the other side of the bed and checked that nightstand: condoms in the top drawer, and old papers, bill stubs, pens, and pamphlets to electronic equipment in the bottom.

She sighed and looked around again. The pain was becoming excruciating.

She went over to the dresser and skimmed the top, then she decided to check that drawer. She opened the top: underwear. She didn't really rearrange stuff, just sort of placed her hand on it and moved it from side to side as she looked. Then she opened the drawer just below it. That's when she noticed them—what seemed to be hundreds of papers, sketches of her.

She flipped through them.

They were intimate. He used only his pencils and the plain white paper and depicted her elegantly. Regally. Simply beautifully. The drawings were full of adoration. The way he saw her—from the inside out. Art was important to him, and for him to incorporate her in it? She knew that meant a lot. The way he saw her was much much different from the way *she* saw her.

She started to breath heavily, almost hyperventilating. She backed up and took a seat on the bed. She began to cry. She knew that Jaye could've come in at any time and seen her, but she couldn't help it.

"J! It's about to start!" he yelled from the roof. At least that let her know that he wasn't near the room.

She got up from the bed and went into the bathroom to wipe her nose and face, and there was the nail clipper—sitting on the sink near *her* side.

She did what she had initially intended and hurried back up to the roof.

"Took you long enough," he said. "Look, it already started."

She didn't say anything. She just smiled pleasantly, took a seat beside him and watched the fireworks. They had a better view from his roof than they probably would've had they tried to go to the Mall.

After ten minutes of listening to him shout, "Wow! Look at that one!" like a little kid, she turned and looked at him. He didn't know it—or just didn't acknowledge it—but she was paying more attention to him than she was the firework display. She realized she *needed* to tell him her now thirty-five-day-old secret. She realized that this was his relationship too and he deserved to know what went on in it. She just didn't know *how* to say something like that, or *when* or *where* to say it.

As she sat there looking at him as he watched the fireworks in awe, she began to wonder what was wrong with him. She couldn't come up with anything. So she figured he was perfect. She had a perfect man. He wasn't insecure about her or the relationship or *himself* for that matter; he wasn't jealous; he had his own things and he didn't have to rely on her for anything; he was loyal to her; he loved her more than anything; and most of all, he was trusting and trustworthy. Though it was hard to believe there could be such a thing, she was finally convinced that Jaye was a good man. However, for the record, she just had to ask, "Jaye, what's wrong with you?"

He furrowed his brow as he glanced at her then back at the fireworks. "Nothin'. I'm cool."

"No, I mean *really*—what is *wrong* with you?" she said. "You can't be perfect. There has to be *something* wrong with you."

He laughed. "You crazy."

"Don't you have any bones in your closet?"

He watched the fireworks as he smiled at her questions.

"Ah… I had a one-night stand with a journalist at my gallery opening."

She sucked her teeth. "That don't count cuz we're together now."

"Well," he thought. "*Hm.*" The smile quickly changed to a look of deep contemplation. He thought about it.

"See?" she said as if her point had been proven. "If you have to think that hard…"

"I mean, come on. There're plenty of things." He was laughing at her again.

"Like?"

"Well, you hate the fact that I ah…" He thought. "Oh! You hate it when I listen to my music all loud in the car."

She started laughing as she realized how much she hated that. He loved Hip Hop, but he hardly ever listened to stuff that she knew like stuff on the radio; he liked that underground, conscious stuff that she couldn't even dance to. Or mix tapes. He was forever buying mix tapes from bootleggers. And he loved to blast it. She hated that.

She said, "That's *one* thing. And that's not a *bone.*"

He turned to her, ironically right when the fireworks ended, and said, "What about you?"

"Please. You *know* I ain't good."

She had said that a little too convincingly. The sad thing was, she meant every word she said. Her perfect man had a not-so-perfect woman. And not only was she not good, she was a lying, deceitful, cheating, not-so-perfect woman. That's what she thought of herself. She wanted to cry again when she looked at him.

He moved closer and laid several soft ones on her lips.

"Yeah, I know you're not a perfect woman, but you're *my* woman. That's why I love you."

She closed her eyes and kissed him to take her mind off of herself and how terrible she felt.

"Even when I clip my nails in bed?" she asked. She had to say something.

"Even when you clip your nails in bed," he validated, smiling. "Even when you comb your hair and leave hair all over my bathroom, I still love you. Even when you eat late at night and have the whole place smellin' like food when I'm trying to sleep, I still love you."

She looked down at her hands because she was beginning to cry and she couldn't hold it back.

He said, "I even love when you leave clothes on *top* of the hamper instead of putting them inside. I love you even then."

She looked up at him with her face filled with pain and disappointment in herself. The first time she began to cry in front of him, she ran away before he could see her. She wanted to do that now, but this time there was nowhere to run.

This was the perfect time to tell him—the perfect time to say, *Jaye I've been unfaithful.* He seemed to be in a loving mood, and loving moods usually meant understanding and forgiving moods.

She looked him in his eyes and said, "Jaye, I am *so* sorry. I'm *so* sorry. I'm a terrible person. I don't deserve you. I am so…"

He hugged her, confused by her apparent overreaction. "J, it's okay. It's not that big 'a deal."

"It's a big deal to me."

He moved back out of the hug so he could look her in the eyes. "J, I *love* you. That means the good *and* the… Everything else." He flashes a boyish smile. "If I didn't want you then I wouldn't be sittin' here right now, holdin' you," he said. "I love everything about you."

He had said all that… Now, she didn't want to ruin his good mood. She couldn't tell him now.

"I love you, too. I love you *so* much."

He smiled and asked, "Even when I ask you where my stuff is?"

She began laughing and wiping her eyes. "Don't make me laugh."

She started thinking about how he always asked her stuff like, "J, where's my keys?" or "J, where did I put my hat?" She would always roll her eyes, suck her teeth and say, "Do I use you're keys?" or "Do I wear your hat?"

"Of course," she said to him, smiling. "I still love you when you ask me silly questions. Yes. And…" She looked at him as she thought about more. As she stared at him, more and more thoughts appeared in her head that coincided with what was being discussed at the time.

"I love you when you overdo it with the sports…"

She thought about how he would watch the pre-game, the game, the post-game, and always—without fail—he would watch ESPN's Sports Center every night. She'd ask, "What's the point in watching the highlights if you *just* watched the same game? They ain't gon' show nothin' new." He always responded, "The highlights make the plays look better, even if I just saw it. And Sports Center shows highlights of all the games I didn't see."

She giggled as she thought about that and continued. "I still love you even after you pay more attention to your art than me. It pisses me off, but I still love you."

Whenever he was creating, he would get into one of his "I'm creating" moods, and he simply could *not* be bothered by anything or anyone. He wouldn't answer his phone, and if she decided to just pop up at his house, he didn't bother to acknowledge her. Not when he was in a creating mood. When he had an idea for a specific piece, he usually liked to work on it from start to finish, even if it took him hours, days… He had to keep going until he was done.

He smiled as he stared into her eyes almost hypnotized—so in love with the essence of her. He placed his hand up and touched her face softly, caressing her cheek with his thumb.

He said, "I'll try not to be so moody. Next time."

She shook her head as she looked down at her hands. "See? No. Don't try *not* to do anything. Just… Don't do anything."

She smiled and sighed as she looked him in the eyes. "See what I mean? You always say… the right things."

He said, "Well… Do you still love me?"

She gave him a love tap to the chest and said, "I will *always* love you."

She knew about his history with women and relationships and she hated to be one of the people on that list of people who had hurt and deceived him. He didn't deserve that kind of treatment from her, and she would've gambled any amount of money that he didn't deserve it from those other women either. He was a wonderful man who deserved nothing but the best.

She realized a lot that night. He liked his toilet paper to go up and over, for some odd reason, instead of down and under like normal people. And he never liked to go and hangout; he always wanted to be at home "Where it's nice and quiet and safe," he'd say. He used miracle whip; she hated miracle whip, she liked mayonnaise on her sandwiches. He liked his fruit fresh; she preferred hers canned and cocktailed. The list went on. He simply had *his* way of doing things and she had *hers*.

She realized that in fact he wasn't flawless at all; however, he was still perfect.

She sat there on Jaye's couch in Jaye's living room with only the company of her own tears; and only the sound of her own weeps. The secret had aged another few days. Six pounds was missing from her frame. It was Saturday now—1 p.m. Before today, she had never really been a religious woman, but she prayed to any God who was listening to her today that Jaye would forgive her.

Instead of calling first, she decided to just show up. And instead of using her key, she decided to knock.

"What are you doin' here?" he asked, stepping aside so that she could come in. "And why didn't you just use your key?"

But he was gone now. She didn't know to where. She didn't know when he would come back.

When she came in, she said to him, "We need to…" She sighed and held her composure. "I need to talk to you."

She was nervous—inadvertently pacing in front of the couch, somewhat avoiding eye contact with him. She wasn't going to beat around the bush; she had to just say it because she knew that the longer she stood around not saying anything, the more likely she would've been to not tell him at all. She would've looked him in the eyes, hugged him, kissed him, and then made love to him. She couldn't do it anymore.

She looked in his eyes and slowly squeezed out each word one by one:

"I. Slept. With. Someone. Else."

Everything seemed to stop for him after she said that. He slowly removed his hand from her thigh and his stare shifted from her eyes to the floor just past her feet. He heard her abundance of apologies, however, he was no longer listening to her. He was still trying to calculate what he had just been told. His girlfriend, his *friend*… had just admitted to being unfaithful. She had given what was his to someone else.

He could no longer look her in the face. In the eyes.

When he finally tuned back in, she was crying rivers and still explaining.

"…when I was in L.A. It was a onetime thing, and it was the worst thing I could've ever done," she said. "I love you so much. And as much as I don't… *ever* want to lose you, I feel…" She sniffed. "I felt that I *needed* to tell you this. I couldn't let you go on thinking that I have always been this… this *truth*ful person when I haven't been.

"Jaye, baby, I'm so sorry."

His face had turned from shocked to stiff and cold. He hadn't looked her in her eyes once since she confessed. He just couldn't. He knew that if he looked her in the eyes he would probably end up crying too.

"Jaye," she said in shaky tone, touching his hand.

He quickly snatched his whole arm away as if her hand was a piping hot iron that could've burned him on contact.

He slowly stood up… and walked away.

"Jaye, where are you going?!" she cried.

He walked to the door, opened it, and walked out.

"Jaye…"

But he was gone.

After sitting alone in his house for another half hour, crying… She left.

* * *

Jaye finally made it back home about three hours later from his walk around the streets of Georgetown. The question—the simple word—that constantly pounded his mind was, "Why?" In his mind he had done everything right, for the most part this time. He couldn't understand why she would do something like this. He couldn't comprehend *how* she could hurt him.

He came in the house and tossed his keys onto the sofa as he made his way to his room. He fell lazily onto the bed with tears in his eyes now. Being back inside the house caused the reality of the whole ordeal to sink in. And it was almost like a little voice inside of him kept saying, "Another one bites the dust."

Jaye didn't belong to any church, mosque, synagogue, or temple because he didn't practice any *one* religion in particular; he had studied many of them and respected most for what they had to offer to their respective followers. So, like in Buddhism and the Hinduism, he believed strongly in karma and reincarnation—the belief that actions in one life will have its effects in the next. After being on the receiving end of heartbreak so many times before, he began to think that probably in a former life he was a man—or maybe even a woman—who took people for granted and played with emotions, broke hearts, and now he was getting his just due.

The news he had received a few hours ago just reinforced that thought.

His birthday was in two weeks, and another failed relationship wasn't something he intended to celebrate it with. He used to see himself married by this point. Part of him had even felt that J could be that woman. He was at his best when he was with her. He had the best conversations with her, the best laughs… Some of the best all around times of his life were spent with her. Not to mention the best sex he ever had. He loved her and he felt that they were *this* close. *Were.*

He had fallen asleep thinking about his life. As soon as he actually realized that he was awake from his nap, all of the indigestible feelings about J came back to mind.

He quickly looked at the clock to see how long he had slept. The clock read 7:32 pm. He had slept for over three hours, though he still felt drained. Lifeless. The blinking light indicating a voice message caught his eye. He was reluctant to push "play." He knew the messages were from her and he was in no mood to hear her voice. He pushed the button anyway to confirm his assumption.

"*You have two new messages,*" a computerized voice said. "*Message one*: 'It's me. I just wanted to-' *Message deleted.*" He was serious about not hearing her voice. He allowed the next message to play, expecting it to be another one from her.

"*Message two*: 'JAYE! Guess what, man! GUESS WHAT!'"

As soon as he heard Keyon's voice, he knew exactly what the call was about.

Keyon spotted it a couple weeks ago when the two of them were in a jewelry boutique in Mazza Gallery.

"Oh my god."

"What now?" Jaye asked.

"Look at that, Jaye. *Look* at that, man." Keyon was in awe. "*That* is it."

"Yo, let me hurry up 'fore you spend all your money up in here."

"No, Jaye. *Look*. This is it!"

"What is what?" Jaye asked, sighing with an inquisitive look on his face, finally deciding to look at what Keyon saw.

"The ring, man. It's the perfect fucking ring," he said, whispering in a monotonous tone as if he were under some type of spell.

Jaye gave the ring a good look. They both stood there looking at this ring—not moving, mouths agape, not blinking… They were both taken.

Jaye agreed in a similar voice, "That *is* nice, man. It's *very* nice."

"You *know* I wanna marry her. I been thinkin' about it for 'bout a month now—how I would ask." He paused, still staring into the glass case. Then he said, "Seeing this and seeing how *perfect* it is... I want her to have this."

They stood there in silence for a moment still taken by the ring—not too little, not too much. Perfect.

So when Keyon called nearly screaming "Guess what!" into his answering machine, he knew what it was about.

The message finished: "She said 'YES,' man! She said '*YES!*' Call me back."

Jaye sighed and fell back onto his pillows. He was more than happy for Keyon. At the same time maybe he was envious.

Sunday, she left another message. He didn't respond.

"Jaye, I just wanna talk to you. *Please*," she begged. "Please, call me back."

That message was the first one he had actually let play completely before pushing the "delete" button. Though it had only been twenty-four hours since he wasn't speaking, or in this case *listening* to her anymore, he had become accustom to hearing the messages as room noise, sort of like the sound a window air conditioner makes. It wasn't something he was actually listening to.

By Monday, she stopped calling him. She decided that she would give him his space to think. But she wanted to call. Every day, several times a day, she would pick up her phone. She wanted to dial…

9 a.m.: she wanted to say, "Good morning, Jaye. I was just calling to tell you that I hope you have a wonderful day today. And... And that I love you. Please call me back."

12 p.m.: she thought she could say, "I hope you have a good lunch. I just wanted you to know that I'm thinkin' about you and that I love you. Call me back, please."

3 p.m.: she really wanted to say, "I miss you. And I love you. Please... Please call me."

6 p.m.: she said, "Umm... I'm thinkin' about you and... I'm *always* thinkin' about you. I love you. Ah... I hope you have a nice dinner. And... I love you and... Call me." But she never dialed his number.

10 p.m.: with tears in her eyes, and a few on her pillow, and the phone in her hand, she would've said, "I love you. Sleep tight. And ah... Please, call me."

Every night she fell asleep with regret in her heart.

* * *

"Aye, everybody? This is ah..." Keyon looked at Jaye smiling. He had his arm around Jaye's shoulder. "This is my best friend, Jaye Cobain. My best man."

Keyon and Ty decided to have an engagement celebration dinner at Keyon's condo so that both families and friends who didn't know each other could get to know each other.

"Hello. Everybody," he said, still smiling.

Everybody said "hi" to Jaye, and then Ty's father said, "Since you're his best friend you should know." Jaye listened attentively to Mr. Aldridge—a fair-skinned, average height, professional-looking man in his sixties. His glasses and salt and pepper hair were what gave him the professional look. He spoke with a thick Jamaican accent.

He looked at Jaye with an expression on his face, which revealed that there was a question on his mind, and asked, "Can this guy make a mean jambalaya? He says that his jambalaya is the best this side of the Mississippi."

Jaye's brows wrinkled and he looked at Keyon. Keyon's jambalaya was good; he had had better. It wasn't bad though.

"I don't know about it being the best on this side of the Mississippi…"

"Aww Jaye!" Keyon shouted.

Everybody laughed.

Jaye just smiled. He wasn't really in the mood to do much laughing. And though he could tell that everybody was nice, he didn't really feel like being there with them socializing. He wanted to go back home and get in the bed.

"Man, you s'pose to be my boy. You s'pose to have my back," Keyon said to him.

Smiling, Jaye tried to redeem himself. "Oh, I mean his jambalaya *is* off the hook though."

"Well, we're gonna have to have a cook off one day to see whose is the best," Ty's father challenged.

"Dad, don't start with the competitions," Ty said.

He said, "What?" as if he didn't see anything wrong with a little challenge.

"Can I talk to you for a minute?" Jaye whispered to Keyon.

"Sure. Excuse us," Keyon said to everybody.

He and Jaye walked back to his bedroom and closed the door behind them.

Jaye said, "Man, you mind if I bounce early?"

"Hell yeah I mind. I'm celebrating my en*gagement*, man. This is *very* important to me and I want my best man to share it with me."

Now that he had put it that way, Jaye gave in and said, "Ah'ight."

"Why? What's up?"

He hadn't told Keyon about what happened a week ago. He hadn't told anybody. He wasn't even sure about what he was going to do. He knew he couldn't ignore her forever.

He sighed and shook his head, looked down at the floor and began to walk to the other side of the room. This was Keyon; he told him everything, no matter what it was or how personal. He felt bad having held on to it for a week, especially with it being so big.

After he revealed the details of the tragedy, Keyon froze, looking at Jaye in shock. He didn't know what to do or what to say. Jaye said, "I don't know what the hell to do. I haven't spoken to her since. And I *know* she's gonna be here." He shook his head. "I don't wanna see her. I'm not ready to see her yet. I'm still tryin' to figure shit out."

Finally, Keyon said, "If you wanna roll, I'll make up somethin'. Go 'head, man." He felt so bad for Jaye. He knew that the last thing he needed was another failed relationship.

J and Kenya stepped on the elevator and Kenya pressed the 8.

"I shoulda told Ty I couldn't make it."

"No you shouldn't have. You know how important this is to her," Kenya reminded.

"Yeah, I know. I just don't feel like being around all these people though." She sighed and looked up at the numbers as they lit up.

DING!

"Don't be so self-centered," Kenya said.

The doors opened and they stepped off and walked toward their destination. J took a deep breath and pushed the doorbell.

By the time Jaye and Keyon came from the room, Ty was introducing Kenya and J to the families.

"And this is J. She's a journalist for *FACE Magazine.*" Ty looked over at Keyon and Jaye as they entered the room. "As a matter a'fact, *he's* her boyfriend," she added, looking over at Jaye.

He smiled nervously and quickly looked over at Keyon.

"You have yourself a beautiful woman, son," Ty's father said to Jaye.

Jaye looked down at his hands thinking about how "beautiful" his girlfriend really was.

Ty's dad said, "I've known her for a long time." He looked over at J with a smile on his face. "She's a really nice girl… Excuse me—*woman.*" He laughed and he looked back at Jaye and said, "Treat her right."

As soon as the words left Mr. Aldridge's mouth, J felt her heart sink to her stomach. And for the first time all night, Jaye looked at her. And if looks could kill…

"Well let's see it," Kenya said to Ty.

"See what?" Ty asked.

"The hardware," Kenya said.

Knowing exactly what Kenya was talking about, Ty shook her head almost reluctant to show off her ring. Not only was she not a flashy kind of person, she knew what the ring meant to her and Keyon. And what it didn't. Its importance was minimal.

The ring was very simple. But it was very Ty; he obviously knew her. It was beautiful.

"Keyon really knows how to treat a woman, doesn't he?" Kenya said.

J looked at the ring and it was nice. She felt disappointed though. Security was starting to feel really good nowadays. She felt disappointed because she felt her own security slowly slipping away. It would've been nice to know that somebody felt secure with her—that somebody she loved felt so secure that he wanted to make her his other half. That would've felt good.

"Yeah," she agreed with Kenya. "That is a very nice ring, Ty. Congratulations," she said, touching Ty's shoulder to assure the sincerity and authenticity of her statement.

Ty smiled and said, "Now see, a year ago your response would've been a little different."

"A *lot* different," Kenya said.

J looked down at her hands to hide her face, somewhat. Kenya and Ty started laughing at the truth behind that statement.

J smiled and said, "Well, that was a year ago."

Happy with the change her friend made in the past year, Ty said, "I'm proud of you."

J didn't ask why; her eyebrows wrinkled implying that she needed an explanation as to why her friend was proud.

Ty gave her one of those you-know-why looks.

Kenya simply looked away knowing how different their conversation would be if Ty knew what had happened. Or once she found out.

Ty smiled at J and said, "Well, thank you," referring to the well wish J and Kenya had just given her.

Everybody ate while telling stories and reminiscing, but mostly listening to tales of Ty and Keyon's fifteen-month courtship. Barely half an hour had gone by. Jaye had decided to stick around for a little while, mostly to save face because he had been introduced as her man. But he kept his distance from her. And once he got his plate, he kept his distance from everyone; he chose to sit alone at the bar between the kitchen and the dining area, away from most of the people who were in the living room eating. He didn't look too anti-social.

J came and sat on the vacant stool beside him, placing her plate on the top of the bar.

He saw her when she sat down, but instead of getting up and walking away like he wanted to, he just sighed and continued to pick at the food.

She looked at him for a moment before she said anything. But once the silence in their area became unbearable, she said, "Jaye... I love you so much."

It was the only thing she could really come up with at the time. That was what she was thinking. Her eyes became watery.

He sighed and placed his fork down on the plate. He didn't look at her once since she had sat down. He just stared at the food so he didn't have to make eye contact.

"Baby, I can't go on like this," she said in a soft whisper. "Would you *please* talk to me? *Please*," she begged.

He looked at her again with those same piercing eyes and said, "You wanna talk? Let's talk."

He got up from his seat and walked toward the back to the master bedroom where he and Keyon had talked earlier. She followed him.

Once they got to the back, she closed the door behind herself. Jaye was on the other side of the room pacing nervously. She watched him for a moment wondering if she should say something first or allow him to think and get his words straight. She went with the latter.

He thought about everything as he slowly walked back and forth by the bed.

When he stopped, she looked over at him desperate to hear something from him.

There was so much that he didn't understand and just couldn't calculate. She had expressed the *extent* of her love to him on many occasions, but how much did that really mean if she was willing to sacrifice... Well in this case *ruin* it for sex with another man? Why did she need to have sex with somebody else? He began to think that maybe he wasn't enough for her since she didn't bother having some type of affair to relieve herself of emotional neglect. It was only sex.

So he asked her in his normal calm, cool and collected tone, "Why?"

She looked him right in the eyes. They held eye contact for about five seconds; it seemed like forever.

"Baby, I..." She had been trying to answer that question herself, but couldn't. "I don't know."

He looked away shaking his head at her laughable excuse. He thought that maybe she would come with something better than that. Not that he would've *liked any* reasoning she had, but he particularly didn't care for that one.

"Is it me?"

"*No*," she said insistently, shaking her head to reassure him that it wasn't him. "No you're... you're the best thing that has ever happened to m-"

"I mean physically."

He thought about the sexual partners situation that came up before. Since he knew that her number wasn't a small number, he started to wonder if he was good enough for her sexually—compared to other guys.

This was her second chance to come forward with something more believable.

"Did you need something more, physically, that I..."

"*No!*" she insisted. "*No*. That wasn't it. I told you I don't know why it happened, it just did. And I'm *sorry*, Jaye. I'm so... sorry."

He looked across the room at her and calmly said, "I can't do this. I can't be with you."

She just stood there as the tears ran down her face like clockwork. She couldn't speak.

He said, "If you really loved me, you wouldn't have done something like that. You don't cheat on a person you love."

"Jaye, I just... I fucked up. I..."

"I know," he said. "You said that before. You fucked up... and you love me and all that... I know that. But me... I can't just *get over* somethin' like that." He sighed. "We gotta end this here."

He held his ground without a tear ever appearing. He had done what he had to do.

She was crying enough for the both of them. She didn't say anything else to him, though. She realized that at that point there was nothing she could say or do to change his mind.

He walked by her and out the door without looking back at her.

"Keyon," he called.

He motioned with his hand for Keyon to come over to where he was.

"Man, I'm gonna go," he said.

Keyon said, "Okay. Everything okay?"

"Yeah," Jaye said shaking his head. After realizing his lie, he said, "No. It's not. I'm just gonna... I can't be here right now."

"I understand, man. Go 'head home."

Jaye said, "Thanks," and they smacked hands. "Yo, congrats and ah... enjoy your dinner."

"Ah'ight, man."

Jaye said his goodbyes and left his excuse for leaving up to Keyon to explain.

* * *

After seeing who it was, she pulled the door open with a perplexed look as she greeted her unexpected guest.

"Hey girl. Wha'sup?"

"Hey," Ty said, inviting herself into her friend's house while holding a plate wrapped in aluminum foil. After J closed the door, Ty handed her the plate and said, "You left before you got a chance to get any cake. I knew you might've wanted some so…"

J said, "Oh. Thanks," still standing by the door.

Ty looked her right in her eyes without any particular expression on her face, which would've otherwise revealed what was on her mind, and asked, "Is everything okay?"

J's eyes never left her friend's. She knew that Ty knew something was wrong. The more she stared into Ty's eyes, the more she could tell that her secret was, in fact, not a secret.

"Ty, I was going to tell you. I wanted to tell you, but…"

"Then why *didn't* you, J? Why?" she asked. "We've been girls for what—"

"I know," J cut in before Ty could think of exactly how many years they had been friends.

"Then why did you feel like you couldn't come to me?"

"Honestly?"

Ty shook her head and looked as if she didn't want anything else besides honesty.

"I was scared." J bit on her bottom lip as she decided not to tell her friend why exactly she was afraid. "You won't disown me?"

"Come on, J." She followed J into her living room, talking behind her. "This isn't the first mistake you made and I'm sure it won't be the last." They both smiled as they thought about past events.

She had gotten Ty's forgiveness, now why couldn't she get Jaye's?

Ty said, "I want to help you out in any way that I can. That's what I'm here for. I want to offer you my ear," she said. "And of course counseling, 'cause you know you need it."

J smiled as she thought about maybe taking her friend up on that offer.

"That's only if you ask for it," Ty said.

J sat in her favorite seat and Ty sat on the sofa perpendicular to her.

"J, I'm not gonna lie—I wanted to strangle you when Keyon first told me. But I thought about it. Slept on it. I'm calm now," she said without a smile on her face. "I've been your friend for a long time and I can't bail out on you now. I want you to know I'm still proud of you."

"I messed up. What's to be proud of?"

"Effort."

J tittered. "Thank you, Ty, but effort couldn't keep my relationship together."

"But you tried, J. You gave it a try. And I have to say that I'm proud of you for that," Ty said. "So like I said: I'm here to listen to you now, and help you in any way I can."

J's eyes got shiny. "You're gonna make me cry," she said.

"Oh and you're crying now?"

Her face dropped as she said, "You would be *too* if you were well aware of the fact that you've fucked up your life. Crying is the only way I can release the pain, at least for a moment."

It was somewhat hard for Ty to separate herself from the memories of J a year ago and the J that sat before her, but she could see that she was a changing woman; she was a changing woman that had just made a bad decision. Ty never lived like J, but she could imagine that it would be very difficult to just up and change the lifestyle she had become so used to. It was like an addiction. She could imagine that it was hard to just stop cold turkey. Those who try usually break the promise to themselves at least once.

J wiped her eyes and sighed. "You know, it's funny how everything can be okay one minute and not okay the next." She paused and got her words together. "I've thought about that every moment since it happened and I can't seem to get it out of my mind."

Her eyes became filled with tears again. She wiped them away with the back of her hand.

"You ever done somethin' that you thought might've fucked up your whole life?"

Ty thought about it. Nodding, she said, "There have been times when I thought I might've made the wrong choice—that if

I had chosen to do something differently I would've had a better outcome." She looked J in the eyes and added, "Yeah, I have. But I don't really think like that. Not anymore. I've learned to believe that everything happens for a reason. Everything, good or bad, that happens… is supposed to. It's something to help you grow in some way."

"So what are you sayin: I was sup*posed* to cheat on Jaye?"

"No, I'm not necessarily saying that." She looked at J wondering how she was going to say what she wanted to say while still sounding sympathetic and aware of her friend's emotions. "I think that there was a reason why you did it—something deeper than you might realize right now. But in order for you to get what you're supposed to get from this experience, you're going to have to figure out why you did it."

She waited a moment before adding, "I also think that you're being a little hard on yourself."

"I *hurt* him!" J said as if Ty had no idea of what had happened. "I'm sup*posed* to be hard on myself. I've never felt more like *shit* my entire life. And the worst thing about feeling like shit is knowing that you've made the person you love feel like shit too." She shook her head. "It's a vicious cycle."

Ty wanted so much more out of the conversation, but she tried to hold back her attempts to be a counselor and stuck with just being a friend; she had to differentiate what job she was doing at the time. But she needed to ask one crucial question. She had been thinking about J's action ever since Keyon told her the night before, after their engagement celebration. She thought about how much her friend had changed her life around—because she did in fact believe that J had made a conscious change for the better. She didn't think that J would purposefully go out and cheat and ruin a great relationship for no reason; she had a feeling that it was more complex than that. And since it was more complex than that, she knew that J didn't do it with just some random guy. She believed that J had matured past that now. A random man was out of the question. Whoever it was had to be someone with more credibility—clout in J's book. However, with J, considering her past life, it would be very hard to try and figure out who the culprit might be; she was never with anybody long enough to say that she had any ties to him.

Instead of treating this like the mystery that it was, Ty decided to just ask her, "Who was he?"

More guilt and pain covered J's face. She didn't have a problem telling Ty who, but she dreaded mentioning his name, which she knew would spark up more thoughts and memories about him and that day.

"Was Marien."

"*Marien* Marien?" she asked, making sure it was the same guy she remembered. She knew exactly who Marien was and who he was to J. Ty had never actually met him, just heard a lot about him—about how good he was in bed and all the freaky things he did. J never shared too much more about him, only how much she enjoyed being with him—for physical reasons only.

"Yeah, *that* Marien," she confirmed.

Ty looked at J who had her head down now, staring at the floor.

"How come you keep doing this to yourself, huh?"

"Keep doing what?"

"J, don't you understand what type of..." She felt crazy calling it this, but she went ahead and said it: "re*lation*ship you and Marien have?"

"Marien is nothing more to me than a..."

"And here we go again," Ty said, staying calm when the subject had actually really upset her. It was more so disappointing.

J said, "Well it's true. He's just a good fuck."

"You've said that so much that you actually believe it." She felt reluctant saying what she had to say because she knew her friend would be insulted. But what needed to be said needed to be said. She continued: "J... I hate to break it to you like this, but... Sweetie, Marien is a lot more than just a sex buddy. I think he means more to you than that."

J didn't say anything, so Ty continued to finally tell her what she had noticed from years of observation.

"Now you know I wouldn't just *say* something like this to you. I'm telling you how I see things," she said.

174

In her own defense, J said, "He and I have an agreement, which we made a long time ago…"

"J, it was an agreement not a contract. You're not obligated to keep doing this, so why do you keep doing it?"

"I was available all those years…"

"But then you weren't. And J you still did it. But this time you hurt two important people. I don't think this thing you and Marien have is worth this much pain."

J was quiet for a moment allowing what Ty said to sink in. She sat gazing at the floor as she thought about everything. "Marien was always nothing more to me than a good fuck with no strings attached. And now he's responsible for helping me fuck up my life. Ain't that something?" she asked rhetorically. She allowed her tears to flow down her face now without stopping them.

Ty's eyes became watery too as she listened to her depressed friend go on about how messed up everything was because of one wrong decision.

"Nah, I can't blame Marien. It was all on me. I can't blame him at all." She sniffed. "I chose to sleep with him. I chose to leave my life with Jaye outside of that hotel room while I fucked it up inside. It's all my fault." She thought about it and added, "But maybe that's the way it s'pose to be, huh? After years of shameless fucking, I get fucked. Fate's a bitch, ain't it?"

* * *

The computerized voice on her machine informed, "*You have one new message. Message one,* 'Ahh… It's me—Jaye.'"

When she heard his voice, she stopped everything she was doing and focused her attention on the machine. She sat down on her bed and looked at it as if she could actually *see* him talking.

"I was just calling because ah… Well. I wanted to tell you to… You can leave my keys with Ty. And anything else of mine that you might… That I might've left at your house…"

The tears immediately started rolling down her face.

"You can leave everything with her. I'll leave your things with her as well."

There was a pause. She just sat there on her bed crying and staring at the machine.

He finally continued. "I guess this is goodbye."

There was another pause before he said, "Goodbye. J."

"End of messages."

When she left out a few hours ago, he was in his art room *seemingly* in one of his art moods. So when she came back in just before 6 p.m. that Saturday, she was surprised to see him sitting on the couch in the living room watching baseball. Meka had barely been back in town a whole day—she got in last night—but unlike her brother, she wasn't a homebody; she was out before noon.

"How was your day?" he asked without looking up from the television. His face showed no expression as he waited for an answer.

"It was nice." She locked the door behind her. "We had a good time together."

She also didn't give any clues as to how she was feeling. And even if she did, he wouldn't have noticed; he was so into the game that he almost didn't know she had responded to the question he was programmed to ask once she entered the house.

With her purse in hand, she walked over and sat on the couch beside him. He immediately looked at her with a perplexed expression on his face. He didn't know whether to acknowledge her or continue watching to see whether the guy at first would steal second. A grimace covered his face as he looked back and forth from Meka to the television hoping that she would explain her reasons for sitting there. It wasn't that he had a problem with her watching the game with him; it was just that she didn't like baseball; said it was boring. Luckily, the game went to commercial before he could interrupt it by questioning her about it.

He looked over at her quizzically, but before he could speak, she said, "I need to talk to you about something."

He figured it was probably something that required his full attention, so he picked up the remote, turned the television off, and looked at her fully attentive.

"What's on your mind?" he asked.

"What's going on?" She assumed that he would just know what she was talking about.

He asked, "What do you mean?" He was buying time. He actually planned to tell Meka about his and J's relationship, but after he picked her up from the airport last night, they spent the entire night talking about other stuff, primarily her trip even though they spoke every other day while she was gone.

What he wasn't counting on was her saying in response to his question: "I was with J today."

He probably forgot just how close the two had gotten. He inhaled and held his breath while she finished saying what she had to say.

All she asked was, "What's up?"

Whether he was comfortable was no longer a concern. The question had been posed so now was the time to address it. "Ah… Well." He sighed. "We aren't together anymore. We broke up." He didn't look at Meka to see her reaction. "A few weeks ago," he finished.

Meka had already somewhat braced herself for what he had to say. She noticed last night when they talked, for two hours, J's name was neither mentioned once nor were there any references to her. She noticed her brother's deportment; his posture was even different.

She had spent several hours with J that day and noticed the trend; she even looked a little skinnier. After listening to J tell her, in detail for the first time, about all her duties at the magazine and about the traveling and all that, Meka said to her, "J, you know, I really admire you."

She remembered J's strange response when she said what she thought was a compliment.

J asked, "Why?" almost as if she couldn't believe that anybody would, or could.

Meka shrugged her shoulders and said, "I don't know—everything. You're a great writer and you're doing exactly what you wanna do in your career. You have your own money and a nice ride and a house. And you're pretty..."

"You're flattering me," J said impassively. All of that stuff Meka talked about used to be enough for her. But not anymore. She would give it all up. All of it.

Smiling, Meka said, "I wanna be like you when I get older."

J quickly began to think about how her life was going at the time—not so good. She had been miserable for the past month or so because of a stupid decision she made.

"No, you don't."

Meka frowned at the response to what she thought was another compliment.

"You should be better than me," J said.

"Why?"

J hadn't planned on being asked "why?"

"Because," she said.

Meka waited for her to finish answering the question.

"You should aim higher," J said. "Be better. I think you can be better than me. I want you to. I have a lot of regrets." She sighed as she thought about some of them. "You can be a better woman."

Meka could see that J wasn't saying that just for the sake of saying it. She was almost *insisting* that Meka live her life differently, as if being like her, even remotely, was a god-awful thing—something she wouldn't have recommended her worst enemy to do. The fact that J advised Meka to "be a better woman" let Meka know that J probably didn't think too highly of some of the choices she had made in life. Or maybe didn't make.

"I understand what you're saying," Meka said. "It's just that I look up to you, that's all."

J decided that there was no way for her to talk Meka out of doing that. She wanted to tell Meka that yes, she could look up to her, but only because she was taller. She wanted to tell Meka to only look at her as a symbol of how *not* to be. But to say either of those things would invoke too much explanation; thus, revealing too much about herself—things she would never want somebody that looked up to her to know.

"I appreciate that," J said. "But you should make your own footprints. Don't step in mine."

Meka looked at Jaye who had not looked at her since he told her that his relationship was over. He just sat staring at the black television screen, tapping the remote on his thigh. Meka was even watching this show called *Nothing* with him.

They sat in silence for more than a whole minute, and he was sure that the game was back from commercial, but he didn't turn on the television. It just felt inappropriate.

Finally, Meka looked at him and asked, "How do you feel?"

He was hating the fact that he was obviously so vulnerable in Meka's presence. She had never seen him like this. He didn't say anything because he knew that if he started talking he might start crying. And he couldn't cry in front of his baby sister.

She asked, "Are you angry? Are you confused? Are you glad? Are you unmoved? What?"

He sighed. Another half minute went by before he said to her, "I don't wanna talk about it."

She sucked her teeth, rolled her eyes and shook her head. She watched him as he continued to twirl the remote in his hand and look at the blank television.

"Is that it? Can I turn the game back on?" he asked without looking at her.

"Why do you always do that?"

"Do what?" he asked, a little upset that her response was an obvious 'no' to his question.

"Keep stuff bottled up," she answered. "You need to stop doin' that…"

He said, "I'm not bottled up. I paint. I get it out that way-"

"No. You need to talk. It ain't healthy. That's probably why you're havin' back problems."

Meka sighed and asked with an attitude, "How come whenever something is bothering *me* you just about *make* me talk to you about it, but when it's you, I can't try to help?" She didn't wait for an answer. "You always want me to talk. How come you don't?"

He stared at the tube knowing that Meka was right about what she was saying. So instead of doing the brother/friend thing and talking to her about it, he did the grown-up thing and told her, "Because I don't have to."

"So you're just gonna sit here and watch TV all night instead of trying to make up with your girlfriend?"

"You don't even know what happened…"

"Well tell me!"

He pushed the power button and just like that, the Orioles and Yankees had his undivided attention.

She got up from the couch and headed to her room. "So stupid," she mumbled.

He heard her and didn't know whether she was talking about him or about his response to her question or what. And at the time, he really didn't care. He didn't want to talk to his little sister about why he and *this* girlfriend broke up, mainly because she actually liked this one. For J's sake, he decided it would be best not to tell Meka what had happened because she still wanted J in her life, which was okay with him. Well it wasn't exactly okay, but he decided not to be petty. Just because J would no longer be in his life didn't mean he should make Meka keep her out of hers.

An hour later he was still thinking about what Meka had mumbled when she got up from the couch. "Stupid" was a word that seemed to describe a lot of things as of late. It described the way he felt, mostly. He thought about his latest relationship to fail and thought that maybe being *stupid* was the reason why.

Some people like to think that every experience is a learning experience. But how much do you need to know before you get it right? Or before it gets right for you? Jaye only seemed to have negative experiences with the women he was intimate with, so instead of trying to figure out what was wrong with *them*, he started to think that maybe something was wrong with *him*. Maybe he was stupid like Meka said.

As he sat there, he realized that "stupid" also described the way he had acted earlier that night. He got up and walked to Meka's room, tapped softly on the door and waited for her to answer.

"It's open."

He twisted the knob and walked into Meka's little lair.

"Hey," he said.

"Let me call you back," she said to the person she was talking to on the phone.

With somewhat of an attitude, she looked at him waiting for him to say something.

"Ah… Sometimes people do things—things that are… that may be unforgivable. These things can change the course of a relationship. Sometimes people do some selfish shit that… that hurt other people, and sometimes they don't even know why the hell they did it. And because of that…" He thought about how he was going to say it. "Because of that… Because of that, people have to separate themselves from each other in order to ah… In order to concentrate on themselves and learn what they need to learn in order to move on."

He tapped the door seal, nervously. "Yes, I'm angry. I'm mad. I'm… pissed." He realized he was saying the same thing. "I'm miserable. Disappointed. Confused."

She knew that he was talking about himself and—as it was given—his *ex*-girlfriend, but because it was appropriate, she took it to also be an explanation for his behavior earlier.

"Apology accepted."

I't's amazing how something can be interpreted differently once it's been slept on—after it's had time to actually sink in and be devoured by the subconscious.

She lay on her back under the sheets staring at the ceiling: 8:56 in the morning, hating the fact that the man who lay beside her isn't the man who should be, and finally realizing what the words, "A woman like you," really mean.

She started to think about what type of woman she really was. Didn't like what she came up with:

She was standing outside fumbling through her keys, trying to find the one to the bottom lock as the telephone came up on ring number three. Several heavy plastic grocery bags dangled from her arms making what seemed like a circus act to get into the house just that much more difficult. She got in and to the phone just before the machine could pick up.

"Hello?" She sounded a bit out of breath from rushing.

A second went by and the person hadn't answered, so she said it again thinking maybe they didn't quite hear her the first time.

"Hello?"

She was already in the kitchen taking the bags from her arms.

"Hi, J."

As soon as she heard the dark, sultry voice, a chill covered her body and she froze right where she stood.

"J," he called again.

"I'm here," she said.

She took the last bag from her arm and then took a seat on one of the wooden stools by the island in the middle of the kitchen.

"I need to talk to you."

Her eyebrows rose, surprised at his statement.

"Talk?" she asked as if he had insulted her by using the wrong word. "So you wanna talk?"

Hesitantly, he said, "Well… Yeah, I mean…"

She rolled her eyes, shook her head and sighed. "Marien…"

He could honestly understand her reaction to hearing from him for the first time, months after they saw each other last. It wasn't like usual when they'd go months without talking to or seeing each other; this time when they remembered the last time they saw each other, they couldn't reminisce about how great the sex was because the last time they saw each other fiancés and boyfriends were introduced—a scene not scripted that was never supposed to be in the movie. So when they spoke now, it was a bit awkward.

"Listen…"

She listened. She heard him exhale, but she didn't bother saying anything. She actually wanted to hang up. *Wanted* to. *Needed* to. But she didn't. She just held the phone at her ear waiting to hear what he had to say.

"I know that what happened at Kenya's party was… I know you wasn't expecting that. And I mean, if I woulda known that I was gon' see *you* there, I woulda never brought her."

As soon as the words left his mouth, she became consumed with a weird feeling. She thought, *If he would've known I would be there, he wouldn't have brought her.* Him saying that changed her attitude about the phone call. For some reason, she wasn't that upset that he called. Not as eager to hang up.

In just that split second, she seemed to have forgotten that she was talking to Marien: *that* Marien.

"You wouldn't have?" she asked.

"No," he insisted. "I wouldn't have. She would've stayed in L.A., and we could've picked up where we left off when you were there."

She thought about what happened when she was in L.A. and how it changed her life for the worse. But what was done was done.

"Now look… I'm sorry that it ever happened. Aw'right? But I don't want it to change what we have. I know it didn't mess anything up," he told her, confidently.

She didn't say anything—didn't give him a response to his comment. He really wanted to know if she would say that things had changed—if he wouldn't still be able to see her for the incredible sex they always had.

He was ready to stop talking, so he decided to just make the proposal he had called to make in the first place. "Well… I just wanted you to know that I'm in town for the weekend. If you wanna meet me later… for drinks or whatevah… I'll be at The Lounge in the Ritz at 7:30."

She looked over at the clock on the microwave and it read 5:47.

"Well, I have a lot of things to do." After she said that, she couldn't remember one thing she had to do.

"I know," he said. He even had no problem with seeing right through her over the phone. "I mean, if you be there, you be there. If you don't…" He waited for a second and continued: "Then you don't."

She didn't say anything, so he said, "See you later, Beautiful."

They both held the phone for a few seconds, and then he hung up first.

She hung up her phone and then proceeded to put her groceries in the refrigerator and cupboards.

She arrived at The Lounge in the Ritz Carlton in DC at quarter to eight and spotted Marien across the room at a small table in the back looking at a menu.

He looked at his watch and said, "You're late," without even looking up from the menu. He felt her approach.

"Well, I'm here."

He put the menu down revealing a smile of delight as he got up to pull out her chair for her.

Once he sat back down, he said—with that smile still on his face—"For a minute there, I thought you wasn't gon' show up." He was facetious.

"I wasn't," she lied.

"But you did. That's all that matters."

After she hung up the phone with him earlier, his proposition nagged her mind. At one point, she contemplated calling Ty just so she could have somebody say to her, "Girl, are you crazy? You better not go to that hotel." But as she slowly watched the clock tick closer to the time he proposed they meet, the more she realized that she, in fact, didn't want to hear her friend tell her not to go. Why did she need to hear that she shouldn't go? As she thought earlier, what's done is done. What else did she have to lose?

They both had one drink before leaving the table to go to his room.

Before he could even close the door completely, they were all over each other, kissing and stripping. And that's when he said it:

"This is why I need a woman like you in my life."

She heard him, but didn't bother to put any thought into why he had said it or even what he meant by it. Not until that morning when she started to think about what type of woman she really was and realized she didn't like what she had come up with, especially considering she was lying in bed next to a man who was engaged to be married.

She felt like bursting into tears as she thought about what type a woman she was—or at least the type of woman she was being at the time. Being there under the sheets of that hotel room bed, she saw herself as a *simple* woman—uncomplicated and easy. Not the type of woman the man who lay beside her would waste any amount of time with other than just to fuck.

The woman he planned to marry though was different, she supposed. She was probably one of those women who pretty much played by the rules—a good girl. She had met a guy, who she thought was great; he was a successful filmmaker, which implied that he was well taken care of. They dated—didn't have sex right away because she's a good girl and good girls don't do that. She probably came from a good home, went to a good school, and had a good career. All she wanted was a good man, like the typical red-blooded American woman, so that she could begin a family and continue the good life. But little did she know, somebody was sleeping with the man she planned to marry. But what type of person would do such a thing? What type of woman? That was an easy question to answer. The type of woman that would knowingly sleep with a married man—or in this case, a soon to be married man—was nothing more than a cheap and dirty heartless whore.

"What exactly did you mean when you said that this was why you needed a woman like me in your life?" she asked, oddly *wanting* to hear his reason for saying it.

He didn't answer right away because he thought for a moment about why she was asking him that. And why now?

He said, "Well, I enjoy being with you." He thought about what else he could say to honestly answer her question. "I mean… there's just certain things that a man don't do with his wife."

She simply nodded and hummed, "Hm," while listening to him and maintaining her composure.

While smiling, he said, "Come on, J. We have an agreement. You know who we are to each other. And that's why we have what we have," he added. "You don't ask for the same things most women ask for. You want the same thing I want. Nothing more." He paused and then said, "You don't complicate things. That's what I like about you."

Just as she thought—he thought she was simple, uncomplicated, easy.

Her aunt once told her that *any* female could be a woman, but that it takes a certain type of female to be a lady. She told J to always carry herself like a lady. If her aunt only knew...

"I'm about to have room service bring some breakfast, you want something?"

She shook her head implying that she didn't want anything. She didn't say much else to him. She got up from the bed, took a shower, put her clothes on, and left the hotel room without saying goodbye to him.

She needed to talk to somebody. She needed to explain herself to somebody and she needed somebody to hear her out. She left the hotel that morning and headed directly to Ty's office, hoping that today was one of her workdays. But it seemed as if she couldn't get there quick enough; every traffic light seemed to stop her and there seemed to be more stop signs than she ever noticed.

"I need to see Dr. Aldridge."

"Okay," the young secretary said. "But she's with a patient right now."

"Well how long is she gonna be?"

The now somewhat irritated woman, who barely looked as if she were out of college, said without losing her professional tone, "I don't know. This appointment should be ending around 10, but..."

"Well can you let her know that I'm here?"

"And who are you?"

J looked to her right at the closed, maple wood door where she knew Ty was, and then back down at the woman in front of her.

"J," she answered. "A friend."

"And what is this in reference to?"

J couldn't believe the girl was asking her that. She said, "It's private."

The woman sighed. "I don't interrupt her sessions unless it's an emergency." She looked at J just waiting for her to say that it was an emergency. It was the typical thing to say since it seemed as if it were urgent that she see Dr. Aldridge.

Instead, J just sighed heavily and looked around the waiting room, then put her hand on top of her head because it was throbbing, again. She didn't look like the usual well-put-together J. That day, she could've easily been mistaken for a woman that suffered from some type of substance abuse or clinical depression. She looked depleted. Her eyes looked dark and had bags beneath them, and not to mention she was acting weird; she was at a psychologist's office begging to be seen. It ain't look good.

She looked at her watch just as the door swung open. It read 9:59.

"So I'll see you next Friday, okay," Ty said, walking a patient out.

"Okay," the barely teenage little girl said as she made her way over to a middle-aged woman with the same brown skin and long hair. "See ya next week, Dr. Aldridge."

"Okay, Kasey. And go easy on the tennis court this weekend, too. Little Serena," she threw in.

"Okay," the girl replied as she and her mother laughed.

Ty almost didn't see J standing in the waiting area. "Hey, what are you doing here?" she asked.

"I need to talk to you."

With a look of worry on her face, especially after examining J from head to toe, she said, "Come in."

J walked past her and into the room, and Ty closed the door behind them.

"Girl, my 10 o'clock must've known you needed me 'cause they rescheduled."

J tried to force a smile, but the smile didn't quite make its way through the pain.

"Have a seat," Ty said as she sat down in the chair designated for her.

"In *this* chair?" J asked, referring to the patients' couch.

Sarcastically, Ty looked around as if she were looking for another seat in the room. There were only two and she was already sitting in one.

J finally got the picture and sat down.

Ty looked up at the clock on the wall, though she already knew it was around the 10 o'clock hour, and asked, "What can I do for you?"

"Please. Don't treat me like a patient. I'm not a patient. I don't have problems. I just wanted to talk to you, okay."

"Okay," Ty said, immediately realizing that something was seriously wrong with J. If not, then she wouldn't have looked the way that she did and she surely wouldn't have made it clear that she *didn't* have problems.

"I'm listening."

J sighed while staring at the floor.

"For some reason... Though as fucked up as I feel... I can't cry. It feels like I need to cry. But can't. Tears won't fall for this."

"For what?"

She looked up from the carpet and over at her friend. She didn't want to say it now that she had driven all the way from the hotel to the office. She felt ashamed.

Slowly. Nervously: "I spent the night... with Marien."

Ty inhaled two lungs full of air but neglected to let it out as quickly as she took it in; she didn't want J to think she was frustrated or mad at her because they had discussed this before. She was J's friend, so she was obligated to just be there for her. She had to hear her out.

"He called me up and..." She shook her head as she thought about it. "He called and told me where he'd be staying. And like an ass, I went running."

J twiddled her thumbs for a moment, still shaking her head. All she could say was, "So fuckin' stupid."

Ty got up and sat down beside her on the couch. "You're not stupid," she said. "You just need to..." She thought about exactly what it was that J needed to do. She reached over and put J's head on her shoulder. She hugged her. "We just need to talk about this."

She didn't say everything they needed to talk about right then and there, but she knew she needed to help J understand her relationship with Marien. She knew there was more to it than met the eye, but J couldn't seem to see it. After ten years, J was still blind to the fact that Marien was no good for her; their "relationship" was no good for her life. And he was a married man now—engaged... Same thing. But this was bigger than that. Regardless of whether he was married, engaged, or whatever, Marien was simply a bad habit that J just could not kick. She needed help.

Ty wanted to help J understand who she was to Marien, but that became much easier once she found out that Marien had already done the honors that morning. The plan was not to *tell* J anything, but to ask the right questions, which would cause her to think—cause her to see and understand through her own words and memories.

Ty managed to help J calm down before her 11 o'clock appointment that day, but they were far from being through aiding this problem. A friend's job is never done, especially when that friend happens to be a head-doctor. Since J didn't want to feel like a patient, Tylia never required that she come back to her office, but she designated time in her off-hours to help her girl.

* * *

One night while Jaye tossed and turned beneath the sheets, he dreamt something: He was in his house—in his bedroom to be exact—and J lay on his bed. Bare. Sound asleep. He just watched her. He just sat on the floor beside the bed looking up at her—watching her as if he could follow the storyline in her dream. He couldn't though. But she was all he needed or even *wanted* to see. She was so beautiful. He sat there the entire time just watching her as the thought of just how *much* he *loved* that woman consumed his heart and his mind. And so he sketched her.

His eyes opened before seven o'clock that morning and he couldn't seem to fall back to sleep after that, even though he had no place in particular to be that early and had stayed up until almost three painting. All he could do all morning was think about her. But he refused to sketch her.

With that dream came nights of many. The dreams seemed so simple, but the significance was nothing more than a reminder. A reminder of what he missed. A reminder of what helped him be happy. Many of those nights, tears came down his face and wet his pillow. Thoughts of her became so overwhelming that they were almost taunting. Six months had gone by and he hadn't lost one bit of love for her, yet she didn't lie beside him.

Hello?"

"Ah… Hi. It's ah… It's J."

His heart skipped a beat as soon as he heard her voice. She didn't even have to say her name.

"Hey," he said back. He didn't know what else say to her.

His tone, when he answered, didn't sound suspicious at all, though if she had seen his face she would've notice the inquisitive look that covered it. He didn't know why she was calling, so he just waited for her to say what she had phoned to say.

"I just wanted to know whether Meka was home yet," she said.

Immediately, he looked at his watch to see what time it was before he said, "No, she isn't here yet. I thought she was with you."

"Well she was. But I took her to the subway at 6:30 and I waited there with her until the train came, so I know she got on. I saw her," she said. "And I told her to call me when she got home." He looked at his watch again; it was 7:35.

She said, "It only takes like five, maybe ten minutes to get to the station near your house."

"Well, did you call her on her cell phone?"

"Yeah, but the voicemail just keeps picking up."

"She always keeps her phone in her pocketbook and she never hears it when somebody calls," he said as if he was sick of that happening. "I told her to look at it periodically." He sighed and looked at his watch again, and said, "Well I'm sure she'll be home soo…"

The door opened before he could finish his optimistic consolation.

"Here she is now. Where were you?" he asked her before she could even get in the house good.

"I had to get a book from my friend's house, so I stopped by there before I came home."

"She went to get a book from a friend's house," he said to J. "And did you bother to check your cell phone that you never hear ringing?"

She reached into her purse and grabbed her cell phone and looked at it to see if she had any missed calls. She had missed two.

"Oh," she said. "It was in my purse."

"It was in her purse," he relayed to J. "I told you about that, Meka."

As she locked the door behind her, she said, "Yeah. I know, Jaye."

"What's the point in having it if…"

"I can't hear it ringing when somebody calls," she finished. "I know."

J heard her over the phone and chuckled at what she said.

Smiling too, he said, "I swear, that girl is gon' make me…"

"Who are you telling all my business to anyway?" Meka asked, wondering who he was talking to on the phone about her.

"None of your business," he said to her out of spite.

She simply smiled and shook her head; she didn't say anything else to him.

He sighed and focused his attention back to the telephone conversation.

"Well ahh… She's here," he said.

"Alright."

"Thank you for your concern."

"No problem."

He didn't say anything else right away, just held the phone on his ear. There was silence for a moment. He wanted to *talk* to her; it just seemed so natural to say more, but it was like he didn't know *what* to say. He didn't want to sound as if he had completely forgotten about everything that happened between them because he hadn't; he didn't want to just start talking to her, sounding all nice, when he was supposed to still be mad! He was supposed to still be hurting. And he was. The entire situation still clouded his mind. But the very thought of her—of how much he missed her—affected him emotionally.

"Well, I'll let you go," she said. "Tell Meka I'll talk to her later."

He felt like asking her what she was doing or how her day was or how she was in generally—how things had been since they parted ways. He should've said something to keep her on the phone and let her know that he was ready to progress past not talking to her, even if they simply spoke to each other as mere associates—not even as close as friends. Even if they just spoke… But instead, he just said, "Okay."

"Okay," she said.

Silence struck again.

Then he said, "Okay," again.

"Bye," she said.

He pressed the "Off" button on the phone without saying any more. He even cursed himself for sounding so silly and keeping her on the phone that long, only continuously saying, "Okay."

"Damn," he said in a whisper.

"Who was that?" Meka asked walking into the living room where he was.

He placed the phone onto the table and said, "That was J. She was wondering why you hadn't called her yet."

"Oh yeah, I was s'pose to let her know when I got home." A second passed, and then she asked, "You were talking to J?"

Pride kicked in quickly and he said, "It was only for about a minute. She called like a minute before you walked in."

"Yeah, but you were talking to her," Meka said, smiling. "What did you say?" She was grinning like a kid on Christmas.

"Nothin'," he insisted. "Look at the call history. She called like one minute before you came in here."

"Why you front'n like you ain't got nothin' to say to her? How long has it been since the last time you spoke to her?"

"Front'n?"

"It's been *five months*, Jaye. Come on. I know you still love her."

He sucked his teeth and said, "You don't know what you talkin' 'bout." He wanted to correct her and say six months, but he didn't.

He flopped down on the sofa, picked up the remote and turned on the television. He always used the television when he didn't want to talk about something.

"I know *you very* well," she said. "That's why I be tryin' to help you."

"Help me?"

With seriousness in her voice, she said, "Don't act like that."

He smiled.

"I'm serious, Jaye. You know I'm always looking out for your best interest."

He could play with her, but he couldn't debate her on that; he knew that Meka had his back.

"Now look… I don't know why ya'll broke up. *I'm* assuming it was mostly—if not entirely—her fault because she said to me one day when we were talking that... when I find a good man to recognize it, and treat him as such." Meka looked at him waiting for a response, but when she didn't get one, she continued: "Nobody just says stuff like that. I could tell regret was in her tone. I pay attention, Jaye. I can read between the lines very well. Now I don't know exactly what she did, but even though she may not deserve it, I know she would *love* to talk to you," she said. "She probably doesn't think I noticed, but she is *very* unhappy, despite the fact that she just got a big promotion last month."

"She got a promotion?" he asked, reluctantly sounding happy for her.

Meka smiled and said, "Call her and talk to her about it."

He didn't say anything. And she didn't say any more about it.

She got up and said, "I'm going to run my mouth on the phone. I'll see you in the morning."

He sat in the same spot on his sofa in his living room for more than two hours watching nothing, thinking about what—or who—had been invading his center of consciousness for the past few weeks. He didn't know whether to listen to Meka or keep convincing himself that they were broken up and that what she had done was stupid and that she had hurt him terribly and that because of what she did they shouldn't speak or even talk casually. But these thoughts were few and far between. She was what was on his mind all the time—those good thoughts of her and of being with her, of laughing with her. Some were simple and innocent and pure. Others were sensual and sexual and just... not so pure. But that was okay. These were happy thoughts. He even caught himself smiling a few times as he daydreamed inadvertently.

He went to sleep early that night. 10 o'clock.

The phone sang, waking her up from a deep sleep. She had retired at 10:30 that Saturday night not expecting anymore phone calls, especially not any at the stroke of mid-night. Without thinking, without bothering to let it ring any longer because of the piercing sound, she just picked it up prepared to tell someone that they had the wrong number.

"Hello?"

"Hello. J." Her already cranky face became even more wrinkled as she fought to keep her eyes open while not believing whose voice she thought she was hearing on the other end. She thought maybe she was still asleep and was hearing wrong.

"It's Jaye," was all he had to say and she had already forgotten that she had been sleeping. She wasn't hearing wrong. But what made him call, and at midnight of all times?

"Hey," she said, making the phone more comfortable on her ear.

"Ahh… I know it's late, but… I yah… I just wanted to know if… if you wanted to talk."

* * *

"So have you set a date yet?"

Ty shook her head. "No," she replied. "Not yet."

"Well what the hell are ya'll waiting for?" J asked, laughing at her own comment. "I mean you *are* still gonna do this, right?"

Smiling, Ty said, "Yes, silly. But these things take time. Everything's gotta be right—the right time, the right place… Everything has to be perfect." She flipped through some more pages in one of the many bridal magazines she had scattered over her dining room table before saying, "The wedding is just a day. Just a ceremony. We're preparing for our marriage right now—our life together."

J thought about what Ty said. Of course, she had never thought about that.

Ty finally said, "We're thinking about maybe sometime in July."

"That's in what—seven, eight months?"

"Yup." She flipped through a few more pages. "And it'll be here before you know it," she said. "Or before *I* know it."

"Yeah," J agreed, thinking about the fact that she and Ty were looking through magazines for a wedding gown.

It seemed weird that one of her best friends would soon be a married woman. Not that marriage would be uncharted territory. J had been through this once before with her, so long ago that it seemed like it'd happened in another life. But that was now something they just saw as a two-year stint about which they preferred not to talk. J always found herself wondering how such an intelligent woman—really, an Ivy League graduate—could fall for such an idiot-asshole (what J called him, even to his face). And that intelligent woman now always felt a little not so intelligent for having been so stupid. In any case, they both maintained this unspoken rule to just pretend like it never happened.

"So where are you gonna do it—here or Boston?"

"Probably Boston. It won't be big though." She flipped by some more gowns, still not finding anything that tickled her fancy. She said, while still flipping pages, "I've looked through about fifty of these books…"

"Probably not counting the fifty we just looked through today," J said. "I'm get'n sick of this. Don't you have somebody to actually take you out and help you do this?"

"No. I thought I could do it myself."

J closed the magazine she was looking at and said, "I don't think this is working."

"Me either," Ty said, closing hers and sighing. "I'll find the right dress though," she said, optimistically.

J looked at Ty across the table. "So this is it, huh?" she asked.

Ty smiled. "This is it," she confirmed. She thought about some of her past relationships. Then she thought about the man she was about to marry. "He is incredible." She looked at J and smiled.

"I am so happy for you," J said, so genuinely that it was almost mushy. While smiling and nodding, she added: "I'm really glad you got what you wanted." Her real smile slowly disappeared as she thought about those words, but she threw on a replacement smile hoping that Ty wouldn't notice.

"Thank you," Ty said. Not even five seconds had gone by before she asked, "But what about you?"

"What *about* me?"

"Are you gonna…" Ty felt weird asking this. "Are you gonna like… date now?"

J smiled and answered, "I don't know. I really haven't thought too much about that."

She had thought about it, she just hadn't told anybody.

"Actually… I *have* thought about it," she confessed. "You know, they say, 'it's better to have loved and lost than to never have loved at all.' It may sound kinda corny, but that's how I feel." She said, "I've experienced love. It was a wonderful experience and I don't believe I could've had a better experience with anybody else, so…"

She thought about what else she had to say—how she could tell Ty that she didn't plan to date.

"I feel like I'm a changing woman, so I'm *not* going back to my old ways. And I wasn't into dating to find love before I met Jaye, so to tell you the truth—I don't plan to get into it now that Jaye is no longer in my life."

In her lifetime, J had probably been involved with—not necessarily slept with—maybe 200 men, and in her opinion Jaye was certainly one of a kind. There were probably a few others that weren't *so* bad; but even so, of the 200, only probably about 5—give or take 1 or 2—were worth spending more than ten minutes alone with; any more time with the others and she would be ready to jump out of a ten story window to get away from them. Well maybe not a ten story window, but definitely one of a women's restroom; she had done that before. So, statistically—by her own experience—only 2.5% were actually worth a damn, which is less than 3 guys per every 100. So, *statistically*, she'd have to date about 40 just to find 1 worth the time and energy, and that *still* didn't necessarily mean that the one guy that's worth a damn would have mutual feelings.

See? That was the reason she never tried to do the relationship thing—too mathematical. She was always a language arts type 'a gal.

"Jaye proved to you that all men aren't the same," Ty corrected.

"True," J said. "But I really don't wanna try and find another man to love. I honestly don't *want* to love another man. I don't wanna go through that. Jaye is one of a kind. I'm satisfied with just having learned what love is with him. I don't wanna tarnish what that experience meant to me by trying to emulate it with somebody else."

"So you're not going back and not going forward... What—you celibate now?"

J had not thought about that at all. And she wasn't about to right now.

"Shut up," she said laughing, realizing that she had backed herself into that corner.

"Well..." Ty said, smiling before she could even get out what she knew was going to be something controversial. "Have you thought about trying to get back with him?"

"Not you too." J sighed. That was one of those questions she didn't feel like entertaining. She had her reasons for not "bothering" to try to move back into Jaye's life, but they were hard to explain. To her friends, she'd just sound like a coward. "You sound like Kenya."

"Kenya asked you that too?"

"Yes, and I told her the same thing I'm about to tell you—I'm not doin' it," she said. "I mean have you ever considered taking somebody back that cheated on you?"

Ty knew J had a point, but after she put in a second or two of thought, she said, "Considered? Yes. But I never took any of them back because none of them ever asked for a second chance. Had they asked for forgiveness and showed that they wanted to give the relationship another try, I might've taken them back."

J sighed again. "Well Tylia... I won't be asking because I think I might've really messed up my chances for that. Actually, I know I did."

"So?" Ty asked again. "What are you gonna do about that?"

"What am I gonna . . ?" She couldn't believe Ty was asking her that. She grabbed one of those gown books and said, "I'm gonna sit my Black slash El Salvadorian ass right here and look for a wedding gown. For *you*," she said, still laughing.

Ty laughed at her silly friend.

Flipping through the magazine, but not really looking, she said, "You know, I think I enjoyed life a little more when I didn't have any regrets."

The reality of her statement hurt her, but it was true.

Ty looked at J inquisitively.

J clarified: "Talking to you these last few months... It's helped me a lot," she said. "I realize who I've *been* most of my life. And now I know who I *want* to be—the *wo*man I wanna be."

Ty smiled—happy to hear the newfound maturity in her friend's words. She liked it.

The moment of clarity came a few months ago in Ty's office. Though J wasn't required to come back to the office, it was convenient. Plus she had gotten used to the patient's chair; it was actually quite comfortable. She had also become accustomed to answering questions she usually preferred not to think about the real answer to.

"Who is Marien?" Ty asked.

J moved in the chair. The question, not the fabric, made her obviously uncomfortable. She sighed. She thought some more.

"He's... He's..." She sighed again. "He's just a guy I yah... He's a guy... You know who Marien is," she said.

Ty said, "I do. But do you?"

J didn't answer that one. She was still focusing on the first question.

"I sleep with him."

"That's it?"

"That's it!" J exclaimed. "I don't do anything else with him *but* fuck. *You* know that."

Maintaining the same calm tone, Ty said, "I didn't ask you what you did with him. I asked you who was he. I wanna know who he is to you."

"He's my fuck buddy, okay."

"Why?"

"Excuse me?"

"Why is he your fuck buddy?" Ty asked.

"Because," she smiled, "he's great in bed." That was easy.

"Why isn't he your boyfriend? You've known him for ten years, so why isn't he your husband by now?"

"Because…"

At first the question seemed easy too. But then it wasn't. First thing to pop into her head was Marien's words: "a woman like you." Women like her weren't girlfriends or wives. They were fuck buddies.

The tears ran down her face without hesitation and she didn't bother trying to catch them.

"Because women like me aren't girlfriends," she said.

She took a few seconds to let her tears run because the emotion was starting to affect the lucidity of her voice.

"All he wants is sex."

Ty could see it slowly coming out. She wanted J to hear herself say it.

"So what do *you* want?"

An even harder question. J must've sat in silence thinking about the question for twenty minutes straight. Coming up with an answer only took half-a-minute; actually spitting it out is what took so long.

"I want… I guess—I want… to be more. More than… more than a fuck…"

Bingo!

Once Ty got her to say that she wanted to be more, helping her see the light was almost easy.

Now, today, J sat across from Ty flipping through wedding dress magazines with understanding. Insight. Consciousness.

"You were right," she said, looking at Ty. "With all of the guys I've been with… I always had in my mind that I wanted to get them before they got me, y'know? My wall is how I protect myself. It was," she corrected when she thought about the changes she was making in her life. "I've been a victim before. I've felt neglect and abuse… I had to toughen up to survive—to not get hurt."

"But you understand your faults now," Ty said.

"I do. But I regret that it took losing Jaye..." She sighed as she thought about him and what he meant to her. She started over: "I regret that it took losing Jaye for me to understand all this. I regret that it took hearing Marien say to me that I was nothing more than a *ho...* for me to see this. It hurt like hell to hear him say that," she admitted. "But it was true."

She looked at Ty who just sat across the table from her, listening.

"Ty, why didn't you tell me I was a ho?"

Caught off guard by the question, Ty shrugged, speechless, trying to find words, but failing.

J smiled. "That's okay. But now," she said. "Now I just want contentment. That's it. I think I can have that being by myself."

* * *

"Jaye," she said as she approached, smiling as usual. "What's up witcha?"

She seemed to have been in a rush before she spotted Jaye on the basketball court stuffing some of his things into his Nets duffle bag, and now she wasn't going to leave before she found out how he'd been since she last saw him.

With a friendly smile on his face, he said, "I'm good. How 'bout you?"

"I'm aw'right. Tired," she threw in. "But good." The teeth-displaying smile slowly turned into just a look of delight as she continued small talk with Jaye. She said, "I've been so busy that I haven't had time to talk with you like I usually do."

"Yeah right," he said. "I think you're just tryin' to avoid that game you owe me."

Her big brown eyes lit up, surprised that he would accuse her of ducking out of the game of one-on-one to which she challenged him a few weeks back.

She gave him a soft punch on the right shoulder, and they both shared a laugh.

"I'm gonna give you that one-on-one," she promised, not laughing as much anymore.

Jaye said, "Okay," as if he didn't believe her, and finished zipping up his bag.

She said, "Look, I got a class to teach right now."

"Aerobics?" he asked, no longer multitasking.

"High intensity, low impact," she said, smiling. "It's fun. You should try it."

Grimacing, he said, "I'll stick to basketball."

Laughing, she said, "I gotta run." She reached over and touched his arm before saying, "I'll see you later."

"See ya."

As Jaye slipped his wristband into the side of his bag, Keyon walked up twirling a basketball in his hand. "Aye, who was that?"

More than a month ago, Jaye followed his Thursday routine, which he finished at the new, state of the art fitness center. Keyon had introduced him to the place just after it opened less than a year ago, and ever since, the two of them had been going at least twice a week, primarily to play basketball. That day as he and four other guys prepared to start a game of what they hoped would be three-on-three, they realized they lacked one person. Keyon would've normally had that spot, but he wasn't there.

Just then, a female walked in with a sports bag on her left shoulder, a white towel thrown over her right, and she was holding a bottle of water. She wore a black sports bra exposing her exceptionally exercised abs, and gray sweat shorts that provided the perfect peek at her muscular thighs and left little to guess about much else. Her legs were slightly bowed, which only seemed to add more curves to the shaven shafts that seemed to disappear into her white ankle-socks that hid inside of a pair of gray New Balance sneakers. She stood just over 5 feet and 9 inches, had a golden brown complexion, dark eyes, and her hair was tied back in a neat, slightly bent ponytail.

She placed the bag onto the bench, took a sip of water and immediately walked over to the court where Jaye and the other guys were.

"Hey, beautiful. How you doin'?" one of the guys said.

She ignored him and asked, "Are ya'll get'n a game goin' or are you just standin' here chit-chattin'?"

Jaye said, "We wanna start a game, but we need another man." He realized she was probably on the court for a reason, so he added, "Or a woman. You play?"

A smile covered her face, but she didn't want to brag or exaggerate her skills; however, she was *good*. She simply said, "I shoot around in my spare time. But ya'll don't mind if I play with ya'll to—you know… tighten my game up a little, do you?"

After they won, Jaye complimented her: "Good game. You're good."

Noticeably blushing at the compliment he gave, though she didn't need him to validate that she had game, she said, "Thank you."

They continued to walk from the court over to the bench where she had placed her things when she came in. He had put his bag over there too.

He pulled a towel out and wiped his face and neck, then asked her, "I'm sorry, what's your name again?"

"Chandler. Chandler Evans," she said, introducing that beautiful smile she would soon become known for. "I've seen you here before. I work here," she revealed.

"Oh," he said with a look of unfamiliarity on his face. He had never seen her before. Or just never noticed her.

"I'm a trainer, and I teach group workout classes."

"Oh okay," he said. "Jaye." He introduced himself as they shook hands.

Politely, she said, "Well it's nice to meet you, Jaye."

From that point on, they had conversations every time he came into the gym.

"Oh, that's my home-girl, Chandler," he said, answering Keyon's question. "She's a trainer here."

Keyon watched her as she jogged by the treadmills in an attempt to get where she was going faster. He said, "She's cute."

"Yeah. *And* she can ball."

"Word?" Keyon watched her until she disappeared into the back. "So you try'n to hook up with her?" he asked.

Jaye shook his head, still looking in the direction in which she ran: "Nah."

Keyon didn't say anything because Jaye didn't look as if he were finished. He could almost guess why Jaye had said what he said, but he wanted to allow him to actually say it.

He said, "I talked to J." He looked at his friend and realized his own vagueness. He added, "I called her and... We talked. Caught up a lil bit."

Keyon nodded. "That's good," he said in a tone that almost sounded as if he were asking instead of commenting.

Jaye considered what he had just revealed to his friend. And as they slowly continued to walk toward the exit of the gym, he looked over at Keyon and asked, "Yo, am I stupid?"

Keyon sighed unnoticeably because the question puzzled him. Was he stupid if he wanted her back? was really what he wanted Keyon to answer. So Keyon said, "No." He really didn't know what to say, but he surely couldn't call his friend stupid. "I mean you love her."

Jaye said, "Yeah, but you know love can make you do some stupid things."

Keyon nodded his head agreeing with him.

Jaye added, "I don't wanna do a stupid thing."

Jaye was too used to making the "wrong decisions" as far as relationships go. He was trying to approach things differently this time. He was older now and not as resilient.

Still nodding, Keyon said, "Jaye, I can't tell you what to do."

Jaye wasn't expecting that answer.

"I know you love her..."

Jaye looked down at his feet almost hating to hear those words leave Keyon's mouth. He didn't like the fact that he could still—after what she did—love her. Like it didn't happen.

"Obviously, something is still there. It's gotta be," Keyon said. "Are you stupid?" he asked rhetorically. "No. Not at all. You're just not over her."

Jaye slowly nodded at the truth that Keyon spoke. It was almost like Keyon was reading him. He knew so much, even though he hadn't actually told Keyon all this stuff.

He sighed and shook his head. "What would *you* do?" he asked.

Now Keyon sighed. He said, "If I loved her that much?" He thought about it for a moment. "Everybody makes mistakes…"

Advice was his wife-to-be's specialty, not his. So Keyon was honest in saying, "You know, that's a hard one. 'Cause it would be easy for me to say what I would or wouldn't do, but this isn't me," he said.

They got into Jaye's car to continue the conversation there. Jaye listened.

"You gotta decide whether you're willing to take another chance."

They had ridden in silence for the entire ten-minute drive. Jaye had a lot on his mind.

They pulled in front of Keyon's building, and just as the vehicle came to a complete stop, Jaye said, "Aye… Do you think Ty is the one?"

Keyon smiled as he thought about where the conversation was going. He asked, "What? You think J is?"

Jaye didn't answer, he just said, "I mean, you know, you're about to get married and all that. I was just askin' if you thought she was the woman who was put here for you."

Keyon answered confidently, "I wouldn't have asked her to marry me if I didn't. I know she is."

Jaye simply nodded.

"Not a doubt in my mind," he said, taking it upon himself to continue. "You know… I spent a whole lotta time trying to find the right woman." He paused and then looked over at Jaye and said, "But when I focused on making me right? That's when the right woman came along." He shook his head, this time slightly smiling, and said, "It's not a doubt in my mind, man."

Jaye always had so much respect for Keyon. He admired his friend's confidence in himself and his choices.

Keyon smiled and said, "You're an artist, man. You think with your heart."

Jaye welcomed the joke into the conversation.

Jaye nodded and said, "I know what I want." He thought about what that was. He said, "But I'm in a place where I feel like… I feel like I can't move forward—move on. There's a part of me that's scared to go back. And I'm hating where I am right now. I'm just confused right now."

"Jaye, you know what you gotta do. You know what the truth is." Keyon looked at him and asked, "Are you really confused because of the situation? Or are you confused because you don't wanna admit the truth and do what's right?"

That confidence that Keyon had that Jaye admired so much? He knew where that came from. Though Keyon said that he spent time looking for the right woman, Jaye remembered him spending more time alone. Just then, as he thought, he figured his friend had probably spent all that time growing as a man without having to worry about the distractions of relationships. And now his friend was a real man with a real lady about to embark on a real lifetime together. Again, Jaye thought about where his friend was in life—confident, secure, happy—and he compared that to where he was—confused, not secure, dis-happy…

When Keyon said, "admit the truth and do what's right," Jaye knew what he was talking about—admitting that he in fact isn't ready for any of his current worries and doing what it takes to become man enough to handle this reality.

Gordon Parks and Maya Angelou have a way of captivating audiences with their art, turning letters into words, words into phrases, phrases into ideas, and ideas into pictures of cross-generational inspiration. She idolized that. So like her heroes, she would paint—with words—images so modestly called "magazine articles" that were so beautiful and so pictorial that readers almost felt like they were there—like they themselves had sat in maybe the soundstage or studio or wherever she conducted the face-to-face talks, and asked those same questions while taking in the world around them. It was easy, effortless even, for her to write a several thousand-word story detailing the feelings, opinions, and personal and professional progression of popular—or sometimes not so popular—players in the world of arts and entertainment. Actors and actresses, singers and rappers, artists of all kinds and even industry higher-ups would all sit down with her and reveal just enough of their life to beguile followers.

But for some reason, this time, as she lay there staring at the blank paper beneath her pen… nothing would come to her. Nearly a half an hour had gone by. Though she didn't look at the clock, she knew exactly how much time had passed because the theme music to her favorite syndicated TV show indicated 10:30 p.m.

She sighed and dropped her head onto the pillow, almost frustrated.

She was walking through one of those big convenient department stores earlier that week—where she got most of her grocery, some make-up, household stuff, music and movies, and even a few articles of clothing all from the same place? Well, as she passed the aisle with all the birthday cards and such, she approached a display of small journal books that had different letters of the alphabet on the fronts of them. Ty had mentioned something like that to her the first time they'd talked. She told her that it would be a good idea to document her feelings and track her progression in a journal as often as she could. "Maybe not every day," she said. "But try to do it as often as you can, especially when you know you're feeling something—anything…" But she had been too lazy—she used the excuse "forgetful"—to ever pick one up. She got the one with the big pink "J" on it; she always liked to see her name on stuff.

She had tried it a few times before—writing her feelings—on loose pieces of line-less paper from the printer, but the more she tapped into her center with Ty, the more she realized that she could've (and should've) been writing more. So tonight, she cracked open her cute little new "J" journal and wrote the words: *Lately, I feel…*

And after thirty minutes, that was all she wrote. Literally.

The buzzing vibration of her silenced cell phone distracted her concentration, startling her as it indicated an awaiting caller.

She pushed the speakerphone button and said, "Hi, Mami."

"Hi, baby. How you?"

"I'm fine. What about you?"

Her mother sighed. "Tired, Jesenia. But I'm okay."

J hated to hear her mother say that. She only threw in that last part of her answer because she knew that J would worry. She always did that. But it never worked; J worried about her anyway.

"Have you thought about what we talked about last week?" J asked.

Elsa replied, "Yes, mija." She took a little longer to express what those thoughts were. Finally, she said, "I have to think some more. I like Chicago."

J wanted to argue again why she thought it would be better for her mother to move and be with her, but she understood and respected that her mother needed time to make a big decision like that.

She interrupted J's thinking by asking, "How did things go with Ty today?"

J recognized the change of subject, but answered anyway: "It went well. We talked about Jaye today."

She had recently told her mother about what she had done to Jaye and why they weren't together anymore; she told her about Marien; she relayed everything that she and Ty had discussed in their meetings… Her mother knew everything about her now. Some things surprised her; she hadn't known those things about her daughter. Some things disappointed her… But she tried as hard as she could possibly try to be supportive. J was her baby. And she understood how her own inadequacies probably had a lot to do with her daughter's current tribulations. So she would sit on the phone almost every night and listen to her only child talk about all the different ways she was growing up—on her own—and she would hate that she couldn't play a more integral role in that evolution. Even if she tried.

J thought about all the things that she and Ty discussed that day. She said, "He calls me sometimes. And I don't say much, y'know. I just listen to him."

"What does he say?" her mother asked.

J smiled as she thought about some of the things he would talk about.

"He loves to talk about art."

She thought about their very latest conversation, which was just a few hours earlier that day. He called her and told her he was in the bookstore and he was telling her that…

"They have this book with a lot of Kandinsky's work in it!" He was so excited. "It even talks about *Composition VII and VIII*…"

He paused. He must've been looking through the book.

"Man, it even talks about *Improvisation 28* in here!"

She just sat on the other end of the phone line smiling, really actually sharing this moment with him. She knew of Visily Kandinsky. She knew that he was an expressionist. She knew that he was Jaye's favorite artist. And because of Jaye, she could virtually see *Improvisation 28* when he mentioned it.

"I hear music when I see his stuff," Jaye said. He had even told her before how he heard music when he painted too—how different colors looked like different sounds to him.

"He paints from his core. It's deeper than just *feelings*," he told her. "This stuff comes from deep deep down inside." He turned a few more pages. "This is spiritual. You can tell just by looking at it that it's just… It comes from a soulful place." He must've pondered his own thoughts, because he added, "I been slackin'. I need to get my spirituality straight."

She and Jaye stayed on the phone for over an hour as he narrated his outing in the bookstore—he got a cup of coffee from the café inside the store, he bought that book on Kandinsky, and decided to finally pick up a book Keyon told him about by Kahlil Gibran after realizing the comment he'd made earlier about his own spirituality. He got one for J too.

"That night when he called me and we spoke for the first time in a long time… I was so taken by the call that I, *me*, *J*… was actually speechless."

Her mother chuckled at that comment. She knew that "speechless" was not a word synonymous with her daughter. She always had *something* to say.

J continued: "He said that he wanted to thank me again for being so concerned about Meka. She's become like my little sister too. I love her. He said that Meka had told him about my promotion at the magazine. He told me that I deserved it and that he was proud of me."

She remembered that conversation vividly.

"I was so excited to be talking to him. I missed him so much. It's still almost… surreal when we talk. I haven't…" she started, but chose to go with: "There's so much I want to tell him. And there's a lot I know he wants to know. But that'll come in due time. The right time.

"We don't carry on about the past. We don't talk about the future. I don't know where we're going. Or what we're doing. I don't call. I let him do that. I'm kinda quiet when we talk; I have to get used to actually being his friend again—being in his life at all. I'm just happy I'm moving into a better place with him."

Her mother asked, "Does he tell you how he feels?"

J thought about all of the conversations they'd had thus far. They all had something in common: "He's never emotional. He doesn't reveal how he feels about what I did to him." She thought some more. "No. He doesn't talk about how he's feeling about that. He hasn't said how he feels about me. I can only assume—since he wants to talk again, maybe he has come to some terms about what happened. Maybe, in his own way, he has forgiven me to some extent."

"How much do you talk to him?" her mother asked.

"We talked for about an hour that first night," J said. "He called a couple days after that. That was a few weeks ago. We talk a few times a week—three days, four days sometimes. Yesterday, he told me that if I wanted to talk to him that I could call. Guess he realized how much control I was giving him." She smiled as she thought about that. Just the thought of getting closer to him again often put a smile on her face.

"So you feel happy, yes?"

J thought about that. She said, "Yeah, Ma. Yeah, I guess I'm starting to feel happy. Lately, I feel less confused about what I want out of life. I'm not as confused about who I am either. I like that," she admitted. "Cuz for a long time I did a lot of things to try to fill this void. All the wrong things." She thought about all those things. She said, "But you know what?"

"What?" her mother wanted to know.

"Now, I'm getting to know J. So everything I find out about her, I'll make sure to tell you. Okay?"

Her mother started laughing. She said, "Okay. *J.*" She felt awkward calling her daughter that. She had never ever referred to Jesenia as "J," but she recognized how much J had embraced this nickname, so she decided to try it.

As she told her mother all this, something started to come to her; she knew what she could write.

"Mama, let me call you back. Are you going to sleep?"

She hummed, "Mmmm... I am sleepy. Call you tomorrow."

"Okay," J agreed. "Have a good night, okay."

"I will. Love you, baby."

"I love you too, Mama. Goodnight."

She closed her cell phone nearly imploding with thoughts and feelings to write.

* * *

He was hesitant about coming in. Being in—reminded him too much of too many things he preferred not to be reminded of too often. So he walked in carefully and began taking his coat off while looking around the place. It seemed like ages since he last been there. Besides the arrangement of the furniture, everything was pretty much the same. And smelled the same; her house held the distinctive scent of sandalwood candles. The aroma would linger in his clothes long after he left, but he liked it because it was a constant reminder of her and her place.

They had just come back from the sports bar up the street from her house. They walked. It was 35 degrees—a brisk, bleak night; and for the first time in months, they shared a meal together. And with that meal, like old times, they shared beers and good conversation.

"A.D.D.?" he asked referring to what they were talking about on the way in.

"Yes. That's why Jazz music has no place in popular culture today," J said, handing him her jacket so he could hang hers up too. "People can't appreciate the art. They want catchy hooks and subjects they don't have to think about."

Jaye walked to the couch. "I agree," he said, looking around. "Same thing with movies…"

"Yeah," she concurred. "What's wrong?" She noticed him taking in everything around him.

He was thinking about how weird it felt sitting beside her, talking, television on… It felt really strange doing so much stuff with her again, but not kissing her. Or making love to her. It felt weird not being able to call her "mine."

He said, "Wow. It even smells the same in here."

"Oh, I lit those candles earlier just so you would say that," she joked.

He smiled and said, "Yeah right."

She sat down beside him with her knee up on the sofa facing him. And she looked at him without laughing, without smiling. Sincere. "I had a really good time tonight. Thank you."

"Me too." He realized what she'd said and responded, "J, you don't have to thank me."

Still looking at him. Still seeing his pain. Still regretting her part in its cause. She said, "Yes I do."

Her statement made him uncomfortable. He swallowed hard. He neither knew how to respond to that, nor how to accept it. He could tell that she had a lot on her mind. But he also could see how careful she had been in saying what she had to say. Though he opened the door and invited her to call and talk—say what she felt she needed to say—he understood the reasons for her reservations.

He hadn't spoken his mind either. He had questions. He had thoughts. But he was always bad when it came to knowing how to actually come out and say things. Not that he thought he would be offensive; he just wanted to say exactly what he meant, and he wanted to always mean exactly what he said. And because of that, he took his time when expressing his heart, verbally.

She looked at him and said, "You know… when you called me that night… I was so scared."

He had called her that night. They talked. That was that. Just being friendly, he supposed, should let her know that he at least wanted to be that—friendly.

He asked, "Scared of what?"

"I don't know. The unknown, I guess. Or the fact that we would talk for the first time in a long time. I wanted to say all the right things to you."

Now he felt awkward. His eyes focused on something behind her instead of her eyes. He wanted to know: "Like what?"

"Like how much I miss you. And how I would like it if we could just…" She thought about it. "Just *be* again," she said. "Honestly? I want my best friend back."

He noticed her candid expression of how she felt. It wasn't accompanied by shame or embarrassment. It was intentional.

She looked over at him. She knew that he didn't have to be sitting there with her. He didn't have to re-extend his hand in friendship to her. He didn't have to ever speak to her again. But he did.

As she continued to look at him, she couldn't believe she had thrown all that away.

"Jaye…"

His eyebrows rose and he looked over at her to show his attention.

"I'm a different person—from the woman you knew eight months ago." She looked down at her hands. "I'm not…" she looked up at him, "the woman that ruined me and you. Anymore."

This was a good time to let Jaye know that he wasn't sitting across from the woman he used to date, but that he sat next to a woman who was a little better; she was a little stronger; she even felt like she was a little wiser and smarter than the woman he fell in love with. She wanted him to know that. And know why. Not because it would win her some potential future girlfriend-again points, but because she wanted to make a good new first impression—for the second time. Because he was her friend again. And because she thought it was something he should know.

He had wondered. There was so much he wanted to know and wanted to ask, but hardly knew how to get the words out. He let her talk. How much would she tell?

"I used to say… that I would never ever be like my mother." She bit her bottom lip, then let it go. "She was sweet," she said. "But she was naïve. 'Stupid' is what I used to call her until I learned some respect." She chuckled at her own comment. "I was a bad ass," she said. "But that was how I felt; I didn't have any respect for her. I didn't think she deserved it. She was so stupid. And people knew that shit. My father—he knew it." She shook her head in pity. "I swore though… that I wouldn't be like that. I couldn't be like women. Stupid. Men had all the fun," she said, implying that she had obviously admired the *typical* man's lifestyle, though understanding its contrariety to Jaye's.

She looked over at Jaye for the first time since she started this explanation and he was looking back at her attentively. He always looked at her attentively when she spoke.

"I never thought it could happen to me. I never thought I'd get caught up. Never thought I would be so stupid." She shook her head just thinking about it. "I fell in love when I was 21. In college."

The look on Jaye's face asked for more, though not a word left his mouth. He wanted to know about the love he never knew about.

She said, "I never called it love though. I didn't know I *could* love. I ain't even know what the hell love was." She tittered. "But I know now. I gave this guy so much of myself for so many years. I… I was in love." She took a deep breath to avoid getting emotional. "But all he gave me was sex. But that was okay. I accepted that because… Because I wanted him to love me. And to me, that's how he expressed his love.

"Time after time. Year after year… Same thing. He call. I run. For ten years." She pushed her hair back. "I wanted to mean something to him. Be somebody," she said. "We didn't have much of anything in common. Never had an intelligent conversation… But I wanted him to want me. I wanted him to care that I was a great writer. Or that I was a good Chess player. Or that my birthday fell on April first." She looked at Jaye and said, "Even after I already had you."

Jaye could see that she now recognized some things about herself that she perhaps didn't always know. She spoke more maturely. She wasn't scared anymore. He assumed that had something to do with an obvious newfound confidence and knowledge of herself. He liked to listen to a not-so-unsure J.

"Jaye, I cheated on you," she said bluntly and comfortably. "And I *hate* myself for it." She shook her head. "You don't understand, I really *hate* that I did that to you," she said. "But I did it because... Because I didn't realize that I didn't need him. You loved me—in ways that nobody else ever had. And probably ever will. But... I was so used to being the J that only felt love through sex and..." She stared at the carpet as if she could see straight through it—like the rest of her sentence sat on the other side.

"I guess... I guess I forgot that I didn't have to be that person anymore," she said, looking back up at him. "I didn't have to be that woman."

Jaye saw an admirable place in her eyes, and in her words. But he didn't know where to go from there.

* * *

"For a guy with such a reserved demeanor, you sure do talk a lot of trash on the court," Chandler complained, playfully.

Jaye simply laughed as they walked over to the bench.

"I only boast when I win one-on-one games."

"I could'a beat you, but my..."

"Yeah, your ankle is sore, right? Or is it your hamstring?" he asked, sarcastically.

She shot him an evil eye with a reluctant smile before sitting down beside her gym bag and taking out a towel to wipe her face and neck.

"This was my first time playing against you," she said. "Next time though..." She shook her head, a gesture replacing her unsaid words that next time she'd beat him.

"So you think all you need is one more try?" he asked with sarcasm again. As he wiped his face dry of sweat, he laughed at his own comment.

Giggling, she said, "You think you are so funny."

"You're laughing."

She didn't say any more, just took her bottle of water from her bag, opened it and took a sip.

"So you been ballin' all your life, huh?" he asked, assuming that because she was so good, she had been playing since she could walk.

"Since I was about twelve or thirteen," she said. "When my parents divorced, my mother and my brother and I moved here from Richmond. All they did was play basketball around here, so I started playing. Got pretty good at it. Went to Maryland on a full scholarship. Blew my knee out in my last year."

"Damn."

"I was gonna go overseas to play, but…" She shrugged her shoulders. "I guess God had other plans for me."

He thought about what she had said for a moment, feeling bad that she wasn't able to pursue her dream. But then he said, "Yeah," agreeing that maybe God had plans for her to do something else. Sometimes things work like that. Chandler didn't seem very upset or bitter about it though. She was a religious woman, so she was content with the fact that her career choice was not a part of the divine plan.

She took a few more sips of her water, put the top back on it and said, "I gotta get outta here." She picked up her bag and threw the strap over her shoulder. "We should hook up sometime. Wanna go to the Wizards game on Saturday?"

Jaye didn't think anything about what she was asking. "Okay," he said smiling.

"I've got floor seats, half court," she enticed.

"Ah'ight. Can't wait." He said, "I'll be in here some time before the end of the week. We'll talk about it then."

She said, "Jaye, you have my number. Use it."

They had exchanged numbers a month ago and neither had used them yet. He knew what his reasons were, but he had no idea what hers were and he didn't really want to know. He was somewhat happy she hadn't called. It had nothing to do with him not *wanting* to talk to her outside of the gym; it was more so because he never really thought they had much business talking outside of it. He *could've* called her just to talk, but the truth was, he had someone to talk to. He didn't really want to ask her out to dinner or a movie or anything because… Well he had somebody to go out with to the movies and to dinner too. But the basketball game seemed so appropriate for their friendship. It wasn't a date at all; it was just two friends who loved the game of b-ball watching it together, live.

After a moment of silence, he somewhat nervously said, "Okay," only because it was the quote: right-thing-to-say.

"I'll talk to you later," she said.

He nodded with an artificial smile on his face as she walked away.

You ready?" he asked as J walked by him and into his house.

She looked at him and said, "I wanna talk to you."

"Okay," he said. "What is it?"

She sighed and lazily flopped down on the couch.

He couldn't imagine what it was that she had to talk to him about.

She started, "About last night..."

Keyon and Ty wanted to live in the city. It was a must that they find a house inside the city boundaries; something about the quaint designs convinced her that it would be a great place to raise a family. And after months of searching for and visiting different homes, they finally found something in Northwest near the border of Montgomery County, Maryland.

The house wasn't too big; it had four bedrooms, four bathrooms, and added sections on the back and side of the house. The people who sold it to them had done a lot of remodeling, but managed to keep the original look. They didn't modernize it to the point where it stood out among the other homes as if it were more significant. It still fit the look of the neighborhood, and it was worth the seven figures they paid for it, considering it was located in the nation's capital.

So last night, to christen the new crib, they decided to have a New Years Eve house warming party. They invited some friends over to see the new place and party and drink to bring in the brand new year. And drink they did. Before the ball dropped in Times Square in New York City, almost everybody in the house was nearing tipsy and still going. Some were far past it—just flat out drunk.

J limited herself to drinks she could handle—ones she felt comfortable driving home after having.

Jaye went far past his usual Budweiser, which was a walk in the park compared to what he was having.

"Keyon told me you were out here," J said, as she joined him on the deck in the back of the house. "What are you doin' out here? It's cold." Neither of them had on a coat.

"It's hot in there," he said before taking a sip of something in a red, plastic cup.

She started to laugh as she noticed that he obviously had a little too much to drink. She had seen him drinking all night, but she didn't know how much he'd actually had.

She walked over and stood beside him, looking into his cup; he was standing by the banister looking out into the night sky. Couldn't see much because of the night-lights in the city, but it was well worth a try.

"What's that you drinkin'?"

He shrugged his shoulders as if to say that he didn't know.

Shocked, she said, "You don't know?!"

He looked down into the cup, smiling. "I mean… It's rum and coke."

"Rum and coke?"

"You don't like rum and coke?" he asked.

"*You* don't like rum and coke," she informed.

A grimace appeared on his face. He said, "No wonder I wasn't drinkin' this shit." He looked down into the cup again.

"You want it?" he asked, putting it close to her face.

"Hell no," she said moving her head back as the stench of the hard liquor invaded her nose.

"Me either."

He walked from his place by the banister and took a seat on the outdoor sofa just a few feet away, still holding the cup.

"Come and sit," he said, motioning for her to sit on the chair beside him.

She sighed. "Jaye, it is cold as shit out here. I'm about to go back in. The ball is about to drop in a min-"

"Just sit with me for one minute," he said.

Trying to hide her smile, she came and sat beside him.

"What's so funny?"

"Nothing, Jaye," she lied. "I'm cold."

"Drink some of this, you'll be warm."

"Didn't I say I don't want none of that," she snapped, still attempting to hold in a smile. He was a funny drunk; she couldn't help but laugh at him.

He started laughing hard.

"You are so funny," he said. He looked at her with somewhat of a straight face and said, "You are *so* funny. That's why I like you."

He was obviously drunk, but his words were not slurred. He spoke with seriousness and what seemed to be honesty to her. He was looking her in the eyes.

But he was drunk?

He took a sip from the cup and then frowned at the taste.

"Give me this," she said, laughing at him as she took the cup from his hand, trying to change the subject. "Don't you think you've had enough to drink?" she asked.

He smiled at the fact that she took his drink from him.

"J, I love you," he said, changing the subject back. "I'm still in love with you, girl."

She couldn't believe he was saying that to her. She had secretly wanted to hear those words for the past few months, and now that he was finally saying it, he was inebriated. But he said it with such sincerity.

"Jaye, you're drunk," she said, excusing him from touching her emotionally.

"Don't you love still me?" he asked. That was wrong. "Me still. Still love me."

She didn't say anything, just stared in his eyes.

He leaned forward and said softly, "J, I still love you. And I think you… Don't you wanna be my girlfriend?"

"Come on, let's go inside," she said. "They already brought in the New Year without us."

She stood up, then she put her hand in his to help him up just in case he started to stumble. He got up somewhat clumsily and stood closely in front of her.

"Hug me," he said.

With no problem, she hugged him, though that was a stretch considering they hadn't touched at all—no hugs, definitely no kisses, hell, hardly any handshakes—since he accepted her back into his life. He hugged her tight.

"I love you," he said.

When they let go of each other, he looked down into her eyes, and slowly… he leaned in and kissed her.

At first, she was hesitant, but then something seemed so natural about kissing him—so right. Until she eventually and quickly began to taste the liquor on his tongue, which was when she realized how fake that moment was—how unintentional. He was drunk?

The kiss lasted no more than four seconds before she pulled away from him and said, "I'm goin' in the house."

Which is why she wanted to talk to him now before they went to the annual car show at the Convention Center. She wasn't necessarily into cars like that, but he was. She was just going to have something to do, and because he asked her if she would go with him.

"What about last night?" he asked. He looked at her waiting for her to tell him about last night.

She looked at him almost not believing that he didn't seem to have a clue as to what she was talking about.

She concluded, "You don't remember anything about last night."

He chuckled and said, "I remember be'n twisted. That's about it. I don't remember too much past that second Mojito. I just got up at two o'clock."

"So, you don't remember anything you told me?"

He shook his head slowly and his eyebrows wrinkled like he was really thinking about what he might've told her. "No," he answered, shaking his head, still grimacing and thinking. "I can't say that I do. Why? What did I say?"

She continued to look at him, trying to see if she could find any clue of him joking with her, but when she couldn't, she decided to go ahead and "tell him what he said."

"You ah… I asked you if you would go to Chicago with me in a couple of weeks," she lied instead. "You said you would go. But I just wanted to tell you not to worry about it. I may not be going now, so I just wanted to…"

The look on his face said that he definitely didn't have a clue as to what she was talking about.

"I just wanted to tell you not to worry about it, that's all. But thanks for saying you would go with me."

Still looking perplexed, he asked, "And you had to sit down just to tell me that?"

She smiled and answered, "My back aches so that's why I had to sit down."

"If your back hurts then you should get somebody to massage it," he said, smiling.

"I should, shouldn't I?"

She could've read between the lines of that statement, but she chose not to. She chose not to start something she didn't think he would want to finish.

"You ready?" she asked as she got up from the seat.

His response: "I'm waiting for you."

* * *

The Wizards defeated the Pacer's that Saturday night in overtime; however, neither of them really cared because they were neither Wizards nor Pacers fans anyway. Jaye, of course, loved his Nets, and Chandler…

"I'm a Celtics fan."

"Just like Keyon," he said, smiling.

"I've loved them since Bird," she said. "And still do. You gotta admit that they have a nice squad." She looked at him, waiting for him to say it.

"Yeah," he said, reluctantly. "They do ah'ight."

They both chortled at his confession.

Since there's never anyplace to park in Chinatown—where the Wizards play—they both decided to take the train to the game and just meet inside near will-call. After the game ended, they found themselves in a burger joint sitting behind ½ pound burgers and fries.

"So, what do you do when you're not doing your art?" she asked. "Or shootin' hoops," she threw in with a smile.

He said, "Well... Well, I volunteer at the Cregar Center three or four days a week."

"Really?" she said, sounding like she wanted to know more about that.

"I help kids with their homework and then we paint. A lot of them kids got me beat."

She laughed. "How old are they?"

He could see that Chandler must've really had a thing for little ones. The look on her face as he spoke about them gave it away; it was warm and affectionate.

"Most of 'em probably are no older than 8 or 9. Some younger."

"Aww..."

"I'm tellin' you, they'll make you smile even on those days you when really don't feel like it."

"I bet," she said.

Smiling, he added, "I remember when I used to try to get my sister to paint."

"Oh, how old is she?"

"She's seventeen now. Just turned seventeen in October."

"Wow, she's a baby," Chandler said, surprised. "So you said she lives here with you, right?"

"Yeah." He took a sip of his drink. "She came to visit me after I moved here and... she never went back home," he said, laughing.

Chandler laughed too.

"So, you moved into a house here all by yourself?"

"Well, I had a girlfriend at the time. She was supposed to move here with me, but ah... Things didn't work out, so..." He shrugged his shoulders and took another sip from his cup. "Now I live in the house with my little sister. She's a good roommate."

Chandler smiled and said, "Well, that's good that you two are close like that. I didn't get along with my older brother. He was only three years older than me, but I remember fighting with him most of the time. But you two seem like friends."

"Yeah, she's my friend."

They both stopped talking long enough to eat a little of their food.

"So how does she react when you date people?" she asked. "I mean, assuming that you've seen women since you've been here."

He thought about how he would answer that question without telling her too much.

He said, "It's usually hard for her to adjust to women because she's very protective of me."

"Protective?" she asked, cutting in. "She's younger."

"Well, she knows how I am, so she's protective," he said. "But fortunately for her I don't really date that much. I don't introduce many woman to her anyway."

Chandler nodded, following him as he spoke. Then she said, "So let me ask you this:" She looked him in his eyes. "Has your sister been introduced to anybody lately?" she asked, smiling, hoping that he understood the question the way she was trying to get it across. But before he could even begin to answer, to be clearer, she said, "This is my way of asking you are you seeing anybody right now?"

If he were lighter in complexion, his blush would have been more obvious. For the past few months—since he first met and spoke with Chandler—the thought that maybe she wanted to do more with him than shoot hoops had crossed his mind every time they came in contact with each other, but he really didn't want to think so arrogantly. He convinced himself that she really only wanted a friendship based off of their common interest in sports—basketball in particular. She was attractive, but he never intended to act on anything. The Wizards game was supposed to be a part of the friendship based off of a common interest thing. And the dinner together in the burger joint thing? Well that just sorta happened. But the conversation, which was initially only about sports, ended up leading to other topics—topics which were intended to reveal his availability for more than just a sports driven friendship.

"No," he said. "I'm single. I don't have a lady right now."

For some reason, he felt like he had just lied to her face. He would've really felt bad about saying that he had a girlfriend because he didn't. However, he didn't want her to think that just because he wasn't involved with anyone that he was available, because he wasn't that either.

"I just got out of a serious relationship not too long ago," he said, as if it were more recent than it really was; it ended months ago.

Looking down at his food as he thought about that relationship, he said, "It ended on somewhat of a bad note and…"

Chandler wanted so badly to ask what happened—how it ended. But out of respect, she chose not to be nosey. She figured if he wanted to tell her all of that then he would.

He sighed and said, "I took it kind of hard." Then he said, "No, actually I took it really hard and it's like I…"

"You're not in a hurry to bring somebody else into your life right now, huh?"

"Right," he agreed. "Right."

He and Chandler left the restaurant after midnight, said their goodbyes, and headed their separate ways on the subway.

No sooner than the doors closed on the train, his cell phone was at his ear as he waiting for J to answer on the other end.

"Hey, you busy?"

"No, not really," she said. "I was just reading this book I picked up today. Where are you?" she asked, noticing the ambient noise over the phone.

"I'm on the train coming from a Wizards game."

"Oh."

"Hey... You mind if I came over?" he asked.

"Tonight?" she asked. "Now?"

"Yeah, I mean I know it's late, but it's just that I'm-"

"Sure." She hated the fact that she had said that so quickly; it made her sound pressed. And though she was already under the covers and only a page away from putting the book on the nightstand and calling it a night, she said, "I mean I'm up. It's Saturday. I could use some company."

He smiled and said, "I know it's cold, but... you don't mind picking me up from the train station, do you?"

After they hung up, she jumped up and threw on some jeans and a sweater and some shoes and a coat and darted down the steps and into her car. She let it warm up for maybe a second before she pulled off to meet Jaye at the station, which was only three minutes away by car. She didn't want to keep him waiting if he was already there.

"Man, it's warm in here," he said, hanging both of their coats in the closet near the front door.

"I knew you were coming, so I turned the heat up," she joked.

He looked back at her and smiled before coming to join her on the sofa.

"So did they win?" she asked.

"Who?"

She looked at him. "The Wizards. Didn't you say you were at a basketball game?"

"Oh yeah," he said, nearly forgetting that he had just gone to the game. "Yeah. They won in overtime."

"Who'd you go with?"

"My friend Chandler from the gym."

She nodded and thought nothing more about what he said. She was only asking to continue the conversation.

"So what made you wanna come over here?"

He shrugged his shoulders and then looked at his watch; it was one o'clock in the morning. "It is late isn't it?"

"Just a little," she answered, sarcastically.

"I don't know," he said. "I mean... I was on the train and it was headed in the direction of your house and..."

She looked at him, not believing his excuse.

He sniggered. "Okay," he said in a confessing tone. "I haven't seen you in like three days. I wanted to see you. I missed you."

There it was again. He was smiling after he said that, but she wasn't. Jaye had been so hard to understand. He would say things, but never actually *said* things. And he'd do things, but never actually *did* anything. JayMahr was never an initiator of complex conversation, so if he did in fact have something to say to her, there was a good chance she'd be waiting a long time to hear it if she didn't bring it up. She decided to bring it up.

"Jaye," she said. "What are we doing?"

To buy time, he thought about asking her to clarify her question, but the truth was: he didn't need clarification; he knew what she was asking. He had actually thought about that question himself.

The answer he came up with: "I don't know."

The smile that seemed to cover his face since he got into her car just ten minutes ago disappeared quickly and a look of perplexity took over.

Silence covered the room for a moment.

"Don't get me wrong," she said, breaking the silence, "I enjoy spending time with you again. I like the fact that we can talk again, and that you..." She stopped and decided to change her wording. "And that it *appears* as if you have forgiven me, but..."

"J..." he interrupted, neither disagreeing about having forgiven her nor agreeing that he had.

"So what now?" she asked. "Is this it? I'm back in your life now..."

"Yes."

"But as what?" she asked. "It's like I don't understand what we…" She stopped and sighed.

"J," he said, softly, almost as if he were hinting that he didn't want or feel like discussing this.

She looked at him waiting for the rest of what he had to say. But nothing came out.

He exhaled and slouched down on the sofa throwing his right hand over his face. Though he wanted and probably *needed* to say more, he didn't. He didn't say anything else. In fact, he found himself looking at the television instead of putting his thoughts together so that he and she could further their discussion because they were far from finished.

After what seemed like an eternity of silence, she got up and said, "I think I'ma go to bed now."

He looked up at her, but still didn't—couldn't—say anything. He watched her walk away.

When she got to the stairs, she said, without turning around, "Blankets in the closet. I'll see you in the morning," and proceeded up to her bedroom.

He knew that because she couldn't call herself his *woman*, she didn't and wouldn't press the issue like his *woman* would. Otherwise, she would've stayed downstairs with him until her question was answered and the situation was discussed and understood. Then again, if she were his woman they wouldn't have this issue.

He grabbed the remote control that she left on the couch beside him and turned to ESPN almost forgetting that he hadn't had his nightly dosage. He noticed them discussing the highlights of the basketball games he hadn't seen, and slowly, he began to think less and less about what he should've been thinking about, until he was no longer thinking about it at all.

Thirty minutes or so into the hour-long show, he realized he had made himself quite comfortable on the couch—had kicked his shoes off and found a good position where he could see the TV without having to move his neck too much—and that the subject he avoided had somehow eased its way back into his system. He liked it when she wasn't saying anything about it. But even though he got away with doing this to her for weeks, he knew that someday soon—much sooner than it would be before he brought it up—she would bring it up. And instead of having prepared answers for her, he still hadn't fully thought about what the extent of their new relationship would be.

He had to go upstairs. He had to say something. So he thought about what he could say—thought out an entire scene in his mind:

He would explain to her in a monotone, "J, I don't know what to call this. I don't know," he'd confess. "Cuz I'm at a point right now where I'm... I'm just..." He'd search for the word. "I'm still trying to figure out what's good for me—what I *feel* I should do... Or what I *think* I *need* to do. And unfortunately, you're stuck in the middle of that."

Confused, she'll ask, "What do you mean?"

He'd take a deep breath and prepare for what he's about to reveal.

"It's like... I do wanna be with you... but it's just that I don't know if I *can* right now. I love you so much. And I can't help that." He'd add, "There's nothing I can do about it."

She'll wait for a moment, hoping he'd have something else to say, but when it seems as if he doesn't, she'll say, "So *be* with me."

He'd sniff, though he won't be crying and don't have a cold. He'd tell her, "It's not that easy." He'd shake his head, still speaking in an unemotional tone. "It's not that easy."

She'll obviously know what was hard about it.

He'd tell her, "I know this might sound selfish. And even crazy. But... I don't want you to see other people. But I don't know how much I can let you have back. How much of me."

She'll understand every word that leaves his tongue and she'll feel like hell as she thinks about why he feels this way.

He'd say, "But I hate the fact that I'm stringing you along like this."

She'll probably say, "You're not stringing me. I'm here because I wanna be here. I just wanna know what this is."

"Why does everything have to be defined?"

"Because it does. It has to be *some*thing."

"It's nothing," he'd answered.

"Jaye…"

"This is nothing. This whole thing… is nothing."

He would want to say that, but he'd realize that he actually has a better answer for her, so he'd choose to use it. He'd tell her, "This is a stupid… place that we are… *together*, where we're not just friends and not… together." He'd hope she understands. "We're just…" He'd think about a good word to describe it. "It's a place I chose to be because I didn't know where I wanted to be. And I didn't know who I wanted *you* to be."

She'd just listen and continue to let him talk.

"But now that I know…" He'd look at her. "Now that I know… I don't know if I can."

"Can what?" she'd ask.

Sighing again, he'd say, "I wanna be with you…"

That would be the second time during this conversation that he'd say he wanted to be with her, but it would be obvious that he was scared to submit.

He'd shake his head and say, "But I can't be hurt again."

Looking in his eyes, she'll definitely say—in a tone that implied that she swore these words on her mother's grave—"I would *never*… hurt you twice."

Their eyes would never leave each others'. She would look into his assuring the truth in her words and hoping that he believed her, and he would look into hers simply because he wouldn't be able to look away; he'd feel that to look away would imply that he didn't see sincerity in what she spoke. Though he'd stand more than six feet away, he would see deep into her and trust that sincerity lay there. He'd know her heart.

She'll whisper, "I miss you."

"I love you," he'd say in return.

The signature Sports Center opening theme music distracted his trance as the show prepared for its second or third run of the night. But he was finished daydreaming anyway. He was prepared to tell her exactly what he wanted to tell her—exactly the way he'd just thought it out.

TAP TAP TAP

Though it was dark in the room, she still turned and

looked at the closed door as if she would be able to see who was knocking.

"It's open," she said, sitting up and flicking on the lamp on the nightstand so she could see him.

He pushed the door open and said, "Sorry to wake you up."

"It's okay," she said, not bothering to go into the details of not being asleep. She had been there in the dark for nearly an hour.

He sighed and stepped in just beyond the doorsill, keeping his eyes on the floor.

Silence seemed to stick around just a little longer than she liked, so she broke it by saying, "Jaye."

Looking up from the floor, he stuck his hands into his pockets for lack of better things to do with them. He was nervous. He took a deep breath and looked over at her sitting on the bed. She was waiting for him to speak. He wanted to do just like he had just thought it out.

His lips parted, but nothing came out.

They could read each other's eyes. Each other's mind. Each other's heart.

He just stood looking at her. And she was looking back at him. And after about a half minute, he walked over to the bed and he sat down within her reach. He looked at her and still didn't say anything. He very slowly leaned in. And he kissed her lips.

He began rubbing her shoulders and removing the thin straps of her silk lavender nightgown.

"Jaye..."

She wanted to talk about it.

He stopped for just a moment and looked into her eyes. They were filled with so many questions. So much pain. So much guilt. But instead of addressing the situation that he knew needed addressing, he just kissed her and continued taking her nightgown off. He knew that words wouldn't leave his mouth—they couldn't! This was beyond metaphors. And no simile could articulate. He knew that he would just have to *do* to her what he was feeling. In order for her to know, she would have to feel his feelings...

And so he held her close. And tight.

He moved his hands up and down her back making sure he rubbed each and every spot. He felt her breast on his chest—soft, succulent. With his eyes closed, he smelled her and she smelled just like he remembered. And he tasted her. And she tasted... Just. Like. He. Remembered...

He moved naturally, instinctively, unconsciously... Because being with her—like this—was so familiar. And so true. So right.

Because being with her—like this... His spirit could understand things that his soul couldn't comprehend. Because the closer he got to her—the closer he got to being back in [inside] that soft, warm place that was pure perfection, and made to fit him and *only* him—the more he questioned his place in this place. The more he questioned... his place.

He looked at her. He looked at her for answers to questions he didn't speak.

She was naked. And he could see everything. He could hear all the colors... And he could see the music that played only in his head. And she saw this music too. T'was like Coltrane on a tenor sax—too complicated to decipher the sound of each note, but too beautiful and too real to deny the art of this complexity.

She closed her eyes as Life came back inside her...

This was the time for her to truly be. For him. She was his and only his, but a part of her knew what she had to do to make this a reality to him. And so she threw away her pride. She turned off her control. And she just let go...

She submitted. Fully. Entirely.

If this meant being uncomplicated—for him... Then she would be that—uncomplicated. For him. She would do anything that it took, just to be—with him.

She even whispered, "I miss you..." More than words. More like a prayer...

He too missed her. He missed his place—this place. And his spirit could understand things that his soul couldn't comprehend. Because the longer he stayed in [inside] that soft, *hot* place that was pure perfection, and made to fit him and only him, the more he realized the familiarity of thinking this before—or assuming this before—and being *wrong*. He questioned his place in this place. He questioned... his place.

He moved—in ways that took her. He had never moved like this before. He had never moved as if he had something to prove...

He did things that made her do things... Like things she never had done before. She felt feelings she had never felt before. She had never had *this* before. She could feel that what they were doing—what *he* was giving to her right now—was a type of passion that came from somewhere not even in his body. It was from somewhere deeper than that. And she could taste the sweet love, but lingering was a tangy hint of something painful.

He had never moved as if he had something to prove.

He knew her. He knew her ways. He knew what was felt inside her and *when* it was felt. He knew what he was doing to her. He put her in this place... And in a place like this, the mind can't lie. He had to know. He *had* to know. He just *had* to *know*... And so he asked, "Whose is it?"

He was flying her to her peak. But she wasn't afraid of heights...

"Jaye!"

But the pain struck her so deep down inside. His pain. She had caused this: a man so right in every way knew not of his rights, but of maybe his wrongs. But wrongs that didn't exist. There was nothing wrong with him. But if she had given what was his to somebody else, then—to him—he had wrongs. And now he wanted not to assume anymore—again—but to know: "Is it mine?"

He moved in such a way... Such a way that asked this question again and again and again... And she had gone as high as she could possibly go—as far as she could possibly go... And that's when she cried.

"Yes! Yes, Jaye... Yes!"

Oh God... And she cried *for* him. And she cried. And she cried... She couldn't hold on any longer, and so she just let go... All of it. Everything. She just let go. She let it go.

And her tears flowed freely and easily... Herself was now his.

"Is it mine…"

"Yes."

He had never shed tears before her before. But his tears came as he did…

He never wanted to ask. But he had to know. He needed to hear it said. For Life, he needed to hear her say it.

And she said it.

She could almost hear her own heart beating. Or maybe that was his.

She knew that her work was far from done. Words meant a lot. But actions meant a lot more. She knew that her words had not purchased her his trust, but rather simply put a down payment on it.

She could taste his tears.

And just so he would *know*. And so that he would never have to ask her again, she said to him:

"It's yours."

She got up from behind her desk and headed straight out of her office and over to Blu's. His door was open, so she walked in and closed it behind her. He was sitting behind his desk finishing off a foot long cold cut sandwich.

Artemus Blu was the Chief Editor—a big, tall guy, in his late thirties who favored uncle Phil on The Fresh Prince, except he was darker. People around the office all called him Blu once they found out that was his DJ name back in the day. That's the type of relationship he had with most of his subordinates; he joked around with them and allowed them to speak their minds, and he always heard them out, but when it came down to business he expected them to follow his rules. He was generally a liked person, but he had no problem with making a person dislike him if need be, particularly when enforcing rules that could be debatable because he always had to have his way.

"Blu, I can't do this."

Sighing as he rested his elbows on the desk and put his face in his hands. "How did I know I was gonna hear this shit?"

Ignoring his complaint, J said, "I thought Sara was supposed to cover this via phone for the next issue."

"J, he is in town *now*. Nobody knows why, but word has it he's working on something new and it's gonna be taking place in the Nation's Capital. We need to be on this shit, pronto."

"Can't no other writers do it?"

"All of your staff is booked crazy, you know that. And I need an interview with him for *this* issue. We need to at least *look* like we got the first fuckin' scoop on this shit! Shit."

She sighed again. There were a million other things— better things—she could've been doing. She was not trying to do this story. Searching for another way out, she said, "We can't go freelance? I gotta lotta shit to-"

"I don't wanna go freelance, Jesenia. I want *you* to do it."

"I am Associate Editor, Blu. All this last minute, running behind people... I thought I left shit like this behind in Oct..."

"This is Marien. Fucking. Scott. Shit like this is never left behind. I want my best person in Arts and Entertainment on it."

With a crooked grin, she said, "And that's me."

He cracked a smile once she noticed the inadvertent compliment. "You got the promotion didn't you?" He didn't expect an answer. "Look, I want you on this story. We wanna know why he's here, and we need verification about why his wedding is being cancelled."

"Cancelled?"

"Postponed. Shit, I don't know. That's why we need you to do this interview," he said. "Now, I've already taken the liberty of calling his manager, who's an associate of mine, and he said he can arrange something for us this evening." He looked at J to see if she was following him.

Her face still said that she didn't want to do it, but he continued anyway.

"Marien is going to make an appearance tonight at some nightclub." He mumbled, "I can't remember the name. He can pick you up in his limo on his way th…"

"No, that's okay. I'll drive."

He noticed her quick answer and asked, "What's up with that? You're not a fan?"

Her face said no, but she said, "It's not that. I'd just rather drive. I don't have time to sit around at some club all night."

"He'd bring you home when you're ready."

Again, she said, "That's okay."

She was already on her way out the door when Blu yelled, "First scoop, J! Remember that."

She said under her breath, "Yeah. First scoop."

* * *

Handing him one of the ice-cold beers she brought with her when she came over, she asked, "What cha paint'n?"

He saw the potential in it being by far one of his most incredible pieces. Though it was nowhere near done, he already knew it would be at the top of his list of picks for the premier display at the gallery's second anniversary celebration. This year, he and Keyon with the help of their publicist came up with the idea of featuring three to five pieces, the Second Anniversary Collection Series. They hadn't come up with the numbers yet, but all of the pieces sold would only have a maximum of fifty prints in circulation, making the original—the selling piece—extremely sought after.

Using his paint-covered shirt to get a good grip on the beer top, he twisted it off and shot it in the little tin trashcan by the door.

"Ahh… This is just something I started on today. It's a…"

Squinting, she cut in, "It looks like-"

"You," he said taking a sip. Smiling.

Her eyes lit up. She took the cold bottle from his hand, swigged a little, swallowed the little bit she had in her mouth, and then asked in excitement, "You're painting a portrait of me?!"

"Well it's not a portrait…"

"But it's me, though," she cut in, boasting almost.

She handed him back the bottle. He smiled and shook his head while watching her blush in excitement about the painting.

"J, it's abstract. I'm using you as a platform, and then I'm gonna add a…"

"But it's still me, right?"

"Yes, it's still you," he said. "In a sense. You see, I'm gonna add a creative…"

Before he could finish, she was straddling him in the chair.

"I'm gonna ah… gonna… I'ma… creative ah… add a…"

He was looking directly into her dark brown eyes, and before he knew it, he had forgotten what it was he was supposed to be telling her. He forgot he was even talking. Only thing he could focus on now were her breasts since she had scooted just a bit closer pressing them on his chest. She took his beer from his hand and sat it on the floor, leaving his hands free. He drove them up from her waist to her breast. He was a breast-man and hers were particularly round and firm. He squeezed them like he was testing the ripeness of some type of market fruit.

He moved his hands back down to her hips and kissed her as she gyrated on his lap. He wore sweatpants making *it* much easier than it would have been otherwise.

He took off her shirt and let it fall to the floor, then her bra, which fell on top of the shirt. His teeth and tongue and lips moved from her lips straight to her breast—his favorite part of her body, along with her soft neck, smooth shoulders, flat stomach, thick thighs, long legs, and ass he loved to grip like a Wilson.

They were in his art-room—not exactly the place to make love; not exactly the place for all the four-play and whatnot, so he stopped sucking her breast as they finished undressing. Sometimes, though he loved her dearly, he didn't want to make love to her. And she didn't want to be made love to. Making love, sometimes, was too sensual and romantic. Time-consuming. Sometimes, less was more better. And this was one of those times.

They lay on the floor afterwards, exhausted.

He looked at the clock. "J, it's almost 8:30."

"Damn." She didn't want to leave. Though she told him that she had to leave at 8:30 to be where she had to be to do the interview on time, she made no rush attempts to move.

"You gon' be late," he said.

She sighed and sat up. "Remind me never to do it on a fucking hardwood floor again. Please." She rubbed the small of her back. "My back is killing me."

He was on the floor beside her, still tired, tempting, in the nude. Every curve on his dark brown skin seemed to be defined by the lights in the room. She looked over at him and contemplated getting up to leave him.

He reached over and began to massage the small of her aching back.

"Who do you have to interview?"

With her eyes closed, enjoying the rub he was giving, she hated having to say his name. "Marien Scott."

"Marien Scott? The director guy you went to school with-"

"Yeah," she cut in. "Him." She knew that if Jaye knew more, then he'd have more to say. A part of her wished that he did know who Marien was—*exactly* who he was. There was still a lot of pain when she thought about what she had done, and what had been done to her. She had done a lot to reconcile her wrongs with herself and with the man beside her. Maybe one day she would be able to explain Marien Scott to Jaye Cobain. But today just wasn't that day.

"He's in town and Blu in*sists* that we get all of this *exclusive* information about his new movie and his marriage and shit for this issue. Talkin' 'bout 'we need to have the first scoop'. I don't feel like doing this shit."

"Then don't."

"Jaye," she said, looking at him. "This is my job."

He stopped massaging her back and she looked over at him like he was crazy and as if to ask, "Why'd you stop?"

She hadn't said a thing before he read her mind and said, "If I keep going, you'll never get up."

She laughed. "I know," she said and finally got up from the floor.

She began to gather her clothes and put them on piece by piece.

"You ain't gon' take a shower?" he asked.

She smiled and shook her head. "I'll wait 'til I get home. I wanna have you on me for a little longer."

* * *

When she got to the club, there was a black limo parked in the back exactly where Blu said it would be.

"Isn't it a coincidence that they assigned _you_ to do this interview?" Marien asked, grinning from ear to ear. "Makes things more convenient. I was gonna call you tomorrow."

"Yeah, big coincidence," she said.

He chuckled. "Not really. I told ol' Blu that I wasn't talkin' to anybody else."

"You what?!"

She knew she was the best person for the job, but for Blu to lie and say that it was his idea to have his best person on it because of the significance of the story and not because of a request, angered her.

Marien said, "Hell, if I gotta do an interview—cuz I _hate_ doing interviews—I figure I might as well knock out two birds with one stone." He found what he said funny, but he was the only one.

"Two birds with one stone huh?" It wasn't really a question, just a thought that she'd said out loud. "Why'd you feel the need to sneak and get me here?"

"I don't have to sneak. I just made a simple demand," he corrected. "I mean, of course, I'm not doubting my ability to charm, cuz you know... I _am_ a charmin' mutha-fucka," he said, popping his collar with that arrogant smile on his face. "But two birds with one stone means less work. That's always my philosophy. Unless of course we're talking about sex, then the whole 'two birds, one stone' thing takes on a different meaning."

Ignoring his last statement, she said, "Marien, let's just get this over with. It's late and I'm tired."

"Is that the way you talk to all the stars you interview?" he asked, grimacing, speaking sarcastically. "Don't make me have to report you." He was smiling again as he joked and flirted with her. His eyes continuously searched her body from top to bottom.

She couldn't help but crack a smile, but it was more so *at* him rather than *with* him.

"See, there's that beautiful smile."

Blushing and trying to hide it, she said, "Let's do this."

Seductively, he said, "Yes, let's do it."

She shot him a look that said that they were not on the same page. That was not what she meant.

She pulled out her tape recorder and began her interview. She didn't have too many prepared questions besides the major ones that everybody wanted to know; all of the others were follow-ups. Come to find out, Marien was producing his first feature film; he was also directing it, and part of the movie would in fact be taking place on location in DC.

She wondered, but not *really* wondered, why his wedding was cancelled. She, of course, had her own idea as to why, but she was curious as to the specifics. Rumors stated that he and his girlfriend of three years were separating because of irreconcilable differences.

"Nah, nah, nah. We just decided that now was not the best time to make that jump. It's mutual pre-wedding jitters, I'll say. We'll work it out."

"So there will be a wedding?"

"No doubt."

She stopped her tape recorder and prepared to leave the limo. "Well, thank you, Mr. Scott."

"So what's up with tonight?" he asked, causing her to slow down in her attempt to leave.

"Nothing is up with tonight," she answered.

When he noticed that she was really about to leave, he rolled his head back and said, "Not this again. Don't tell me I gotta go through this shit again."

She opened the door and got out.

He jumped out behind her.

"Come on, J. Do I really have to go through this? We're right here. *Alone*," he emphasized. "I know you want to."

"Marien…"

"Come on. Don't make me beg. I hate begging," he said. "But I'll do it," he joked.

She smiled and shook her head. They had just finished discussing his marriage and how indefinite it was, and here he was putting the moves on her again.

"Marien, I'm finished what I came here for."

"No, you're not."

"*Yes*. I am," she said with force in her voice.

He said, "You are so sexy when you try to be demanding. I like it."

He placed his index finger on her chin and moved in for a kiss.

This time, she found it. Maybe it was in her purse or maybe in her pocket, but she found the strength somehow to move her head back and prevent his lips from touching hers. Then she simply removed his finger from her face and began to walk away.

He gently grabbed her arm to stop her from going far. She looked down with an expression on her face that made him remove his hand quickly.

"Why you doin' this to yourself, huh? Why?"

"Marien, I can't be fuckin' around with you anymore."

"'Can't'?"

"I *won't*. I'm *not*," she reworded.

He sighed. "Is it because of this wedding shit? I told that bitch this would fuck up my reputation."

She ignored the fact that he had just called his wife-to-be a bitch.

"What is it?"

"It's me," she said quickly. "I'm not simple. Anymore. I want things," she said. "I *am* like most women, okay. I wanna complicate things." She sighed. "It took fucking with you for me to realize that, but… I know now."

"That was *six* months ago," he said, smiling, not believing what he was hearing from her.

"Yeah. I learned a lot in six months."

He just stood there shaking his head, honestly thinking that she was crazy.

She said, calmly and seriously, "Don't call me. Don't try to contact me in anyway."

But she wasn't crazy; she was serious.

He looked at her waiting for her to break. After seconds, which could've been mistaken for minutes, it finally looked as if she wouldn't.

She felt victorious. It was one thing to *say* that she was a stronger person, but it was another to prove it. She had just proven to herself that she could withstand one of the hardest temptations of her life.

She turned and began to walk away.

"J," he said, stopping her.

She turned and looked back at him and they held eye contact for a moment. Again he wanted to see if she would break; he wanted to see if she was really about to walk away from him like that—like she had never done before.

He didn't seem to have any reason for stopping her, but she was glad he had because she had forgotten to say, "Goodbye, Marien."

"Are you fuckin' serious?" he asked. "J!"

She ignored him and walked away, proud of what she had just done. Or better yet, *didn't* do.

* * *

Jaye and Marien exchanged handshakes.

They had met before, but Jaye didn't want to rely on that brief meeting as his proof, so he professionally reintroduced himself.

"How're you doing, Mr. Scott. I'm Jaye Cobain, the co-owner…"

"Jaye Cobain," Marien repeated with narrowed eyes as if he were trying to remember him from somewhere. "I know you."

"Yeah," Jaye said. "We met last year at-"

"Kenya's cookout."

Jaye smiled and said, "I guess you do remember."

"I don't forget much," Marien informed.

He had come in for a painting, but he'd be lying to himself if he said that his visit had nothing at all to do with him wanting to look in the face the reason why his good ol' reliable fuck buddy of the past decade suddenly did not want to… well, *fuck* anymore.

He said, "I had a lil' free time in my schedule today. I thought I'd come down to Black Girl and check shit out. See what I can splurge on this evening."

"This your first time comin' here?"

"Yeah," Marien said. "Yeah. Every time I come to DC I always seem to get tied up some how," he said, looking at Jaye and smiling. He knew that Jaye didn't get it, which was the funny part. "I always have *things* to do when I'm in DC, y'know." He chuckled after that comment too. "I've just never been able to make it."

He took a few steps while examining a sculpture that stood before him on pedestal.

"But yeah man," he continued, "this is a nice lil' set up you got goin' on here," while giving the gallery a once-over, starting with the ceiling.

"Thanks," Jaye said, taking the statement as a compliment.

"I used to fuck with paint a lil bit back in the day," he said, still looking around. "Didn't think painting was a real career so I dropped it."

Marien's tone was nonchalant, but his eyes revealed that he couldn't deny that Black Girl was beautiful from its appearance on the outside to the exquisite art that decorated its walls and floors on the inside. Even the carpet was nice.

Jaye ignored his comment and accepted it as simply his opinion about where art stood in his life. Or didn't stand.

"So did you come just to check us out or are you..."

"Oh, I'm tryin' to buy, brotha."

They shared a laugh.

"Yeah, I came in here to spend some money, y'understand."

"I got you." Jaye asked, "Well is there anything in particular that you're looking for or... Anything that you like?"

"I like 'em all, that ain't no lie," he said. "But I'm lookin' for somethin' that's a little on the..." He maneuvered his hands as if that would help Jaye to help him figure out exactly what it was he was trying to say. "Something that's..." He gave facial expressions and body movement, but still, couldn't quite explain it. He didn't know exactly what he was looking for.

"I'm lookin' for something that's..." He snapped his finger as he tried to think of the word. "Sexual," he said. "But oh," he interjected, "gots to keep it classy, my man. I'm a man who exudes class."

Jaye noticed Marien's haughtiness, smiled, and continued to show him a few contemporary expressionist pieces he had in mind, some of which he chose to give somewhat of an explanation; he allowed Marien to see what he wanted to see in many of them.

Marien picked out the one he wanted, which was an oil painting on a canvas made of wood imported directly from Italy, done by an artist from San Francisco.

"So where do you plan to hang this—living room, office..."

"Bedroom," he answered confidently with that infamous crooked, cocky smile of his.

"Ohhh, okay," Jaye said, catching Marien's insinuation. He decided not to ask anymore about the painting for the sake of not wanting to know more.

"If you want, we can have that delivered wherever you want, free of charge."

"Actually, you know what? My driver is parked right outside, so I can take it with me."

With a suit yourself look on his face, Jaye said, "That's fine."

Outside, Jaye said, "I appreciate your business, man. Thanks."

Marien said, "No prob'm, brah," as they smacked hands. "I bet you can use it, huh. Can't make but so much in an art gallery."

By now, Jaye had already concluded that this guy was an arrogant ass; he only continued to show respect because it was good customer service. He could've told him what the gallery pulled in last year—more than he can say about his last movie—but he didn't. He wasn't a man that bragged about his possessions or put down others.

He simply smiled and said modestly, "We do ah'ight."

"Well I guess you do. You just got me for a few thousand," he said, laughing.

Jaye didn't really find his joke funny.

"Well aye man, let me get outta here."

Yeah, let you, Jaye thought. "Okay," he said.

"And oh… Tell your girl J I said wha'sup. I mean—that is still your girl, ain't it?"

Instead of answering yes or no, the first thing to pop into Jaye's head was the thought of what difference it made to Marien.

"Well…" he started.

"Please. You ain't gotta explain," Marien interjected. "You seem like a very personable guy. Nice," he said. "You gotta watch yourself with a girl like that, man."

Jaye grimaced and his eyes squinted 'cause he couldn't believe he had just said that.

"A woman like what?"

Marien smiled; he could see he was finally getting to Jaye. He could tell he had hit a soft spot.

"You know…" he said as if Jaye was supposed to catch on to what he was implying. "I've known her for a while and ah… I don't know. You just don't seem like the type of guy that would go for a girl like her."

Jaye's facial expression said that he still didn't understand what Marien was trying to say, but that he didn't like where he had gone thus far.

Marien chose to elaborate. "Don't get me wrong—she's fine as hell. But I mean you seem like the wife-wanting type. And believe me, she ain't no wife type."

Jaye could almost feel his entire face tightening up, but he stayed calm. He wasn't going to say anything negative.

"Well, thank you for the ah..." He searched for the word. "The information," he said, calmly. "But I think I can take care of myself."

"Aye bro, you ain't gotta get all defensive, I-"

"I'm not getting defensive, I'm just saying: I don't need you to advise me about my personal affairs."

Marien said, laughing almost, "Aye, I'm just a brother tryin' to look out for another. *Nah'mean?*" he asked, rhetorically. He had noticed Jaye's northern Jersey accent and was now mocking him a bit. With the smile gone now, he said, "Because I'm sure she fucks ya' brains out—rides it hard, don't she? Sucks ya' dick so good make ya' fuckin' toes curl..." He shook his head thinking about it. "Oh, I know all about that shit, man." He looked Jaye in his eyes and said, "Cuz she does it to me."

Jaye wanted to walk away—didn't want to hear what Marien was saying—but something compelled him to stay there. It was almost like he couldn't move. He just stood there staring Marien in his eyes as he talked—having a good ol' time telling him things he didn't want to hear.

Smiling again, Marien said, "But I guess you don't want me to advise you about your personal affairs. Even if they involve the same *bitch* that was fuckin' *me* in L.A. while..."

Before Marien could completely finish his thought, phrase, sentence... he was pulling himself from off the side of the car with a bloodied nose.

Before Jaye could pour on more punches, Keyon, from nowhere, was holding his throwing arm—his left arm.

Not loud, Jaye continuously said to Keyon, "Let me go, man. Just let me go. I'ma kick his ass."

A small foreign man—probably of African descent—had jumped out of the driver's seat of the car and run around to the side where they were, yelling, causing more of a scene than the scene did itself.

"What the fuck is going on here?! What the hell do you think you're doing!" he yelled at Jaye, who probably didn't hear a word he said. "Mr. Scott, are you okay?!"

"Did you hear what he said? Did you hear what this mutha-fucka said?" Jaye asked Keyon in his quiet, but pissed off tone. "I will fuck you up," he said to Marien. Probably only Marien, Keyon and the driver could hear him. He didn't yell, though he was steaming mad.

Marien was standing up straight now. He managed to squeeze a smile through the blood that covered his mouth as he looked at Jaye. He had succeeded.

Keyon was trying to hold Jaye back, but he continuously made his way toward Marien, trying to get just one more hit in. He wanted to knock that stupid ass smile from his face.

"Let me go, Keyon. I'ma fuck him up."

"Let him go, Keyon," Marien said, laughing.

Keyon contemplated letting Jaye go, but he had valid reasons for not wanting to let things escalate.

The little driver opened the car door for Marien and he got in, closed it and rolled down the window.

"Hey, Jaye…" he called.

Keyon was no longer holding him, just trying to convince him to go back inside.

"Tell ya' *girl* I said thanks for the interview the other night."

Which is why when Jaye stood there in J's house holding an oil painting on a canvas made of wood imported directly from Italy, painted by an artist from San Francisco, he nearly lost his breath. And the note that said, "I have no use for this. If your boyfriend fucks anything like he punches, call me if you need me. You know the numbers," didn't help the situation at all.

He wanted to throw the painting up against the wall, but he held back. Those were not his walls.

It was wrong to open other peoples' mail—illegal even—but at this point, he really didn't care. He had seen who the package was from. He immediately noticed that it was very close in shape and size to the painting purchased yesterday. So he opened it.

The carrier had arrived just as the cable guy was leaving. He asked for Jaye's John Hancock and handed over the package. As Jaye closed the door and looked around for a place in the living room to put it, he happened to glance down at the return address and the name read: M. Scott.

Jaye had come over to her house because she needed him to be there when the cable guy arrived. So he decided not to go to the gallery just so he could sit around at her house because she couldn't. The cable company said that someone would be out between 9 a.m. and 2 p.m., so Jaye got there before 9, just before J left to go to the office. Of course, they had made these plans a couple days ago, before the situation at the gallery, and since he wasn't a man that went back on his word, he did as he promised her. He hadn't said much of anything to her since then because he really didn't know what to think, or what reaction he should've had to Marien's words about her. He didn't know whether to believe it.

It was 2:30 when the cable guy got there.

It wasn't his mail to take. But now it wasn't hers to have. He broke the painting in half—frame and all—over his knee. He shoved the two halves back into the box and took it with him along with the note.

He found the closest dumpster in the closest alley and disposed of it.

If she ever asked about it, he'd tell her what he'd done.

* * *

"You said you were gonna call me earlier."

She came in holding a bag, which obviously contained food, and a cup. She sipped some of the drink and asked, "What happened?"

Before he could say anything, though it didn't seem like he was making any attempts to anyway, she said, "I didn't know what you wanted to eat, so I just got you a sandwich and some chips. And a lemonade," she added, sipping some more.

He was painting when she came in and he proceeded to paint as she spoke.

She assumed he probably didn't hear her when she said it when she came in, so she asked again: "What happened to you earlier, Jaye? You were s'pose to call me when the cable guy left."

Taking his time to finish his thought on the painting, he finally said, with his eyes still on the canvas, "I forgot."

"You forgot?" she asked. That was a strange answer, considering Jaye almost never used that as an excuse. He never claimed to have the best memory, but he usually remembered things when it came to her.

He looked at her for the first time since she entered his painting room and repeated, "I forgot," to assure her that he didn't stutter. And then he proceeded to paint.

She stopped moving and eyed him for a moment, giving him one of those who-the-hell-you-talkin'-to-like-that looks, but since he wasn't looking her way it didn't quite have the effect she wanted.

She decided to drop it. "Here's your food." She made room on the table where his containers of paint were and placed the bag on it, then just stood staring at him.

He continued painting until her stare became unbearable. He looked up at her with a "May I help you?" expression on his face.

She sighed and switched her lean from her right side to her left. She had her arms crossed too.

He sighed and looked back at his canvas.

"Jaye, what's wrong with you?" she asked, throwing away the attitude she had just formed and becoming more worried, trying to understand him. Something must've been bothering him; he had been quiet and mysterious for the last day.

With his eyes on the canvas, he said, "I'm *try*ing to paint," implying that she was bothering him.

She didn't say anything to him. She didn't have to take that, especially when she didn't know why she would be taking it. She turned, opened the door, and walked out.

He stopped, put the brush down, sighed, and went after her.

"J," he said without raising his voice. "J."

He grabbed her arm and she turned around and looked at him.

He didn't bother telling her about the little discrepancy that took place yesterday at the gallery; he didn't want her to know what had happen or *why* it had happened. He also didn't tell her about the painting that came to her house earlier. That was irrelevant.

Instead of apologizing as he should've or shouldn't have done, he just said, "I had a long day." He pulled her close and kissed her forehead. He hugged her without closing his eyes, without any emotion, sighed and said, "I had a… I had a really long day."

He hugged her because he was confused—because something inside of him made him feel like holding her close was the emotion he wanted and *should've* been experiencing, when in reality that wasn't what he was feeling at all.

The guy from college. The guy in L.A. The guy she fucked and ruined their beautiful relationship. It all made sense now.

He held her because he was confused. He wanted to hold her and say that it would be okay because he was there for her. But at the same time he felt like he wanted to push her away like she was dirt. Tainted. Like she should've never been in his life because she only added to the list of women who had fucked with his head, lied and deceived him. He could've thought this way, but instead, a day ago, he had defended her honor and her title as a woman. Some arrogant *bastard* had called her out of her name and it was his responsibility as her m… As *a* man to punch him in his face. Put him in his place.

But he contemplated whether it was worth it—whether defending her name was worth the bad publicity of his own and his business'. His life.

He didn't really think of J as *not* being his woman until just now, though technically she wasn't! They weren't "together;" they were still in the "trying" stage of the reconciliation, and this situation didn't help the process one bit. It was already taking long enough; this encounter with this Marien character only hindered their progression.

He wasn't ready for J to be his woman again just yet, but at the same time, he really didn't want her to be with anybody else. So what bothered him the most was the *possibility*. If she did, in fact, sleep with Marien the other night when she said she was interviewing him... Other than it simply being unethical because he was engaged to be married, she had every right to do it if she pleased. She was a single woman.

That really bothered him.

He kissed her because he was confused.

It takes a lot to forgive *and* forget. Many people choose to say that they've done the former in situations, but what is the former without the latter? How can you truly forgive if you haven't chosen to forget about the situation? Now of course, to forget doesn't mean to suddenly be struck with amnesia and not physically be able to remember anything; to forget is to accept the error of a person's ways and not hold it against them; it is to understand their fault and extract it from their character as you know it. To forgive is not just a statement, but an action.

But sometimes, forgetting may be the hardest part of the forgiving process. True, forgiveness can be in the heart, but the mind won't seem to let go—won't seem to forget. The mind may choose to go as far as allowing you to let your guard down and bring the assailant back into your life, but the *back* of the mind is the part that always seems to be the most paranoid. The rest of the mind chooses not to worry, but the *back* of the mind is what keeps you thinking; it keeps you suspicious. The back of the mind is the home of insecurities.

Sometimes insecurities can be more detrimental to the mind than the thought of the acts that caused them.

He made love to her because he was confused.

Technically, he and J were not exclusive. Signals had been sent, implications had been made, and lines had been read between. But technically nothing had been said. So technically, they were both unattached.

Peeking his head into the room, he said, "Hey, Chandler."

"Jaye!" She was surprised to see him. Happy, but surprised. She walked over to greet him. "What's up? What are you doing back here?"

She had never seen Jaye in that part of the gym before—where all of the classes were held.

"I was looking for you."

"Me?" she asked.

"Yeah." He looked around noticing that the class was preparing to start. "What class do you have right now?"

"Aerobics, but it doesn't start 'til 6," she said. "These people are just a little early."

All he could do was nod and say, "Oh." He looked at his watch to see what time it was; it read 5:50.

"Why? What's up?" she asked, chummy. Before he could answer, she said, "We don't have to stand here," smiling. She walked out of the class. "I have a few minutes I can spare for ya."

He snickered at her comment as he followed her away from the room.

"So what's goin' on with you? I haven't seen you in a few days?"

Still smiling, he said, "Yeah, I've been avoiding you."

"What?!" She shoved him in the arm as they both laughed. "Why are you avoiding me?"

"I'm jokin' with you," he said. "I just been busy, so I haven't been in here. My friends' wedding is coming up and I'm the best man, so... You know how that goes."

"Oh yeah," she agreed. "My best friend just got married on me last year." She shook her head. "Lets just say that was quite an experience. For all of us."

"I know what you mean. I'm just ready for all of this to be done with and I'm not even the one jump'n the broom," he said. "Gotta go all the way to Boston. Gotta do the bachelor party thing..."

"Well that should be fun. You guys love to watch a bunch of naked women dancin' around..."

Laughing, he admitted, "Yeah. But... it's tradition. I gotta do it because it's a traditional thing."

"Yeah, you better, or you'll have more to worry about than just the wedding—a bunch of angry guys."

"I know."

They shared another laugh before Chandler looked him up and down and said, "I see you're all dry; I guess you haven't been hoopin' today."

"Nah not yet. I came to see you as soon as I got in here."

"Oh. Should I be flattered?" she asked, playing with him.

He didn't say it to flatter her; he said it because that's what he did. To play along though, he said, "Yeah, you should be."

"Well thank you for coming to see me before you got all stank and sweaty."

He gave her a fake smile and said, "You're welcome."

She looked at her watch and said, "I think I'd better get back to my class. I almost forgot—people like to ask questions before we start."

"Oh, okay."

"Don't have too much fun playing without me today."

He smiled.

He watched her walk away and he thought about what he *could* be. He could be *not* Jaye for once. Since forever, he had been good ol' Jaye and the only thing he had to show for it was a wounded heart. Something inside of him wanted to be someone else at that point; he wanted to do something *Jaye* would never do for reasons *Jaye* wouldn't think of doing.

He caught up with Chandler before she got back into the room.

"Chandler, may I ask you a question?"

"Sure." Her face was inquisitive as she awaited the question.

"Ah… would you like to have dinner sometime? With me," he threw in, in case she was confused.

"Of course."

She had asked him out a few times after they went to the basketball game in January, but he always made up something as to why he couldn't go with her.

"Are you free tomorrow night?"

"What's tomorrow—Thursday?" she asked rhetorically, thinking. "Yes. I'm free tomorrow. What time?"

"Seven."

"Okay," she smiled. "I'll see you at seven tomorrow."

* * *

"So are you ready to do this?"

J filled Ty's glass with wine as she awaited the answer to her question.

"Well…" Ty began, sipping before she completed her thought. "I'm as ready as I'm gonna get."

The official date was set.

Kenya asked, "You're nervous, aren't you?"

Ty smiled. "No. Actually, I'm not." The smile never left her face as she added: "I mean it's crazy because it's only a few weeks away…"

"I know," J agreed, sitting down on the other end of the couch beside Kenya.

"But I'm not nervous at all," Ty said. "I'm ready to do it. I'm ready to marry him. I love him so much and I can't wait until he's my husband."

J and Kenya both looked at each other and they both began to pretend as if Ty's words had touched them more than they actually had.

"Aww… I'm gonna cry," Kenya said.

"Me too. Hold me, Kenya."

They reached across the sofa and held each other, playfully.

"You two are so silly," Ty said. "But I'm glad the three of us are doing this and not having some rowdy bachelorette party."

J and Kenya looked at each other.

"Should I tell her?" J asked.

"Tell her, girl. She gon' find out anyway," Kenya said.

J said, "Ty, Sweetie… Kenya and I just wanted to have a lil' something for us three before you get married, okay. But this doesn't make you exempt from a bachelorette party."

"No," Kenya added. "You're not exempt, honey. You're having a bachelorette party."

"But I don't want a bachelorette p-"

"What did we say?" J asked rhetorically; she didn't expect an answer. "You're *gonna* have a bachelorette party with lots of food and loud music and alcohol and butt-ass naked men…"

"Hey," Ty said, stopping her from continuing. She couldn't help but smile from ear to ear at what J was saying.

"How many did you get, Kenya?"

"I think it's like three or four?"

"Would you two cut it out?" Ty was always the least outgoing of the three.

J looked over at her and assured, "You're *having* a bachelorette party."

Each of them seemed to get thirsty at the same time; they all took sips from their glasses concurrently.

Then Kenya, though they had been at J's house for the past hour, decided to compliment J on her attire. "That is a very nice New Jersey Devil's jersey you got on over there. Where'd you get it?" She smiled and looked over at Ty who was catching her drift. "You ain't from New Jersey."

J smiled at their little joke and said, "It's not mine. It's Jaye's."

"Oh, it's *Jaye's* jersey, huh?" Kenya asked.

"Yeah, it's Jaye's jersey." J was still smiling. She said, "You know I'm not a hockey fan."

"Right. I *do* remember that," Kenya said.

She and Ty were still laughing together; J was trying to hold hers back simply because the joke was on her.

"What's up with Jaye, anyway?" Kenya asked. "I mean how is he?"

"He's fine. Why do you ask?"

"Because," Kenya said, "I haven't seen him in a while, but every time I call you, he's over here."

"Mm-hm," Ty agreed, smiling.

"I call ya cell phone and you're with him…"

"Mm-hm," Ty agreed again.

J threw on a phony smile and took it upon herself to tell them, "We're not back together."

Ty's eyebrows furrowed and her face filled with perplexity.

Kenya said, "Nobody said you were. But since we're on the subject…"

"We're not on the subject."

"I don't understand," Ty interjected. "I was under the impression that you two were seeing each other again. You told me that he spends the night."

J smiled, modestly. Forcing a smile on her face was the only way she could keep from exposing the way she really felt.

"That's just what we do. We aren't back together."

"So what is it?" Kenya asked.

J looked over at her hesitant to answer; she was looking for something to say, but all she could come up with was the truth: "I don't know."

Ty slowly took in two lungs full of air and let it out even slower for lack of words to say.

J said, "I thought we were discussing Ty's…" She sighed. "The wedding," she said. "I thought we were talking about the wedding. How did we get on me?"

"We got on you when you looked at that phone for the hundredth time tonight wondering if it had a signal cuz you haven't heard from your man yet."

"I was not looking at the phone because of that," J said.

"So he is your man?"

Kenya and Ty waited patiently for J to say that she and Jaye were not together because they knew that's what she wanted them to believe for some odd reason.

"J, what's goin' on? I thought you were back in there," Kenya said.

J said, "*I* thought I was in there." She sighed again because the thought of it confused her. "But…" She shook her head. "But I don't know."

Kenya and Ty weren't laughing anymore; they were listening attentively as J spoke. Her tone was serious now. She wasn't sure if she wanted to tell her friends about her suspicions because they *could've* just been that—suspicions. But she felt she needed an objective third party perspective. So she took her chances:

It was lunchtime—the first opportunity she'd had all that day to just sit behind her desk and not be obligated to do any work. She took the hard plastic container from the bag and placed it onto her desk in front of her. She had gotten a small sushi platter from the Asian restaurant down the street and was ready to dig in. But before she could make herself completely comfortable, she pressed the speakerphone button and dialed Jaye's cell.

He answered by simply saying, "Yeah."

"Ah… I have your little PDA thing," she said carefully, trying to decipher his mood through the phone. "You left it at my house last night."

"Thanks," he said. "I was looking all over for that thing this morning. Thank you," he said again, relieved.

Though he couldn't see her, she smiled and said, "You're welcome."

He seemed to be okay that day. He was okay the day before too when he had left the gadget at her house after dinner together. So she asked, "You wanna go out later—see a movie or something?"

"Well… I actually planned on staying in tonight. Chillin'," he said. "Meka is staying at one of her friend's house, so I was just gonna stay in and watch the game."

"Oh," she said. "Well maybe I can just come by later, you know… I can drop it off then."

"Yeah, that'll work. Yeah," he said. "Anytime after eight. I should be there."

When later came, she was standing at his door with expectations of coming in, getting comfortable, drinking a few beers, and staying there until tomorrow. Then maybe tomorrow, Saturday, they could do something like catch that movie. But when he opened the door, she quickly realized that her little plan would probably have to be rescheduled.

"Jaye, I left the ice pack in my car," the stranger said, preparing to leave out and get it.

J was still standing on the outside and hadn't the chance to say anything more than "Hi" to Jaye, who had just opened the door. The woman standing behind him was wrapping her scarf around her neck, obviously getting ready to go to her car to get an ice pack.

A nervous silence invited itself between the three. J looked from Jaye to the woman and then back at Jaye for some answers.

He said, "I'm sorry. Chandler, this is my friend J. J, this is Chandler."

Chandler? Who the hell is Chandler? J thought. He introduced *her* as his "friend," but Chandler was just "Chandler," which left room for the imagination to get to doing its work, as it should. What was she to him? Why was she at his house?

All of this quickly ran through her mind as she stood there, but all she could actually do was return the handshake and simply nod to the "Nice to meet you" greeting that the Chandler character threw out.

"I'll be right back," Chandler said to Jaye, and walked past them and out the door.

J looked into the living room and saw the basketball game on the television; two beers sat on coasters on the coffee table, and chips and chicken wings accompanied them.

"I sprained my wrist playing ball," he said.

She looked at him through narrowed eyes. He would've been better off not saying anything, but to try and explain? His half-explanation left her suspicious. She nodded slowly, keeping eye contact with him for just a few more seconds.

Lately, she found herself wondering who she was to Jaye now—what she meant to him. She was confused about her place in his life. Whatever it was, she didn't like it—she hated it—because it reminded her too much of another "situation" she had been in. She wanted to be with him so badly—and by any means, almost—but she couldn't deny the feeling she had inside: they were having less and less of a friendship/relationship, and more and more of a physical/nothingness. She wanted things to change, but had absolutely no idea how she would go about making that happen. But she knew she didn't want to spend any more of her time trying to figure out who she was to a man.

Backing away, she said, "I'll see you later," and turned and left.

She told her friends, "That was two *days* ago."

"So you didn't ask him about it—her?" Ty inquired.

J sighed. "I wanted to." She thought about it. "I mean… I wanted to," she repeated. "I couldn't bring myself to ask him about her. I couldn't."

Reluctantly, Ty asked, "Why?"

"Because I..." She stopped and began to really think about why she didn't feel comfortable asking Jaye a question she wanted to know. She had never had this problem before; any other time she wanted to know something, she would talk with him with no hesitation in her questions. But now: "I'm honestly afraid of what his answer might be. And on top of that, I don't really feel like it's my place to ask:" regretting why it wasn't. "If this chick is somebody who is into him like that, and who he's interested in as well, then... Then, I mean, he can do what he wants because we aren't together. He's not committed to me, so he has the right to see whomever he wants. If that's what he wants to do."

She hated the sound of that.

"You know he's not like that," Ty said.

"I know," she said.

But her tone had so much uncertainty in it that Ty had to say something else to reassure her. "He's not interested in anybody but you. You should know that."

J didn't say anything. She just accepted Ty's words as those of optimism and not necessarily realism.

She wondered if things would ever be anywhere near like they used to be, like months ago when they were happy. Now, insecurities hovered in every corner of the relationship. She was insecure about the future because now it seemed as if something was always keeping them from succeeded—from completely getting back on track. She didn't know whether it was *supposed* to be this hard or whether this was a sign trying to tell her that "it" wasn't supposed to be... *at all*.

She had continuously tried to think optimistically like Ty, but the truth was: Jaye had been scarred deeply by her. So she was skeptical of his moves—unsure of what he might do as a hurt man. And anything that he did do, she would tie back to herself.

She loved Jaye; therefore, she accepted this pain simply because she felt she deserved it.

I t seemed as if the time to submit his choice for the Black Girl Second Anniversary Collection was approaching fast and he just couldn't finish this piece he was sure would be his choice if it were done. Day in and day out, he worked on it—sometimes until 6 or 7 o'clock in the morning, and then he'd wake up after just three or four hours of sleep and start on it again. But it never seemed right to him.

He hadn't been out of the house since Monday, so he decided to go out today and maybe get some new sneakers, but before he went back home to face the music (and the colors that created it), he stopped at the Center to see the kids—his babies. He hadn't been in almost a month, so when he walked through the door they bombarded him—happy to see him.

"Mr. Jaye!" they all yelled.

They hugged him and kissed him and hung onto his legs as he tried to walk... One little girl told him that she knew she would see him today—that she *knew* he would come. She, with the help of Crayola, had made a special drawing at school today for him. And it touched his heart.

He was stressed out before he went there—worried about finishing the painting; worried about how he would handle his situation with the two women with whom he was involved; he was bothered by the thought of being the type of guy who would be involved with two women concurrently; he was troubled by thoughts of J and his insecurities. But when he got around the kids all of that disappeared. Not once during the two hours he was there did he think about any of this. He smiled the entire time, and laughed even more.

That afternoon, he ordered pizza for them and they had a pizza party. He stayed with the kids and played and talked with them until 6 o'clock when the last one left.

* * *

He had been sitting on his bed Tailor style simply staring at the canvas for over an hour. He had moved the entire easel from the art room to his bedroom for more comfort. The piece needed something—he could see that much—but he couldn't quite put his finger on what it was. It wasn't finished though. Close, but not complete.

A tap on the door broke his concentration.

"It's open."

The door crept in slowly and J, almost cautiously, walked through. The room was dark except for the low-light lamp that sat on his nightstand less than a foot away from the painting, providing just enough light for him to see what he was trying to see.

"You're painting in here now?" she asked.

He simply shook his head "no" and continued to stare, even squinting as he studied it.

It was nearing 5:30 p.m. that evening. She had come over to take Meka shopping for a prom dress; graduation was just over a month away (and she was set for college at Columbia in New York). She told J that she'd probably be home around this time, give or take ten minutes. So because J was a bit early—purposely—she sat on the bed beside Jaye and joined him in the stare at the painting. She watched for about a minute before she was ready to not watch anymore. She liked art, but she couldn't see (or not see) things in it the way he did.

She reclined back on the bed and stared at the ceiling. Lately, that's how things had been. She didn't know if he was *genuinely* so involved in his *big* painting, involved with *other things*, or whether he just wasn't interested in being involved with her anymore. But that was one of those questions that remained unasked for the sake of not wanting to know the answer yet.

She lay there still wondering who Chandler was. It was three days ago she shook hands with a woman who could possibly have taken her place. Well, the place that she wanted. That used to be her sitting on the couch with him drinking beer and pretending to watch the basketball game, and now some other chick was doing that. She wondered what else this chick was doing. She used to talk to Jaye for hours, now it seemed like he didn't have too much to say to her—like he was holding back; but maybe he had just run out of things to say because he had already told it all to *this* chick.

She lay there on his bed thinking about all of this.

She turned her head and looked over at him; he was still studying the painting—hadn't moved much since she lay beside him. She sat up and continued to look at him. After about ten seconds, he realized that her eyes were on him and not the painting, so he looked at her with an inquisitive expression just to make sure it was he at whom she was looking.

When his eyes hit hers, she didn't look away. She was only about a foot away from him to begin with, but she decided to scoot closer. She leaned over and began kissing the side of his face and his lips.

He closed his eyes for a moment, wanting so badly to just submit to her; he could've taken her right then and there on his bed. But he didn't. Instead, he just told her to, "Stop."

She ignored him because he didn't really sound like he meant that; it sounded like the type of "stop" that really meant, "go."

So this time, he moved back a little and said again, "Stop it, J. I don't…"

She sighed cutting him off. She didn't want to hear that.

She couldn't remember the last time they made love, or made whatever it was supposed to be. If she really put thought into it, she would come up with the guess about two or three weeks ago. He would either keep his distance from her, which he had being doing a lot lately, or say something crazy like he just had—stop.

She said, "Jaye, we really need to talk."

She got up from the bed and walked around the room giving him time to respond to her statement. It wasn't a question, but it definitely deserved some type of answer. She stopped at the window and looked out for a moment, then turned and looked at him. She was directly behind him, just on the other side of the bed, and from behind, it looked as if he was about to respond; he took a deep breath and dropped his head, then looked back up at the painting.

So now, because she assumed he wasn't completely ignoring her, she continued with what she had to say. She spoke deliberately and almost delicately. She wasn't attacking him.

"I'm really confused right now. I don't understand *what* this is. I don't understand what the *hell* we're doing," she complained. "I *wanna* know, Jaye. I *need* to know," she stressed. "Because *this*..." she said, referring to their relationship thing. "I don't understand this. I really don't understand *you*."

She ran her hand down her face and looked over at him.

"Jaye," she said. But got no response.

He held a very thin brush. Knowing he had no business painting in that room under that light, he touched the palette and then gently tapped the canvas.

"I *can't*... keep doing this." She paced her words. "It's driving me *fucking* crazy." She bit her bottom lip and walked back and forth in a three-foot radius. Her hands expressed her emotions. "You're all I think about. Every time you get like this, I always... I keep thinking it's me—wondering what I might have done, now."

He held the brush away as he examined the art, wondering what he would touch next.

"I feel like I'm walking on thin ice here. Like I have to be careful of where I step. Because I don't know... what I do...

to make you like this."

A single tear ran down her face, but she quickly wiped it away.

"Jaye."

He looked down at the palette to see how much more black he may have needed to add to get the right gray for a particular section.

"I am trying so hard. I swear I am," she said, shaking her head. "I'm trying so damn hard to make things right between us."

She bit her bottom lip again, fighting tears. She didn't want to cry. She didn't really know what she wanted to say to him, or whether he would eventually say something to her. But she knew she didn't want to cry.

"But this is so difficult. I feel like you're *making* this difficult," she said, calmly. "I wanna believe that this isn't about what I did in the past. I want to."

She sighed and the tears ran down. She wiped them though.

"I wanna believe *so* much…"

She was thinking about the Chandler girl. But she didn't want to jump to conclusions.

"But it's so goddamn difficult to do that right now," she continued. Wiping her tears, she said, "It's *so* hard to do this."

He continued to stare at the painting.

"Jaye, are you hearing me?"

He didn't respond, but she went on anyway.

"I'm not expecting things to be easy. I'm not," she said. "But I don't want to be doing this in vain." She looked at him, and then down at her feet as her eyes continued to fill with tears.

"What are we doing?"

She waited and waited for a response, but got none.

"Jaye…" she called in an almost pleading tone.

He had placed the palette onto the small table that was right beside his easel and was now staring down at his hands. There was that question again, and again, he didn't know how to answer it. He heard everything she said, but he didn't know how to accept it. He didn't know how to respond to it.

"I hear you," he said with absolutely no emotion in his voice. He didn't even look back at her.

She waited for him to turn around and finish saying what he had to say, assuming he hadn't finished. The sound of the front door opening didn't interrupt anything, per se, just served as a silence breaker. There was more he *could've* said; there was a lot more on his mind. But before he verbalized anything, he wanted to be sure that what he was saying was what he wanted to say—what he needed to say.

Instead of looking her in the eyes and being honest and saying to her, "J, I love you, but I need some time right now." Instead of telling her, "I thought I'd had enough time. I thought I was ready to do this again. But I'm paranoid as fuck right now and this paranoia is driving me crazy." Instead of opening up and letting her know that, "I do want you in my life, but I need to move slowly."

Instead of saying all of that and instead of talking to her and asking her truthfully about the things that were causing his insecurities, he simply stared at his painting and said to her, "I really need to finish this."

She stood there and looked at him for about ten seconds, though she couldn't see his face. Meka was waiting for her downstairs and she didn't want to keep her. She left from the room without saying another word to him.

She had a prom dress to shop for.

* * *

"Oh, come on! Did you see that?! That was a foul! That man was all over him!" she said, as the whistle blew indicating a timeout.

"Did you see that?" she asked, turning to him as she awaited an answer.

Jaye threw on a smile and said, "Yeah. Yeah, I saw that. Yeah, they should've called that."

He was watching the same game she was, but he wasn't as into it. He wasn't really into anything. He was sitting on the couch facing the television with his left ankle resting on his right knee. His right arm was on the back of the couch and Chandler sat *right* beside him just within his reach—considerably close considering they were only watching a basketball game.

Almost as soon as the game ended, Jaye finished the only beer he had had all night and then got up from the couch, ready to leave. He was ready to go home so he could get in his bed and feel miserable alone.

"Why're you leaving so early? It's only ten o'clock," Chandler said as she got up to show him to the door. "You sure you don't wanna... stay a little longer... tonight?" she asked, suggestively.

He didn't answer immediately, not because he had to think about his answer—he knew his answer—but because he really didn't want to tell her what it was.

"Nah. I think I'ma... I'm just gonna head home. Turn in for the night."

She nodded and didn't give him any flak. "Well okay," she said, just smiling as she looked at him.

The door was about a foot behind him. He dropped his head and was now staring at the floor—not at anything in particular, but just not at her. He couldn't because of the way he felt. He didn't want to look at her.

He was ready to leave—actually, "run" may have been a better way to describe what he felt like doing—but instead, he stood there for just two seconds longer than he should've, because no sooner than he lifted his head preparing to tell her "goodnight," she moved in for a "see-ya later" kiss. He quickly moved his head back before she could land it... But that was before he realized how appropriate it might've been.

Lately, he and Chandler had been seeing a lot more of each other. Just yesterday, reservations had been made at a little Italian restaurant downtown. Italian was Chandler's favorite. This was the third time the two of them had gone out on what would actually be considered a date.

"You were right—the food there was *incredible*," she said, walking into her apartment holding a white Styrofoam container. "I might knock off the rest of this before the night is over."

"Yeah," Jaye agreed, closing the door behind himself. "I knew you would like it."

Jaye intended to come in for just a minute, but they started talking and before either of them knew it, it was 1 a.m. and they were still sitting in her living room running their mouths.

"But, I mean, that's just how he was," Chandler went on about an old boyfriend. "He just couldn't deal with a woman that wasn't needy." Joking, she said, "I bet you're one of those cavemen, aren't you?"

Shocked that she would say that, he revealed, "I like a woman that's doing her own thing. I don't want somebody who *needs* me, but a woman who wants me."

"So you wouldn't mind if your woman made more money than you?"

"Nah," he answered with a grimace on his face, as if her question was absurd. "Definitely not. I mean, if it just so happened that her career—what she wanted to do in life—paid more than what I wanted to do… So be it. As long as we're both happy with what we're doin', I ain't got a prob'm with it."

"Hm," Chandler hummed, nodding as if she was taking a mental note of his words.

"What?" he asked looking at her.

He thought she had something more to say, maybe even something else to ask; it seemed as if she wasn't finished. But all she said was, "Nothing."

She still had that look on her face though, as if she was really thinking about what they had just talked about.

"*What?*" he asked again, hoping that she would share the secret thoughts this time, because he knew they were about him.

She looked over at him and said, "I just enjoy listening to you. You always surprise me."

His eyebrows dropped, wrinkled. He was flattered—even blushed—but had to ask, "Why do you say that?"

She shrugged her shoulders: "You're just… Even though I haven't known you for a long time, I can just tell that you're just…" She started smiling before she finished.

"I'm what?"

Still smiling, trying to be careful of her choice of words, she said, "I don't know. I guess you just seem kinda different to me. Different from most of the guys I meet."

His face seemed to melt when he heard that because at that moment he didn't feel different. At the moment he knew that in fact he *wasn't* any different. So wanting—but mostly *needing* now—to hear more, he asked carefully, "What makes you say that?"

She sighed. She looked into his dark eyes before saying, "You are an incredible man, Jaye Cobain. And I think I'm falling for you."

Since it seemed as if she had his unsaid permission to do so, she slowly moved in for a kiss. And he let her kiss him. He wasn't very *involved* in the kissing process, but she didn't seem to notice. Either that, or she didn't really care. Since he didn't run, she assumed he obviously wanted to be there.

He eventually began to participate, and the kiss lasted just seconds before she moved over, cradling him beneath her. She wasn't very aggressive, but take-charge enough to let him know what she was going to do. And again, since he didn't stop her, she continued. He sat on the sofa allowing her to take advantage of him as she hovered over him with her knees planted into the cushions on either of his sides. She tattooed an earth toned lipstick on his lips... then his face... next his neck... then his chest...

There were no reasons why she *couldn't*...

So, when she went in for just a kiss *this* time as he stood at her front door about to leave, her action wasn't entirely inappropriate. His reaction though caused her to look at him funnily, almost wondering whether she had bad breath.

He took a huge bit of air into his lungs and then let it out slowly. He knew she wanted answers, so he was trying to think of the best way to explain this:

"Chandler..." He looked at her and said, "I can't do this."

She didn't want to assume the worse—didn't want to jump to conclusions about exactly what he meant by what he said—so she asked, "Can't do what?"

He looked her in the eyes now before continuing the

conversation. Actually, it was more like *his* explanation. He took a deep breath again and said, "*This*. I can't be with you. I just can't. I can't be in a situation with you."

Her hand was already resting on her hip when she blurted, "You wasn't sayin' that last night!"

He couldn't believe what she was trying to imply. He was only telling her this *again* because he wanted to reassure her that he couldn't and didn't want to be in relationship with her, assuming that that's what she wanted or *thought* they were on the verge of having. He wanted to make sure they were on the same page.

"I told you a long time ago I wasn't tryin' to-"

"And that was a *long* time ago! So what was last night about?" she asked, looking at him, expecting him to come up with an excuse to help his case.

He asked her, "You don't think I was seeing you just for that?"

"I don't know *what* to think about you?"

He felt awful because he had apparently made her feel this way. He didn't like the fact that her perception of him had obviously changed for the worse in a matter of minutes. But even though he didn't really think he had done anything wrong, because he had told her how he felt before, he apologized genuinely anyway: "Chandler, I am sorry if I made you feel…"

"I'm sure you are," she cut in, glaring at him though narrowed eyes. She was furious.

He looked away not really knowing what to say.

"That was her last week, wasn't it?"

His heart nearly stopped at the sound of the question—at the thought of who Chandler was asking about: J.

When she first met J, she didn't think *too* much about who she was. But now she had all kinds of thoughts running through her head. Now, to her, J was probably some other girl that he was seeing. Probably one of many.

As he stood there thinking about J, Chandler shook her head and continued with her assumptions. "No different from the rest of 'em."

He hated to hear that, but he couldn't deny that—to the

naked eye—he would really look that way right now. He couldn't say much more in his own defense at the moment.

"Chandler..." He felt awful. He sighed and said, "It's not like that."

She bit her bottom lip like she was holding back thoughts about him that she would've otherwise verbalized. She chose not to say anymore about the situation. She was finished with him.

"You can leave."

Nothing he could say now would have any effect on how she felt. He just stood there wanting to explain things. She just stood waiting for him to leave.

So he turned, opened the door, and walked out without saying any more.

She pushed it shut behind him.

J aye sat in his art room in his comfortable red leather, painting chair holding a palette and focusing on the canvas in front of him. He was wearing sweat shorts, a Nets home basketball jersey and slippers. And he smelled good; she could tell he was wearing the *Contradiction* she liked (or maybe didn't like so much now). He was just sitting there, content, painting, not even explaining himself or making any attempts to get up and prepare so that they could leave.

They were supposed to be on their way to an advance screening of some highly anticipated blockbuster fantasy sci-fi movie that he said he really wanted to see—couldn't wait 'til it came out—and it was only being screened this early in three cities in the entire world, so with her position in the media, she was able to get these special tickets to the DC viewing… For him.

She stood around waiting. He was halfway prepared, so she knew he hadn't forgotten.

His back was to her. He was concentrating on the painting. It needed to be finished. He had been working on it for a while now, but for some reason, it never seemed to look done to him. Complete. He continuously touched it up. He *really* wanted to use it as his piece for the Second Anniversary Collection; he believed it was just that damn good. Well, it had the potential to be. Which was why he kept picking with it. He wanted it to be perfect if it was going to have *his* name on it.

There were two small wooden stools in the room. He didn't really use them for anything—mostly just to sit stuff on. So after standing for several minutes and continuously checking her watch, she chose to sit. She sighed and looked at the watch again. It read 6:35. And he still wasn't dressed. Still hadn't budged. And if they planned to get there without missing any of the opening scene, they needed to be leaving five minutes ago. She had been in the room with him in silence for fifteen.

"I take it we're not going now," she said.

He didn't respond; he simply squinted his eyes and moved his head closer to the painting as if he were trying to get a close-up view of a spot he may or may not've missed. Then he moved back into his original position and continued to dab the brush into the gray color on the palette he had mixed himself.

She rolled her eyes and sighed louder. Not loud, just louder than before.

"You know what? This is some bullshit. I mean, come on, Jaye."

He slid around and looked at her hoping that the eye contact would stop her from continuing to talk like she did a couple days ago when they were in his bedroom.

"So what? We're not going now?" she asked.

He sighed and slid back around. With his back to her, he said, "Damn, can you give me a minute?"

His attitude annoyed her. She said, "I gave you *ten* minutes already. I'm ready to go."

He thought about it for a second, then he turned around in his chair again and said, "Then why don't you?"

He turned his back to her again before he could see

the "excuse me" look on her face and the body language that accompanied it. She felt like saying to him, "Maybe I should. Your fuckin' attitude is get'n on my nerves. You actin' like a lil bitch." But she didn't. She calmed herself, took a breath, and sat back down on the wooden stool. She checked her watch again and sighed.

Another minute or so went by before she started looking at the back of his head and thinking. Boy, did she love that man. She knew love was a complicated thing; she knew Jaye was complicated, but damn. This was a puzzle she wasn't sure if she'd be able to figure out. She thought about all the crazy things that invaded her mind every night before she went to sleep. That yellow brick road she once used to see the two of them walking down together wasn't quite that yellow anymore. It suddenly turned from yellow to an ugly brown to a dusty black. She thought about all the things that caused it, and then she tried to think about what was stopping them from moving past it. Or *who* may have been stopping them.

Right then, she had to ask, "Jaye, who is Chandler?"

That question quickly drew his attention, but he didn't stop looking at the painting. In a way, that was a question he was hoping she would have asked a long time ago. Not because he was anxious to tell her who Chandler was, but because it would reveal what was on J's mind. It would reveal that she had been thinking about this—that it bothered her. That maybe it made her insecure. On the other hand, he realized that no matter what answer he gave, a person who had developed insecurities would not believe it. Insecurities meant that the mind was pretty much already made up. If she was insecure then she already had in mind who Chandler was, and just wanted confirmation. A conversation he really wasn't in the mood to have.

He sighed.

"Jaye… You know what?" she asked. "I won't even get mad. I just wanna be clear."

Her words were preposterous to him, and the expression showed on his face. He kept his cool, though he was beginning to burn inside. It wasn't like she should necessarily have been hurt by the fact that there could have possibly been another woman in his life besides her. He thought it was a bit self-centered of her to say she wouldn't get mad. Who was she to even be questioning him about the goings-on in his personal life? Who was she to ask—and with a bit of an attitude at that—who another woman was? *Yeah, an old friend from college, my ass,* he thought.

Chandler was no longer even a friend, but J didn't need to know all of that.

"She's a friend of mine..."

J simply bit her bottom lip because she could sense that he had more to say. She began to gnaw her bottom lip as she waited.

He seemed finished, but...

"That's it?"

He turned and looked at her, pissed off now because her tone said that she didn't believe him. He was burning up. He could feel his blood pressure rise in just a matter of seconds.

Looking at her as if he was offended, he said, "Yes. *J.* That's it. I have other friends besides you."

That statement said too much to her: either he only thought of her as nothing more than just a friend, or he was having the very same sexually complicated relationship with this Chandler chick and was calling that a friendship too.

"What do you mean by 'other friends' besides me?"

He sighed very hard to purposely show his frustration with the conversation. It wasn't that he had gotten sick of talking about it, because she had never really brought it up; he just really didn't want to talk about it now. Or ever.

"I mean what I said: I have other friends." He looked at her. "Just like *you* have other friends."

"I don't have other friends," she answered quickly, becoming very irate.

"Are you sure 'bout that? Because a very *close* friend of yours came into my gallery a few weeks ago. Even purchased a painting."

She quickly started thinking about what friend he could possibly be talking about, but before she could ask, he said, "He makes movies for a living."

She realized that Jaye was talking about Marien, and his attitude let her know that he knew more about Marien than she had ever told him. But she quickly moved past that. She knew what he was implying and she didn't like it.

"The fuck is that supposed to mean?"

"It means what it means, J: I have my friends, and you have yours. I do what I want with mine and you do whatever it is you do with yours."

She couldn't believe the insinuated accusations. Her eyes squinted as she became both insulted as well as very curious. She said, "The only friend *I've* been doing *anything* with is *you.*"

"Oh, come on, J. You…"

He bit his bottom lip still assuming that she must've been doing something for her friend to send her a several thousand dollar painting—like she didn't know a thing about it.

"What?! What are you talkin' about?" she asked, still confused, and now very aggravated by the fact that he was being so vague.

He shook his head and looked back at the painting he was trying to complete. "Does it even matter?" he asked.

"Obviously. If it didn't, you wouldn't have brought it up." She stood up and looked at him awaiting an answer.

"Don't act like you don't know what I'm-"

"Jaye…" she said, cutting him off in a calm tone. "If I knew what you were talking about, I'd *say* I knew what you were talking about." She looked him squarely in the eyes and said, "I don't know what you're talking about!"

He was convinced that she had to have known.

He picked up a paintbrush like he wasn't going to say any more to her. So she asked, "Why do you always do this to me?"

Ignoring her question, he looked over at her and asked, "Why do you wanna be with me?"

Her eyebrows wrinkled as she thought a little about exactly what to say: I love you? She came up with, "Why are you asking me a question you obviously know the answer to?"

"So what's with all this secretive shit?"

Perplexity filled her face. "What secretive shit? What secrets? What are you talking about?"

"Why the hell didn't you tell me who Marien was?"

So that's what this is all about, she thought. She nodded her head as she concluded that the past was in fact what was hindering the future. Marien must've visited the gallery and made it a point to tell Jaye things he really didn't need to know right now.

"Jaye…" she said, with a tone to her voice that revealed the explanation she was about to give. "I honestly didn't think you would care *who.* I told you what I did, I didn't think you *wanted* to know all that. And you never asked me-"

"Don't *give* me that *bull*shit!"

His tone shocked her, causing her to focus more on the fact that he had raised his voice—something she had never heard him do like that—instead of focusing on the conversation at hand. She was speechless.

"Why wouldn't I want to know that if you still see him?"

"I *don't* still see him! I *had* to interview…"

He placed the brush down hard on the rest and it made a loud smacking sound.

"How am I… supposed to have some type of…" He looked at her and said, "Some type of relationship with you if I don't know whether you're interviewing somebody or fuckin' him?"

Her mouth dropped.

"You still don't trust me," she concluded. She wasn't completely shocked, but shocked, nevertheless, because he had told her that he was past that situation. She thought she had revealed to him her newness. That was the old J. Why couldn't he see that?

He simply slid around in his chair to face his painting again because he was not about to entertain that statement. It was obvious what the answer would be had it actually been a question.

With his back to her, he said, "For all I know, you probably had something to do with the reason why they didn't get married."

"I didn't have a…" But she shut up because for all she knew, she might've.

She felt like crying, but she didn't. She actually became very infuriated when the thought of how much time had passed and he was just now saying all of this. Their current relationship—or lack there of—made a little bit more sense to her now; though, at the same time, it was very surprising. It was hard to accept—very hard to believe—that Jaye had been carrying on in a sex-only relationship with her.

"I wanted to give this a try, you know? I wanted to make things right. I thought I had a second chance," she said. She shook her head. "Look... I can apologize for what I did to you." She said, "I'm sorry. Okay? I was stupid. I admit that. But what I *won't* do is kiss your ass forever because of this."

He was still facing the painting. Her words caught his attention, but he neglected to respond and continue this argument. As far he was concerned, it would be one sided for the rest of the night. He had said his piece.

"I fucked up!" she said. "I fucked up. You can either accept my apologies for that and work on moving past it, or you can fuckin'... sit around here staring at that goddamn... *painting* all day long-"

"Look, I didn't ask you to kiss my ass, okay. *You're* the one that acted like you wanted to get back in..."

"I did want us to get back together, but what I *won't* do is allow myself to be taken advantage of..."

"Taken advantage of? What the fuck are you talking about?!"

"I've had relationships before that were based solely on sex..."

"So now *I'm* takin' advantage of *you*?!"

"Yes. Jaye. And I'm not havin' a relationship like that no more," she said. "I ain't doin' that for nobody. I'm not doing that with you."

"I didn't ask you to do that for me."

"You didn't have to ask, it was implied."

"It was implied because it was what *you* wanted."

"It was implied because it was what *you* wanted!" She said, "The *only* fuckin' thing!" She hated that she was telling him, of all people, this.

She was heated. And while she was clearing her head...

"And I'm not gonna be some other woman either."

"What are you talkin' abou-"

"You *know* what I'm talkin' about—Charles, or whatever the hell her name is."

He sucked his teeth and sighed.

She was so upset that she was compelled to ask, "So are you fucking her too?"

"What if I-"

"Fuck you."

He turned his back, annoyed, and began poking at an area on the painting with his brush while shaking his head. He wasn't going to entertain what she had just said to him.

She finally realized that talking to him was probably pointless right now. She looked at her watch and also realized that looking forward to seeing that movie was pointless as well.

He was looking down now, thinking probably.

She bit her bottom lip and then looked over at him and asked, "Is this goodbye, Jaye?"

She was really sick of him not answering her questions— ignoring her like she didn't exist. All he did was breath hard. So then she said, "Do you still wanna be with me?"

She wanted an answer to this question, so she stood and waited for one.

Inside, he believed her; he believed what she said about not being with anybody else. She was never a liar. She even admitted to cheating when she did. So, for that reason, he believed her words over those of Marien. But he needed time to think about where *he* himself stood in all this.

"Jaye."

He was going to tell her. He was going to say that he didn't *not* want to be with her, but that he needed some time. But before he could turn around and look at her or say anything, he saw the red write across it as if someone or something invisible with an invisible knife cut into the painting making it bleed like it had a heart that pumped blood. Like it could hemorrhage from wounds.

He looked down at himself and at the floor, which was covered in red spots now, and there rested the small glass container. That must've been what hit him hard on the shoulder just before the crimson streak invaded the masterpiece.

He didn't answer her when she called his name again; so to get his attention, she grabbed a small container of red paint from the table of many colors—the first one that caught her eye. And she threw it at him, intending to only have it hit his back so that he would turn around. Instead, it grazed his shoulder, the loose top flew off, and red paint was on him and the painting.

Before she could get the words out to apologize for the accident, her back was pinned against the wall. The shoulders of her jacket were in his hands. His palms kept her there, pressed against her clavicles.

When he realized what he had done, he slowly loosened his grip. She helped him remove his hands from her by pushing him away.

She turned and opened the door and walked out.

With tears running from his eyes, he went after her, but he didn't call her name. He couldn't! He wanted to apologize, but words wouldn't leave his mouth.

He followed her down the steps, through the living room, and to the door.

She left, but he didn't leave out behind her.

Keyon had been standing in the same spot in Jaye's art room for twenty minutes staring at the masterpiece. He didn't even turn when he heard Jaye come back into the room, freshly showered now and in his uniform—wrinkleless white tee, blue jeans and crisp white sneaks.

"It's crazy cuz it's like… I can't look away," Keyon said.

Jaye looked from Keyon to the painting, and then back at Keyon. Keyon squinted and turned his head to the side, still examining the painting. Jaye didn't say anything, just allowed his friend to continue studying the work. He took a seat in his favorite red leather chair and joined Keyon in the stare.

"So are you still gonna use this one?" Keyon asked without looking Jaye's way.

"Are you serious, man? There's fuckin' red all over it," he complained.

Keyon said, "So," with his eyes still on the painting. Jaye sighed. "I don't know." He continued to look at it. "Man, I don't know."

"You don't know?" Keyon asked. "This one definitely has my vote."

Jaye kept his eyes on the painting. "I don't know, man."

"Why do you keep saying that?"

"Because I don't know," Jaye said, looking at him for the first time during the conversation. In a low, almost melancholic monotone voice, he said, "I was so sure that this would be it. Just the idea I had in my mind of how it would be once I was done... It was going to be a signature *Jaye Cobain*, y'know."

Keyon smiled because he could see why Jaye could say that about it.

"But look at it," Jaye said, shaking his head as he stared at the "ruined" artwork. "I put myself into this thing and look at it."

Keyon looked at. He said, "It's incredible."

Jaye looked at him like he was crazy or like he was waiting for the punch line to this joke. But Keyon never gave one. Jaye looked down at his hands. One part of him still saw the undeniable beauty in the thing; the other side of him was reluctant to try to see it because he was blinded by the red accident.

Jaye twiddled his thumbs as he thought about things.

"I'm telling you," Keyon said, "They gon' go crazy over this thing. I'm jealous."

Jaye smiled for the first time all day. Blushed even.

Keyon said, "You *gotta* use this one."

Jaye didn't say anything.

Keyon just continued to look at the painting. He then looked over at Jaye and asked, "Have you talked to her?"

Jaye didn't have to ask whom.

"Nah." He shook his head and said, "I called her. And I left a message. Can you believe that?" he asked about the irony of him actually leaving a message. "I didn't ask her to call me back. I just apologized. I didn't mean to do what I did. I just got so mad..."

"I told you to stop holding that shit in," Keyon said.

Jaye smiled again. That was twice.

"I know. I'm working on that," he said. "I'm used to avoiding conflict. I never faced my problems head on. I just waited for them to dissolve themselves." He shook his head. "See where that got me with J." He thought about how that had worked out for him. "And then there's the whole Chandler situation."

Keyon waited for him to explain.

Jaye slowly shook his head. "I wanted to trust J again because I love her so much. But then there was dude." He thought about punching Marien in the face. He'd do it again if he had to.

"I guess I thought she would betray me again. Though she's not a liar. She told me it was mine..." He didn't mean to tell Keyon so much. But he realized that it didn't matter.

"I was so insecure," he revealed. "So insecure cuz I was never clear with her, just made assumptions."

He thought about how stupid that was. He said, "I wanted her to be insecure too. I wanted her to feel what I felt. So I brought another woman into my life."

Pain and regret filled his dark eyes. "I never been so malicious."

He looked back up at the painting almost getting lost in it.

"I didn't sleep with her," he said.

This was news to Keyon.

Jaye looked at him and said, "Honestly?" He sighed. "We fooled around," he admitted. "*You* know." The animation of his eyes told the rest of the story. "She wanted to. I wanted to. But I just... I couldn't do that, man."

Keyon nodded following him, happy that Jaye didn't stoop so low.

They continued staring at the painting, admiring it and everything about it, even the bleeding wound.

"I love her," he said. He just stared at the painting, almost in a trance.

Keyon looked from the painting to Jaye.

"It's not flawless. But…" He looked at Keyon and said, "This is the one."

Keyon was confused. He didn't know whether he was talking about the painting or…

"The one?" Keyon asked.

"This is the one I'm choosing for the gallery," Jaye said. He looked back at the painting and said, "I tried to fix it. I tried to make it perfect. But this is the way it is. And it's right. This is the one, man."

He knew what he wanted to say about her, but he didn't know how he wanted to say it. He knew he had to get it out though. He had to release it.

"I feel like I tried my best with this one." He stopped and thought about what he'd just said. "I think it is my definitive effort."

He spoke slowly as he analyzed: "The absolute greatest thing I've ever laid a brush to."

As he stared at it harder, his words came easier. "I feel it speaks bluntly. I feel like everything about it is utterly remarkable, from its mix of black to its detailed complexity—the gray areas.

"I feel it is rebellious… But I feel it is a martyr. It exemplifies femininity and talks words of poetry expressive of all kind. I feel it is a masterpiece filled with an uncanny inner beauty that is only defined by its tone.

"I feel it has a quality unlike anything I've ever seen because it makes me open my mind and explore it—not only for what it appears to be initially, but what it reads. It shares stories with me filled with regret… and sorrow…" He stares at the painting as he thinks about what he's saying. "And sufferance…" he adds. "But instead of just insisting to only be what it was when I started… It changes. And continues to."

Quietness filled the room as Jaye continued to look at the work of art that was:

"Tough. And *brazen*… And I feel it doesn't surround itself with a frame—doesn't need one, though the edges may be rough. And though it has blemishes, it allows me to see them. In red… plain view. So I feel it is honest. Its story is very… I understand it. It says enough for me to understand."

He nodded because it was so clear now.

Keyon agreed with everything Jaye said, and he even nodded his head too as Jaye went on.

"Keyon," he said. "This painting took me longer to complete than any other I've ever done. And it *still* has room to grow," he said as if the thought of that was unbelievable to him.

"It challenges me. Makes me think. It slowed me down—didn't allow me to rush it. I had to take my time, y'know. I had to be… I had to be careful with it." He thought about how much he valued that now. He couldn't understand it before. He couldn't see the value in pacing himself. But now he got it.

"It made me appreciate everything it has to offer. The good. The not so good. The complex shit… Everything. And once I got it? That's when she opened herself up to me… And she allows me to love her."

He bit his bottom lip.

"She deserves a lot of love."

He realized: "She isn't perfect though, Keyon. She's… She's not perfect by far, man, but… This painting—flawed, scarred, complicated… But I love it anyway. But I love her anyway."

Keyon nodded. He asked, "What do you call it?"

Jaye looked at him to make sure he was talking about the painting.

"The painting—did you title it?"

Jaye looked back at it. He hadn't thought of a name yet. Hell, he just realized that he wanted it to be his.

But considering his muse, he thought it would only be right to call it: "What else? 'Tenth Letter.'"

Blu walked into J's office, closed the door behind him and took a seat in one of the chairs facing her desk.

"Black Girl Art Gallery," he said. "You know the second anniversary is tonight."

She just continued munching on chips, not really paying him any attention because she already knew everything he was saying.

"I heard they're adding this huge thing—the Second Anniversary Collection Series... Five paintings. I could buy a Cadillac with what they're making off one of those things."

He shook his head just thinking about it.

"Everybody is going to be there. It's supposed to be bigger than last year *and* the year before when they opened." He looked at her, smiled, and said, "I *know* you're gonna take it."

She was eating lunch, but hadn't touched her sandwich since he entered the office.

Because she didn't answer right away, he said, "You were the first person I thought of. I figured you would've wanted it since you covered the other two."

She sighed. "I yum… I'm gonna pass," she said. "I've assigned it to someone."

"Are you *sure* about this?" Blu didn't understand. "Everybody's gonna be there."

"I'm sure," she said.

"I mean I would personally want you to take it, I mean…"

"Blu," she said, cutting him short of explaining. "I said I got someone."

Blu didn't understand. But he didn't question her. He said, "All right," using the arms of the chair as a crutch as he got up. "Enjoy your lunch."

And that night, the Second Anniversary Collection Series went over big with the media and potential buyers. Just as many people, if not more, were there this time as there were at the grand opening two years ago. Real art lovers and perpetrators packed the place with the hopes of being the highest bidder of one the very exclusive pieces in the collection series.

Again, Jaye and Keyon found themselves entertaining questions from writers of all walks of life, from newspapers to magazines to websites…

A hard pluck stung his left ear, doing its job of getting his attention.

Rubbing his ear and grimacing, Jaye said, "That shit hurts."

"You'll be alright," Keyon said, knowing the pluck wouldn't kill his friend.

He stood with Jaye for a moment as the media people focused more on the art now than the two of them.

"You better get yourself some wine now while you have the chance," Keyon advised. "I don't know how much longer the art is gon' keep them occu-"

"Excuse me," a female voice interrupted.

"Pied," Keyon finished before turning around.

Jaye reluctantly followed suit. He knew standing behind

them was another writer ready to ask the same questions hundreds of other writers just asked.

She said, "Hi, my name is Tonya Gray. I'm from *FACE Magazine*. Got a few questions."

Keyon looked over at Jaye, and just as he thought, Jaye's face was filled with bewilderment. And disappointment. The woman may not have noticed, but Jaye couldn't hide it from Keyon.

"Sure. Go ahead," Keyon told her.

"Wait a minute," Jaye interrupted. Everything about talking to the stranger felt wrong. She was from J's magazine, but she wasn't J. She was J's replacement. To him, there was no such thing—not even for asking a few questions about the gallery.

He hoped she would come. But he knew she wouldn't. He still had to ask, "Where's ah… J Llaureano? She usually covers our events… I mean, not that *you* wouldn't do a wonderful job of covering the story," he said, not to offend the young woman.

She smiled and blushed implying that no offense had been taken.

"It's just that… we kinda got used to her," he lied.

"Oh, that's no problem. I understand," Tonya said. "J couldn't cover this story. With her workload, I don't see how she gets much of anything done."

"Oh okay," Keyon said, accepting her explanation.

"But I hope I can do just as good of a job as she has, so maybe you can get used to me," she added, smiling. She was flirting with Jaye now.

Jaye noticed.

And nothing about this was right. It was all wrong. Everything was just wrong. So:

"Excuse me," he says to the journalist and walks away.

He pardons his way through the crowd of people who all seem not to want to move as they stand gazing at the artwork in a trance.

"Excuse me… Excuse me, ma'am. 'Scuze me," nearly knocking the camera from one woman's hand. "Sorry. Excuse me, sir."

He finally makes his way to the front…

"Jaye Cobain! A picture for the Afro-American!"

"Sorry." He can't help the man. Dashes out the front entrance.

"TAC-*SAY*!!! Taxi!"

One zips by him. And then two. Three. Four...

"TAC-*SAY*! Tax..."

Before he can finish the word, one is right in front of him.

Through the passenger window to the driver: "I'm going to Arlington."

"What's in Virginia?"

He knows that voice. Almost afraid to be wrong, he takes his time and slowly... slowly looks from the careless eyes of the Indian man driving the bright yellow car to the passenger making her way out the rear.

She climbs from the backseat.

His eyes must lie!

No. He stared at her with his mouth open for a second. He wasn't at a loss for words, he just genuinely couldn't talk at the moment. He reached over the open car door and placed her face in his hands. He just held her face, looking at her. He saw her *differently* as he stared... He wondered why. Was it him? Or was it her? And so a kiss on the lips of this unfamiliar woman was perhaps inappropriate.

He finally let go long enough for her to close the cab door. And he just stood there looking into her eyes. He was so apologetic.

"I thought you wouldn't come."

Looking in his eyes: "You came to me when I fucked up. I owe you one."

He shook his head still trying to believe that it was true—that she was there for him right now.

"J, I'm..." He looked her right in her eyes. He had so much to say to her; he wanted to apologize again for what had happened; he wanted to explain himself... He just looked at her and said, "I'm... I'm not used to this."

"Used to what?"

"Needing forgiveness. Being the sorry one."

"Trust me. I know what you mean," she said.

He had forgotten that the love experience was new to her too.

"I'm sorry. I'm sorry about everything. Everything I ever put you through—I apologize for." He thought about everything: his impatience, his distrust, his insecurities... shoving her into a wall. Everything.

"Look... I'm evolving right now, J—into a new man. A better man." He looked into her brown eyes as she hung onto every word—every letter—that left his tongue. "Being with you... I was able to open my eyes and see parts of myself that... that maybe I knew was there, but just always tried to ignore." He told her sincerely, "I can't do that anymore. It's not right. Not to myself. Or to you."

Those words were new to her. And she could feel Jaye's effort. And she admired everything about it. She admired it because she could relate. Just like she... he needed fixin'. She too was experiencing some natural mutation and knew that she needed to take time to get to know this new woman—this new *lady*—whose name was also Jesenia Lorena Llaureano.

"So where do we go from here? What do we do?"

He shrugged, though he had answers. "What can we do? Try again," he said, answering his own question. "J, I love you. And I wanna try again." He shook his head. "One day. Not today. Maybe not tomorrow," he said. "But one day." He made sure she was following him. "We will try again."

She smiled. Even though they met in this very same place a few years ago, two completely different people stood in this place now. And next time they stand here, even better people will have this place. Two new people knew what they had to do to get where they needed to go.

"But right now," he told her... "Let's get better."

For the first time, he said everything that she knew needed to be said.

And so she reaches up and wraps her arms around his neck. Hugs him tight.

Whispers: "I like that."

"But J," he says, "giving up... just ain't a option."

The End

thank You